FIREFIGHT

A VIET NAM WAR NOVEL

DAVID ALLIN

Table of Contents

ONE

It was an extremely hot and steamy day, which, truth be told, was pretty standard for Viet Nam. Concerned about sunburn, Harry Masters stood up to put his shirt back on, pausing to gaze at the dark yellow bar embroidered on the collar. It signified his rank as Second Lieutenant, the lowest of the officer class. Some argued it was even less prestigious than a Private E-1, but Masters wouldn't let that bother him. He was hopeful, however, that he would soon get to exchange it for the black bar of a first lieutenant, and he would also get his Combat Infantryman's Badge to sew above the left breast pocket. He had only been in Bravo Company for two weeks, and in Nam for three weeks, but he was proud that he was starting to feel comfortable in his new role as a platoon leader. He had quickly learned to call it Nam instead of Viet Nam, and picked up some of the other catch phrases used by the men under him as he tried to assimilate. He wore the same uniform for several days in a row and deliberately scuffed his boots so he wouldn't look so much like a new arrival. He really wanted to fit in.

But it was still difficult assuming his proper role as a leader of men. It didn't help that he looked like he was still in high school— thin, five foot ten, curly dark brown hair, and a very boyish face. He hadn't really started shaving until he was a sophomore in college, and even now he shaved every day only to keep up the pretense that he needed to. Unlike most of his peers, he had not yet developed a deep voice, essential to giving to commands, making him sound like a ten-year-old playing war when he did so. He was pretty sure some of the men mocked him behind his back, but he steadfastly refused to acknowledge this ridicule, for he knew that to do so would only make it worse.

Sitting back down on the ammo crate strapped to the top of the M-113 armored personnel carrier, he straightened his boonie hat and looked around. His platoon—*his* platoon—was deployed beside the dirt road to Tay Ninh, the four armored personnel carriers—tracks, as the men referred to them—facing the points of the compass, ready to provide rapid response security for the convoys that would be rolling down the road soon. Rice paddies stretched away from either side of the road, with women and old men wading in them tending to the young rice plants, and water buffalo grazing along the dikes. Close by, his men were relaxing, their shirts off, their weapons left inside or on top of the tracks, and their attention mostly diverted by the crowd of local Vietnamese that surrounded them. Harry made sure that each of the 50-caliber machine guns on top of the tracks was manned, but the rest of the platoon was taking it easy, buying cold sodas from the Coke kids and food from the sandwich mama-sans, and negotiating with the pimps for the services of the boom-boom girls.

Harry felt uneasy about the lack of military decorum his men displayed, but his platoon sergeant, Staff Sergeant Maxwell, had assured him that this was standard practice when outposting, as this duty was called. All through his training, in ROTC—Reserve Officers Training Corps—at the University of Indiana and at Officer Basic at Fort Benning, his instructors had impressed upon him that as a new lieutenant, he should depend on his platoon sergeant for guidance. The sergeant, they told him, had years of experience and knew the ways of the Army, and would never lead him astray. And Harry had seen other platoons outposting and allowing the civilians to come close, so apparently it wasn't a big deal. Maxwell had told him that it was encouraged as a way to win the hearts and minds of the people, and that sort of made sense. Outposting was boring duty, after all, and with the rice paddies all around, it was almost impossible for enemy soldiers to sneak up on them, so giving the men a chance to take it easy for a few hours seemed only reasonable.

One of the drivers had lowered the wooden trim vane on the front of his track to a horizontal position, propping it up with a shovel, and then draped ponchos and poncho liners over it to create a small low tent. Harry had seen the Vietnamese girl duck under and disappear inside, and then one after another some of the men had gone in, to come out a few minutes later smiling and buttoning up

2

their pants. Sergeant Maxwell had told him the price was only five dollars, or 500 piasters, and offered to let him go first, but Harry had declined. He had to admit he was intrigued, but felt it would demean his already-shaky standing as the platoon leader. He had been warned, as well, that his platoon had the highest rate of VD in the battalion, and he didn't want to be part of that statistic.

The sound of a vehicle approaching cut through the din of children and soldiers who were playing baseball in the road, and they all scattered to either side to allow the vehicle to pass. As it came closer, Harry saw that it was a jeep, one that was remarkably clean and complete with the plastic-coated canvas roof, something he rarely saw in Viet Nam. He also saw the outraged scowl of the passenger as the jeep skidded to a halt right beside the track Harry was sitting on. Harry immediately stood up and straightened his uniform, a lump of dread forming in his stomach as an unfamiliar lieutenant colonel climbed out of the jeep and locked eyes with him.

"Are you in charge of this cluster-fuck?" the colonel demanded, looking up at Harry with an expression that combined anger with an anticipation that Harry didn't understand.

"I'm the platoon leader," Harry answered, jumping down. "Second Lieutenant Harold Masters, sir." He resisted the urge to salute, knowing saluting in the field was prohibited due to the danger of enemy snipers using that to mark the highest ranking targets.

The colonel stomped over to him, fire in his eyes. He was shorter than Harry, with a noticeable paunch, and his small eyes glared through wire-rimmed glasses. He had the black oak leaf of a lieutenant colonel embroidered on his left lapel, and the symbol for the quartermaster corps on his right. According to his name tape, he was LTC Tarreyton, a name Harry was unfamiliar with. Since he had been in the unit for only two weeks, however, that wasn't really surprising. Above the colonel's left breast pocket he had a black metal CIB pinned, which puzzled Harry for a moment. The Combat Infantryman's Badge, highly prized by officers for promotion purposes, was supposed to only be awarded to soldiers with an infantry Military Occupational Specialty or officers in the infantry branch, and then only when they had served in an infantry unit in combat for at least thirty days. He wondered how someone in the quartermaster corps could get one, but his questions were immediately plowed under by the squat colonel's tirade.

Sputtering and spitting, the man got in Harry's face and yelled. "What the fuck do you think you're doing, lieutenant? Don't you have the slightest clue what Division policy says about this kind of shit? Allowing civilians to gather around your vehicles, letting your men walk around out of uniform and without their weapons, and failing to maintain a heightened state of readiness, are all court-martial offenses in my book! You are a total disgrace, unworthy of being called an officer! Look at the example you are setting for your men! I cannot believe what is going on here! What have you got to say for yourself?"

"Well, sir," Harry began, but was not allowed to continue.

"I don't want to hear your lame excuses, lieutenant! You're wrong, wrong, wrong! What unit are you with?" The little man took a notebook and pen out of his breast pocket and prepared to write.

Harry gave him all the information he demanded, including the names of his company and battalion commanders.

With a vicious smirk the colonel took it all down, snapped the notebook closed, and returned to his jeep. "Get your shit together, lieutenant," he called. "You'll be hearing about this from your commander, if I have anything to say about it." He motioned to his driver, and the two sped off.

Sergeant Maxwell came over, looking a little sheepish. "Oh, shit," he remarked.

"Sergeant, get the men into uniform and get these civilians away from the tracks. You heard the colonel."

"Right, sir," Maxwell replied, perhaps a little sullenly. "Okay, guys, get your shirts and helmets on and pick up your weapons," he yelled at the men. "Make the civilians stay on the other side of the road. Come on, hop to it." With no particular sense of urgency, the men complied. Harry watched them, retrieving his own weapon and helmet, and shook his head, worried about what might happen when the captain found out. The men of the platoon avoided Masters,

4

some looking guilty, others sympathetic. They probably weren't used to seeing their leader chewed out like that.

The next day, as he had feared, he was called to the company commander's track at the fire support base. Sitting across from each other in the close confines of the track, Harry felt very uncomfortable with the way Captain Ashcroft was studying him. Finally the commander spoke.

"You don't look like a hardened criminal," he remarked.

"Sir?" Harry was totally confused.

"Well, that's what Colonel Tarreyton suggested when he reported his encounter with you. He said you threatened him, you were outrageously disrespectful, and had violated countless Army regulations and division policies. He demanded your court martial, and I gather he would also like to have you horse-whipped and run out of town on a rail."

Harry just stared at his commander, flabbergasted and overcome with dread. He knew he was in trouble, but this was sounding really serious. Then Ashcroft snorted and smiled.

"Tarreyton's an asshole," Ashcraft told him, "but he's a high-ranking asshole, and he apparently has the ear of someone at Division. Our battalion commander met with him this morning, and talked him down to an Article 15. I'm sorry, Harry, but that's the best he could do."

"An Article 15?" Harry bleated. While it was technically only minor non-judicial punishment, an Article 15 stayed on your record forever, and would almost certainly delay his promotion, if not prevent it entirely. Harry's heart sank.

"But here's what we're going to do," Ashcroft said. "We're not telling Tarreyton, but we're suspending it, so that if you manage to finish your tour without getting in any more trouble, it will be shit-canned. And to keep you away from Tarreyton, you're going to be transferred to A Company. You're going to be their XO."

"Executive Officer? Me?"

"Yeah, I know, it sounds like a promotion, but it really isn't. You're just being kicked upstairs. You'll stay at company headquarters in Dau Tieng, and won't be in charge of anyone except the first sergeant and the company clerk. It sounds like a more important job than it really is. Stay there, keep your nose clean, and maybe in a few months Tarreyton will be gone and we'll sneak you back in as a platoon leader. Okay?"

"I guess so," Harry replied, even more conflicted than before. He knew he was getting off light, but wondered what the long-term effects would be. "Thank you, sir." His gratefulness was heartfelt, for he knew he had just dodged a big bullet.

"And whatever you do, stay away from Tarreyton."

"Yes, sir."

"Get your gear and get ready to go. A Company is sending a jeep to pick you up. Dismissed."

TWO

First Lieutenant Stephen Carr put down the paperback novel he had been trying to read and gazed out the open back of his armored personnel carrier. The other three tracks of his platoon were deployed in a standard defensive perimeter, with A12 on his left and A14 on his right. A11 was directly across, and he could see his platoon sergeant, Sergeant First Class Aaron Samples, sitting on top writing a letter, which was unusual for the man. Carr knew Samples wasn't close to his family, and he was separated from his wife, more so than just by the thousands of miles across the ocean. While stationed at Fort Ord, California, after his first combat tour in Nam, Samples had caught his wife in bed with a young lieutenant, and he hadn't been the same since. The sergeant had refused to give his wife a divorce out of spite, and had immediately volunteered to return to Viet Nam for a second tour. He normally received very few letters, and he wrote even fewer.

Samples had set his helmet down beside him, letting the mild breeze ruffle his dark blonde hair. Beyond Samples was the Ben Cui rubber plantation. The platoon had spent the morning providing security for some engineers sweeping the road to Dau Tieng for mines, and then set up here beside the road as a ready reaction force in case the gooks tried to ambush the convoys somewhere.

Samples had posted men fifty yards inside the rubber as OPs, observation posts, in case any Viet Cong or North Vietnamese Army soldiers tried to creep up on them, and the rest of the men were at least pretending to be alert, keeping their shirts and helmets on, and their weapons next to them. When they had first set up at this location, the usual crowd of Coke kids and sandwich mama-sans had descended upon them, but he had shooed them away, and now only five or six remained in the area, camped out across the road. Everyone had heard what happened to Lieutenant Masters, their new

7

XO, and were now following the rules, more or less. Carr had told the men they could go over and buy sodas or sandwiches across the road, but only one at a time, and to come right back, especially if they heard someone coming.

At the moment the only soldier across the road was young PFC Rancy, who was arguing with one of the mama-sans about the watch he had bought a week ago. At the time he had been very proud of his new Rolex, purchased for the bargain price of only twenty dollars. Two days later the watch had stopped running, and when Rancy popped the back off with his pocket knife, he found that the inner workings were stamped, "Made in China." Now he was trying to get his money back, but the older Vietnamese woman just kept shaking her head and holding her hands up to ward him off. Carr had warned the young man that he was wasting his time, especially since he wasn't even sure if that was the same woman who had sold him the watch, but to no avail.

Carr checked his own watch, a cheap Timex. It was now after five, and typically they would be back to the fire support base or a night laager by now, but one of the convoys had been delayed for some reason. So here they sat, sweltering in the heat, even when the scattered clouds blocked the sun. Carr reached in his shirt pocket and withdrew the latest letter he had received from his wife, Sarah, who was staying with her parents in Tulsa, Oklahoma. He had married her during their junior year at the University of Oklahoma, and he missed her terribly. She had become pregnant just before he left for Fort Benning, which meant she was due in about a month. Carr had definitely mixed emotions about their separation at this critical time in their marriage. He desperately wanted to be there for the birth of their first child, but also feared the complications that would ensue. He could probably get emergency leave to fly home for the birth, but then he would still have to come back to Nam and finish serving out his tour. That meant another tearful heart-wrenching good-bye, a longer time till he was home for good, and probably a whole new assignment when he got back in country, with new men under him and new duties to learn.

He knew Sarah was in good hands, and he trusted her parents to see that she and the baby got the best care possible. There was no military base close to Tulsa, so she would have the baby in a civilian hospital. That would cost him far more money, but he felt that she would probably get better medical care that way. Although he hated to admit it, the idea of being here in Nam during the birth relieved him of the constant worry and endless preparations leading up to the birth. When he got home, he would have a child, without any hassles. It was kind of like taking your broken-down car to an excellent mechanic and getting it back the next day in excellent running condition, rather than spending hours in the driveway trying to fix it yourself when you didn't really know what you were doing. Then he chastised himself for comparing such a blessed event involving his lovely wife to automotive repairs, and flicked his ear as punishment.

Regardless, before he had left for Nam he and Sarah had discussed the issue, since they knew the child would be born while he was little more than halfway through his tour. They had both agreed that it was better that he stay in country, to finish up where he started, rather than risk the long trip home and the possible problems that might entail. "Go there," she had told him, "get it done, and come home." He had already told her he did not intend to make the Army a career, so this would be a "one and done."

In her letter she had described her bulging belly, and avoided complaining about the physical toll of the pregnancy. Instead she had slyly hinted at the growing size of her breasts and hoped he would still find her desirable when he returned. He had assured her that his love for her was unassailable, no matter what she looked like, and had suggested she meet him at the airport with a mattress strapped to her back. He smiled to himself as he thought about her, and daydreamed about their honeymoon. A fly landed on his nose, bringing him back to reality. He swatted at the pesky insect, and looked around at his platoon's weary deployment.

Carr watched Samples fold his letter and add it to a stack of printed documents, sliding them all into a large manila envelope and sealing it before dropping it in the platoon's outgoing mail bag hanging inside the cargo hatch. He put his helmet on, and then picked up his rifle, jumped down, and strolled over toward Carr. Samples was a little less than medium height, but wiry and strong.

9

He walked with a quiet confidence that was well-earned. He had taught Carr a lot, especially when they had been forced to depend on each other while trapped behind enemy lines in the Crescent.

"Still no word?" Samples asked when he reached to edge of the ramp. Carr picked up his own rifle and helmet and stepped out on the ramp, shaking his head.

"Nope," Carr answered, wiping his forehead on his sleeve before plopping the helmet on. "I guess when the convoy finally passes us, we'll be allowed to head back. Meanwhile, it's hurry up and wait."

"Well, it's done," Samples announced seriously, apropos of nothing.

"What's done?"

"My marriage. I just signed the divorce papers." Samples' face was grim but determined.

"I thought you weren't going to give her a divorce," Carr commented carefully. Although Samples had said he had declined to divorce her just to punish her, Carr suspected Samples had actually hoped for some sort of reconciliation. His reaction after receiving the occasional letter from home had led Carr to believe that Samples' wife was not similarly inclined.

"Changed my mind," Sample replied simply. "Time to move on."

"Probably for the best," Carr told him. He didn't want to say too much on the subject, for fear of saying the wrong thing.

Samples turned and squinted at the sun getting low in the western sky. "Convoy better come by pretty soon," he remarked. "Don't want to be here after dark."

"Roger that," Carr agreed. They were currently very near the location where the gooks had set up an ambush back in May, two days before the big battle in the Crescent, and the rubber plantation provided easy unobserved access for the enemy. This was definitely not a good place to spend the night. Carr remembered the nights he and Samples had spent in the Crescent together, when they had gotten separated from their unit and had been presumed dead in an APC that had caught fire. Their trek through the enemy-infested woods back to American lines had been harrowing, but it had created a very strong relationship between the two men. Carr stepped off the ramp and walked around to the front, where his driver, Fred Aiello, had the trim vane down and the engine cover up, checking the engine for the fourth time today. Samples followed him.

"Problems?" Carr asked Aiello.

"No, I don't think so. But I think we're going to need new injectors before long." Aiello lowered the engine cover and latched it shut. The two of them walked back around to join Sergeant Samples in the center of the formation. All the tracks needed maintenance, even the one-four, which had replaced the one burned in the Crescent. The one-four, he had been told, was an in-country rebuild, so much of it probably had many miles on it still. Technically the one-four was the platoon's heavy weapons squad, but all that really meant was that they carried the platoon's 90mm recoilless rifle, a bazooka-like weapon that was almost never used. With constant missions and no good location to work on them, the tracks were being worn out. Carr suspected that the long-rumored withdrawal from Viet Nam might be lowering the priority for investments in maintenance and repair.

All three looked up at the sound of a helicopter coming from the east. Everyone was a little gun-shy about senior officers surreptitiously inspecting their operations. While Masters had been caught by a guy in a jeep, it was more common for colonels and generals to be flying around in choppers, looking for something to criticize.

"Huey," Samples announced, long before Carr could determine the type of chopper by either sight or sound. Senior officers always flew in the Light Observation Helicopters, which the soldiers called "loaches," from the abbreviation LOH. The bigger Hueys, sometimes called "slicks," were mostly used to haul troops or casualties. A moment later Carr spotted the bird, and it indeed was a slick. It didn't have a red cross on the nose, so it wasn't a medevac. It was headed southwest, from Dau Tieng to probably Cu Chi, and would pass well south of Carr's platoon as it flew over the Boi Loi

11

Woods. Lacking anything better to do, the three men just watched the helicopter buzz through the sky, like a brown whale suspended from an almost invisible disc of spinning rotors.

"Oh, shit!" Aiello blurted. Carr had heard it, too. The chopper's engine song had skipped a beat. For a moment Carr thought it might just be a hiccup, but then the roar of the turbine ceased abruptly, and only the whoosh of the blades could be heard. The chopper wobbled and began settling, the fuselage rotating horizontally it sank toward the forest below. The rotor blades continued to pinwheel, but as they lost speed the helicopter dropped more rapidly, until finally it disappeared from sight. Carr heard the distant sound of tree branches breaking, and waited for inevitable fireball and smoke, but those never came.

"Did you see that?" Eberhart shouted from the top of the track. Spec Four Earnie Eberhart was the platoon's RTO, or radio-telephone operator.

"Call it in," Carr ordered him. "Tell them it went down straight south of our location, about three miles out. No fire or explosion." Carr dug into his pants cargo pocket and pulled out his lensatic compass. Unfolding it, he raised it to his eye and shot an azimuth toward where he had last seen the chopper. "One-seventy-five" he said, more to himself as a reminder than to anyone standing near him.

While Eberhart jumped down through the cargo hatch to use the track's radio, Carr continued to watch the area to their south, hoping he wouldn't see a belated puff of smoke.

"Think they landed okay?" Aiello asked nervously.

"That's the middle of the Boi Lois," Samples said judiciously. "Not a lot of good landing zones there. But since it didn't blow up or burn, there might be survivors."

"Man, I would hate to have been on that chopper," Aiello said. "Those things just aren't safe."

"Yeah," Samples said sarcastically, "not like an APC dodging mines and RPGs all day."

"APCs don't fall out of the sky," Aiello retorted.

12

"Good point," Carr agreed. "I guess."

Eberhart stuck his head out of the cargo hatch and called, "Battalion says to stand by and be ready to move. They're checking with Higher."

Carr turned to Samples. "Aaron, get the men mounted up and fire up the tracks. They're going to have us go to the crash site."

"You think so?" Samples asked, and then said, "Yeah, you're right." He turned slowly around the center of the site and yelled, "Mount up! Get ready to move out!" Rancy ran back from across the road and headed to the one-four, still clutching his fake Rolex.

Aiello raised the trim vane and locked it into place, then climbed up it and dropped down into the driver's compartment to start the engine. Sergeant Montoya, A13's squad leader, ran back from A14 where he had been talking to Spec Four Reyes, that track's squad leader. Spec Four John Allman, the platoon medic, was in the machine gun turret, but he dropped down to get his aid bag. Carr knew that PFC Merrill would soon return from his OP in the rubber.

"We going after the chopper?" Montoya asked.

"Probably," Carr told him. "Waiting on Higher to make a decision."

Montoya nodded knowingly. Carr stepped away from the track to a position where he could see the entire platoon. All of the tracks had dark smoke coming from the exhausts, and the last few men were climbing aboard, including Merrill, who arrived breathless.

"What's happening?" Merrill gasped as he climbed up the side of the track. Having been in the rubber, facing the other way, he had not seen the crash.

"Chopper went down in the Boi Loi," Montoya told him succinctly. "Take the fifty." Merrill climbed over the cupola and took his position behind the fifty caliber machine gun so Allman could get his medical supplies ready.

Eberhart popped up again and looked around for Carr. When he saw him, he yelled, "Battalion says to go for it."

13

Carr nodded, and ran to climb up onto his seat atop the track. He exchanged his steel helmet for the CVC—combat vehicle crew—helmet with built-in headphones and keyed the mike. "We're heading south, on line," he told the rest of the platoon. "Let's go bust some jungle."

*****

"*Di-di mau!*" Samples yelled at the Coke kids and other civilians milling around along the road as the one-one track lined up with the others at the edge of the road. As instructed, the Vietnamese scattered to either side of the formation to watch the platoon roar across the road through the low brush and grass along the verge and plunge into the wood line. Samples held his rifle across his lap with one hand and pressed his helmet down with the other as the track bucked and rolled across the uneven ground and crushed the smaller trees and bushes of the Boi Loi Woods. The squad leader, Sergeant Art Jamison, sat in front of him with a CVC helmet, using the intercom to pass instructions to PFC Dale Gunn, the driver. Spec Four Simon Greenberg was in the turret, clutching the dual handles of the fifty-cal, with PFC Roland Sweet standing in the cargo hatch behind him ready to pass him more ammo if necessary. Spec Four Greg Hicks and PFC Bob Crosby sat on ammo cases along the other side of the cargo hatch.

To keep in sight of each other in the thick woods, the four tracks maintained an interval of about thirty feet. Samples had told Jamison to take the far right side of the formation. To their left was the undermanned one-four, with Spec Four Carlos Reyes as the acting squad leader, and then the one-three carrying Lieutenant Carr. On the far left was Sergeant Rich Reedy's one-two. The roar of the diesel engines, the clatter of the track blocks over the road wheels, and the snapping of limbs made conversations impossible, but talking wasn't necessary—everyone knew what to do. Sergeant Samples, just like the rest of the platoon, was sweeping his eyes back and forth, searching for any potential danger while simultaneously staying on line with the other tracks and seeking out the best path

14

through the trees. Busting jungle was fun, but probably the most dangerous thing they could do. Not only was it possible to rush right into an enemy ambush or become a target for snipers, they risked getting hit by flying tree limbs, or, even worse, hitting a mogator tree. Mogators were a particularly vicious species of large red ants that nested in trees instead of the ground, and when disturbed they all dropped down and attacked anyone they could find with their huge sharp mandibles. They didn't sting, they just bit like hell, and their instinct was to climb and bite at the same time.

The platoon had gone only a couple hundred yards into the woods when the one-four track became today's first victim of mogators. Suddenly the track stopped and all the crew jumped off, swatting at their bodies and ripping off their shirts. While sympathizing with their plight, Samples joined the rest of the platoon in laughing at their antics. PFC Rancy, one of the newest members of the platoon, dropped his pants to brush off the ants crawling up his legs. Samples gave them a minute to rid themselves of their tormenters and put their uniforms back on, then yelled, "We don't have time for this shit! Mount up and move out." The one-four's crew reluctantly climbed back on their tracks, brushing ants off the seats and top of the track and occasionally yelping as the residual insects found their marks. The platoon resumed it's slow, difficult push through the heavy forest, crashing through the brush and pushing down the smaller trees.

Through the passing trees Samples caught glimpses of Lieutenant Carr checking his compass and then relaying course corrections to the platoon's drivers and squad leaders. The platoon didn't have enough CVC helmets for Samples to have his own, but he could hear some of the radio traffic blaring up from the wall-mounted radio inside the track. The platoon shifted a little to the left and kept on driving forward. Samples looked up, trying to see through the canopy of leaves and judge the color of the sky. The blue was fading. Either the sun was setting, or clouds were moving in. Probably both. He heard a helicopter zoom overhead in the same direction they were going. He guessed that there would be all sorts of choppers circling the crash site, unable to land because of all the trees. At least the platoon had immediate air support if needed. That is, until it got dark, which wouldn't be very long now.

Samples heard the distant sound of a rifle being fired, followed by the drawn-out "brrraapp" of a minigun returning the fire. "Shit!" Samples muttered. Sweet shot him a worried look, and Samples just nodded morosely. There was garbled traffic on the radio below, and when it ended, Samples tapped Jamison on the shoulder. "What did they say?"

Jamison half-turned and told him, "The choppers see survivors, and they're taking some ground fire from gooks about five hundred meters from the crash site. They want us to hurry."

"Easy for them to say," Samples remarked as their track pushed its way between two massive tree trunks.

There seemed to be more light ahead of them, and Samples hoped that meant the forest was thinning, which would allow them to increase their speed. But as they approached the lighter area, the tracks actually began to move slower. While the trees were smaller here, the brush was thicker, and the ground was softer. They broke out into an area that was almost devoid of trees, a long strip of clearing covered with thick green leafy plants and the definite scent of water.

"It's a fucking creek," Greenberg noted loudly as the tracks slowed to a crawl.

Samples nodded. Although they couldn't actually see it, he knew that somewhere under all that brush was a small stream, probably a tributary of the Saigon River that flowed to their east.

"Hold up," Carr said over the radio. "One-four, proceed slowly. Let's see if we can get across."

Samples shook his head. A few days earlier they had gone into a different section of the Boi Lois and brought a bridge-laying tank to cross a similar stream, perhaps this same one. The bridge-layer got stuck before it ever got close enough to scissor the bridge into place. This was the rainy season, and the streams had all left their banks and soaked the surrounding terrain.

Samples jumped down and ran over to the one-four, putting himself in front of it to act as a ground-guide. The track began edging forward as Samples led it through the few remaining trees.

16

He could feel his boots sinking an inch or so with every step, and water began seeping into the drain holes on the side of his insteps. In theory an M-113 could ford a stream, and even float, but these tracks had lost that ability with the removal of the side skirts and bilge pumps. And even if they hadn't, that ability depended on having a firm bank and stream bed. This area, however, was more of a swamp, and despite the track blocks spreading the weight of the vehicle over a greater area than wheels would, there was a limit to how far they could move through such unstable ground. And sure enough, they quickly found that limit.

Samples turned around to see the fountain of mud being thrown up behind the one-four as its treads spun without moving the track forward. The belly of the APC was now resting on the ground while its treads dug a muddy trench. The one-four was definitely stuck. "God-mother-fuckin'-damn!" Samples cursed. He signaled to Knox, the driver, to cut the engine.

Lieutenant Carr ran up, his feet making squishing sounds as he arrived next to Samples. "Not good," he remarked, surveying the situation.

"We ain't gonna get across this son-of-a-bitch," Samples warned him. "Not with the tracks, anyway." He looked up at Knox, who had stood up in the driver's compartment and was looking to Samples for orders. Reyes had jumped down and was inspecting the mud-encased road wheels. "Have the one-one hook up and try to pull you back out," he told them.

Carr was looking up and down the long clearing as shadows grew longer. "Maybe we could find another place to cross that's better," he suggested doubtfully.

"Yeah," Samples responded, "and maybe we can get more tracks stuck, too. Meanwhile we're wasting time. It's going to be dark soon." From here they could see the helicopters circling over the crash site, at least another mile away. Samples saw a loach, a slick, and a Cobra gunship, all staying fairly high because of the occasional ground fire. As he watched, the Cobra made another pass with his minigun, the stream of red tracers raking the woods below.

17

Eberhart, the radio antenna bouncing over his head, ran up while listening to the handset. "Colonel wants to know what the hold-up is," he relayed to Carr.

"We're taking a coffee break," Carr said, obviously annoyed by the question. He scowled. "Tell him the area is impassable for tracks, and we're continuing dismounted."

Samples nodded his understanding, and ran back to the edge of the clearing where most of the crews had jumped down, either to help hook up the tow cable from the one-four to the one-one, or to form a hasty perimeter. He signaled the men to listen up. "Okay, we're moving on dismounted. We'll leave the driver and one TC with each track. Art, you're the TC for the one-one, and acting platoon sergeant. The rest of you guys get all your gear, your canteens, ammo, and some C's. Everybody grab some smoke grenades and frags, and some star shells and flares. We don't know how long we'll be out there without the tracks." Each man, other than Crosby, carried an old Claymore mine bag filled with magazines, usually fourteen or fifteen, each loaded with nineteen rounds. Crosby, their sole M-79 gunner, had an ammo vest filled with the large stubby rounds his "bloop" gun required. Samples hoped that would be enough.

Samples waited until Gunn had swung the one-one around and backed up toward the one-four before he joined the rest of the men in loading up with the equipment they might need. Meanwhile Jamison and Reyes hooked up one of the braided steel tow cables to the tow hooks on the back of the tracks, connecting the one-one to the one-four. Samples watched as the two squad leaders expertly guided their drivers to begin the process of pulling the one-four out of the mud. Samples joined Carr and the rest of the men on the edge of the clearing as they watch the one-one edge forward until the tow cable was taut, and then both tracks increased their rpm slowly, the one-one's automatic transmission in Drive, and the one-four in Reverse. With black smoke pouring from the exhaust pipes on the top right front of the tracks, they slowly began to move, mud flinging in front of the one-four in twin sprays from the spinning treads. Suddenly the tow cable went slack as the one-four gained traction.

A cheer went up from the men, and Carr told Samples, "Let's go." But before they could all get started, Samples heard a shout from Dale Gunn.

"I think I broke it!" the one-one driver yelled.

"Broke what?" Samples yelled back at him.

"The transmission. It won't go into Drive anymore, just Reverse."

"Are you fucking kidding me? Jesus H. Christ! What else can go wrong?"

"Don't ask," Carr told him. He gave Samples the look that told him he should calm down. "He'll just have to back it out. They can't stay out here in the dark anyway. Once they get to the road, a couple of them can tow him to Dau Tieng where the mechanics can fix it. Then they can come pick us up in the morning."

While Carr went over to give Jamison the plan, Samples got the dismounts organized and gave them their marching orders. He looked across the clearing at the now-gloomy woods beyond and shook his head. A quick headcount told him they had only fourteen men to now go to the crash site, armed only with rifles and a single M-79 grenade launcher. The platoon had three M-60 light machine guns, but rarely used them. One was mounted on the one-four in front of the driver, and the other two were stowed inside the one-one and one-three. Samples had considered bringing one along, but the extra weight of the gun and its ammo would slow them down. These were mech guys, and unlike Samples, not accustomed to patrolling at night on foot. He would have to keep a close eye on them, and give them a lot of OJT—on-the-job training.

THREE

Lieutenant Carr looked up and tried to judge how much daylight they had left. Discouragingly he estimated it was only an hour and a half or two hours until full darkness. He rejoined the men clustered at the edge of the clearing, where Sergeant Samples was giving them advice on how they would be operating.

"Don't we need to spread out?" he asked Samples. The wiry sergeant shook his head.

"Not till we get across the creek," he said. "We ought to go single file, so if one guy gets stuck, the others can pull him back out. I'll go first." Before Carr could object, Samples plunged forward into the waist-high foliage of the clearing. "Sir," he called back over his shoulder, "why don't you be tail-gunner, make sure everyone makes it across." Carr sighed. He wondered who was really in charge of the platoon, but acknowledged that Samples was right. He watched Samples push through the leaves, at first striding purposefully, but gradually slowing down as his boots started sinking into the muck. One by one the other soldiers followed. Carr looked back to watch the tracks departing, with Sergeant Jamison sitting behind the one-one's driver, facing rearward so he could give Gunn directions as he backed the boxy vehicle back down the trail they had created as they arrived. It had taken several minutes for Gunn to get its rear end pointed the right way.

When it was finally his turn, Carr fell in behind Doc Allman and waded out through the plants, seeking firm footing that he couldn't really see. Within a few feet he felt the ground soften and his boots making deeper and deeper impressions in the wet soil. Soon it was like walking through peanut butter, the mud sucking at his feet and clinging to his boots until his feet felt like they were incased in lead. It was a struggle to maintain his balance, but he could see that the men ahead of him were having the same problems. He heard water splashing, but never crossed what he would call a stream, just a patch of mud that was wetter than the rest of the mud. Finally, as he neared the line of trees that marked the other edge of the clearing, the footing firmed up and he was able to scramble onto solid ground again. The other men were waiting for him, taking a minute to scrape the mud off their boots against the tree trunks or with sticks they had found. Carr stomped his feet to knock the worst of the mud off, and then took out his compass to check their bearings again.

"Okay, spread out," he instructed the men. "We're heading that way." He motioned in the direction indicated by his compass. It was going to be difficult to maintain their bearing, since here in the woods there were no distant landmarks to key on, just random trees and bushes.

"Move quietly," Samples added, "and keep a sharp eye out. We know there're gooks out here somewhere."

"Mogators, too," Sergeant Reedy added with a chuckle.

Carr gave the hand signal to move out, and the men expertly spread out on line and began walking forward, their weapons at the ready, their eyes constantly moving. Eberhart, with his PRC-25 backpack radio, moved next to Carr on his right, and Doc Allman was on his left. Samples was farther down the line, ensuring that all the men were in sight of at least one of the two leaders. The undergrowth was thick here, impeding their movement, but as they gained some distance from the stream, it began to thin out a little at ground level, while the canopy overhead grew denser. As silently as possible, the men slipped through the woods, avoiding vines and spiny bushes, and dodging around tree trunks while maintaining their course and staying on line with their buddies. Every five minutes or so Carr would check the compass again, and gave minor course corrections with hand signals. The noise of the helicopters circling over the crash site really helped, in more ways than one. Not only did the sound help guide them through the dense forest, it also masked the sounds they were unavoidably making as they pushed through the woods: the crunching of feet on fallen leaves, the thump

21

and clink of equipment, the muttered curse when someone got caught by a wait-a-minute vine.

Judging by the sound of the choppers, they were getting close, Carr decided, but the light was noticeably fading as well. Not for the first time, he hit the bottom of his rifle's magazine with his left palm to ensure it was properly seated, and then hit the forward assist button with the heel of his hand to make sure the bolt was locked in place. With his right thumb he found the firing selector lever, checking to see that it was on SAFE, but could be switched to SEMI quickly if needed. Thus he was prepared, if not really ready, when he heard a shot ring out.

Carr dived to the ground, clicking the lever to SEMI as he looked around for the source of the shot. Analyzing the sound, he realized it had been an M-16 that fired, not an AK-47, and immediately feared that one of his men had fired by accident, revealing their location to the enemy. But that first shot was followed by several more, from different weapons.

"Gooks!" a voice shouted, and Carr was pretty sure it came from Sergeant Montoya, the third squad leader. He had been on the far left of the line.

A burst of automatic fire from their left front was clearly an AK-47, and Carr, like all the rest, opened up in that general direction, firing single shots closely spaced. It was called suppressive fire, and was Army doctrine in Viet Nam. Keep the enemy's heads down, and keep so much lead flying that maybe someone will get lucky. Carr couldn't see anyone, but that was normal in these jungle firefights. In his training, his tactics instructors had always insisted that the proper response to an ambush was to launch a frontal assault. Carr had always thought that was suicidal, but in this case it seemed the only possible solution. They had to keep moving and get to the crash site, so there was no time to withdraw or employ fire and maneuver. In an instant the decision was made. He pushed himself up into a crouching position.

"Wheel left!" he shouted. "Advance on line! Keep firing!"

After a brief hesitation, the other men joined him, and the line swung like a gate hinged over by Sergeant Montoya. Carr and the men fired as they walked forward, keeping up a steady stream of bullets that pierced the bushes and thudded into the tree trunks. When they had gone fifty yards and received no further return fire, he halted the advance.

"Over here," Sergeant Reedy called out. "We got him."

"Wait here," Carr told the men around him, and then hustled through the trees to where Reedy and Samples stood looking down. Between them was a Viet Cong soldier crumpled on the ground in a fetal position, his black pajamas soaked with blood, and his AK-47 lying beside him, its wooden stock shattered by a bullet.

"By himself?" Carr asked doubtfully.

"Not likely," Samples replied. "Maybe the rest di-died."

"We haven't got time to look for them," Carr said. "They're probably headed for the chopper, too. We need to get there first."

As he turned to give the men the order to regroup and head toward the crash site, he heard a screech and yelps of pain from the other side of a large clump of bushes. Cautiously Carr darted around the right side of the foliage, while Samples and Reed went around the other side. Carr closed up behind a thick tree trunk and leaned forward with his rifle to take a look. In a semi-clear area under a small young tree was another VC, this one writhing on the ground hitting himself all over his body, his AK-47 abandoned a few feet away. Samples and Reedy appeared a few feet on the opposite side of the man, and stared at the man rolling around like he was on fire.

"Mogators," Samples commented, nodding. Looking closer in the fading light, Carr now saw the horde of red ants that were attacking the man. When the VC finally got to his hands and knees and tried crawling toward Samples and Reedy, they backed away, not wanting to get any of the ants on themselves.

"Should I put him out of his misery?" Samples asked, pointing his M-16 down at the man.

"No," Carr told him, "let him squirm." The fact of the matter was that he didn't want to be responsible for shooting a man in cold blood like that. A prisoner would be a great inconvenience right now, but he might be useful later. They watched the man struggle to

23

his feet, still slapping and brushing at his body to rid himself of the tormenting insects.

"Chieu Hoi?" Reedy asked the man, keeping his rifle trained on the man. The South Vietnamese government's Chieu Hoi program gave special privileges to Viet Cong and North Vietnamese Army soldiers who voluntarily surrendered.

The VC ignored the question. Carr noted that the man was stockier than most of the Vietnamese he had met, and this face looked somehow different. He was definitely Oriental, and only about five foot two, but not typically Vietnamese. He wasn't really concerned, since he knew there were a lot of mixed-race people in Viet Nam, whose ancestors included Chinese, Japanese, and French. As the man flicked off the last of the ants, he looked at the three Americans who surrounded him. His expression was a mix of anger, disdain, and humiliation, but Carr detected no fear or acceptance of defeat. The man reached over with his left hand and gingerly probed his right shoulder, and only then did Carr notice the wetness of the sleeve of his shirt. Blood was soaking the thin black fabric around a small hole in the shoulder of the garment.

"He's wounded," Reedy noted unnecessarily.

"Bring him with us," Carr ordered. "Have we got something to tie him up with?"

"I've got some spare bootlaces in my pocket," Samples said, reaching down.

"That'll work." Carr whistled to bring the other men over while Samples quickly tied the man's hands behind his back, slapping the back of his head when he initially resisted.

Eberhart ran up, the handset of his radio pressed to his ear, and announced, "Eltee, Battalion has contact with the choppers now. They asked if you can pop smoke."

"I got it," Reedy said, pulling a smoke grenade off his pistol belt. He pulled the pin and tossed it over to where the mogators were still swarming. Immediately yellow smoke began billowing out of the cylinder and drifting up through the trees.

Carr took another quick look at this compass, and then motioned the men forward. Reedy got behind the prisoner and prodded him with the barrel of his M-16 to get him moving. The other men looked at the prisoner with undisguised curiosity, but without any anger or hate, Carr was glad to see. Once again the patrol moved out, threading their way through the undergrowth toward the crash site.

"They see it," Eberhart told Carr after acknowledging a radio message. "They say we're about four hundred meters out."

"Have they got contact with the downed chopper?" Carr asked. "Can they let them know we're coming in?"

"I'll ask," Eberhart replied, and began calling. Meanwhile the men continued to shove their way through the forest, alert to any possible attack from the dimness of the woods. Carr kept glancing over at the prisoner, who was reluctantly cooperating and occasionally twitching as lingering ants found a place to clamp their sharp jaws on his skin.

Eberhart said, "Roger, out," into the handset and then told Carr what he had learned. "The crashed chopper still has a working radio, so they know we're coming. So far they haven't received any incoming, but the crew chief has got their M-60 ready." Eberhart paused. "They said 'the girls are okay.' I don't know what they meant by that."

"Girls?" Doc Allman blurted. "What girls?"

"Want me to ask?"

"No," Carr told them, "we'll find out soon enough."

The mysterious mention of girls quickly spread up and down the line of young men until Sergeant Samples finally ordered the men to shut up and pay attention. Carr wasn't surprised at their curiosity. Most of his soldiers were still in their teens, and their interest in females was at its peak.

Within twenty minutes Carr heard the strong baritone voice of Dupar Johnson over to his right. "I see it," he announced. "Over this way." The formation shifted to the right and pushed on, with

Carr peering through the trees in the fading light until he, too, saw the glint of bare aluminum torn loose from the olive drab fuselage.

"Hey, guys," Carr yelled, "we're coming in. Don't shoot."

"Come ahead," a voice responded.

*****

Aaron Samples pushed a leafy limb out of his way and let it flip back behind him. Only then did he see the helicopter, which was standing mostly upright, wedged between trees and covered with leaf debris. Its landing skids were about a foot off the ground. The next thing he saw was a large burly soul brother holding an M-60 machine gun like it was a toy, the belt of ammo draped over his shoulder. Despite his menacing size and weapon, he had a friendly smile on his face. He was wearing a flight suit, and Samples surmised he was the chopper's crew chief/door gunner. On the ground just under the nose of the chopper was the inert form of a dead man wearing a flight suit and a flight helmet.

Still inside the cabin of the chopper, peeking around the bulk of the door gunner, Samples saw three small faces staring at him with fearful curiosity. From their features, Samples guessed they were Japanese, and their long hair and bangs marked them as female, but the oversized flight suits they were wearing masked their small bodies. He guessed they were in their twenties, but he had never been good at estimating the ages of Asian women. One of them, incongruously, had blond hair. Standing next to the door gunner was a short balding man with wire-rimmed glasses, clutching a thick brown leather briefcase to his chest. Samples saw the black oak leaf on his collar that identified him as a lieutenant colonel. Through the shattered Plexiglas of the pilot's compartment he saw a mass of red hair bobbing around, but couldn't identify the person.

Having taken two seconds to survey the situation, Samples went into action. "Form a perimeter!" he bellowed, waving his arm in a circle that encompassed the aircraft. "Reedy, sit the prisoner down on the skid and secure him somehow."

26

While Lieutenant Carr approached the chubby colonel, Samples went to the door gunner and nodded a greeting. "So what's the situation?" he asked, pausing to read the name tape on the man's flight suit and note the E-6 rank pin. "Sergeant Pastorini?" He asked to make sure he was pronouncing it correctly, and also because it seemed inappropriate for a black man.

"Copilot's dead," the man replied in a surprisingly gentle voice. "Pilot's got his legs trapped. The nurse is trying to help him."

Samples checked to make sure the men were deploying properly, and then looked over Pastorini's shoulder. He raised his eyebrow at the man as he nodded toward the three girls in the cabin.

"The Girlfriends," Pastorini explained with a shrug. "USO. They did a show at the 'O' club, and were heading back to Cu Chi. Their band and roadies went in a truck."

"The girlfriends?"

"That's the name of their group. They sing Motown and girl group songs. Don't speak much English, though."

Samples looked over and saw that Lieutenant Carr and the colonel had stepped a few feet away to have a deep conversation of some sort. Samples tilted his head toward them and asked, "Who's he?"

Pastorini rolled his eyes a little. "Just catching a ride. I don't know him, but I can tell you he's not a friendly guy."

From the way Pastorini said it, Samples inferred that Pastorini's opinion of the colonel was very negative, for some reason. He couldn't hear what the colonel was telling Carr, but the tone of his voice came through, and combined with his body language, Samples knew he was giving the lieutenant a very hard time.

The nurse stuck her head out of the pilots' compartment. Samples saw a mass of frizzy orange hair, a plain face sprinkled with freckles, and piercing green eyes. "Hey," she said in greeting to Samples. Looking over at Pastorini, she said, "Preacher, can you and him come help me up here? This fucking instrument panel's not moving."

Samples was a little surprised, and shocked, by the nurse's language, but he had seen the captain's bars on her uniform, so he wasn't going to say anything to her about it. Instead he looked over at Pastorini and said, "Preacher?"

"My nickname," the man replied simply as he set the machine gun down and coiled the ammo belt around it. Samples laid his own rifle down next to it. "Come on." Together they climbed into the chopper and moved aside as the nurse crawled out to let them have room to work. Samples gave her a quick once-over, noting that her name was Gaither and her jungle fatigues fit well around a decent, but not spectacular, figure. Then he followed Pastorini through the opening to the pilots' compartment. The black man was so big that Samples could only get part way in. He could now see the pilot, his helmet off and his eyes squeezed shut with pain. A tree limb had crushed in the side of the chopper right at the instrument panel, and the pilot's legs were wedged beneath the aluminum and bleeding badly.

"I'll try to lift it up," Pastorini said, "and you try to pull him out."

"Roger," Samples said, reaching out to grasp the man's shoulder and bicep. His safety harness had already been unhooked, and the man leaned toward Samples in an effort to help. He was very young, blonde, and slight of build. His flight suit had a striped bar insignia that indicated his rank to be some kind of Warrant Officer.

Pastorini squirmed around, seeking the best leverage position, then grunted as he tugged at the panel, making it creak in protest. Samples pulled on the pilot's shoulder and tried to find some way to brace his legs. The pilot screamed through gritted teeth as he pushed on the seat to help Samples pull him free. Pastorini let out a powerful groan as he tugged harder, and suddenly the pilot was loose. Samples fell backwards as he dragged the pilot through the opening into the main cabin.

"Careful, Sergeant," the nurse commanded him.

"Doing my best, ma'am," Samples apologized as he regained his footing and slid the man over by the door. Looking down, he saw that the young man's eyes were closed, and at first he feared the man had died, but he saw the man's chest rise with a slow breath, and was relieved. "Here," he asked, "or move him outside?"

"Let's get him away from the bird," Pastorini suggested as he climbed out of the front. "It could still go up if the gooks start shooting at it." Samples hadn't considered that possibility, and suddenly had an urge to get back into the woods. Together he and Pastorini gently lifted the unconscious pilot and carried him a few yards away, laying him down on the brown leaves covering a bare patch of earth near a large tree trunk. The nurse squatted down by the man's legs and began probing them with her bare hands.

Doc Allman appeared and squatted down beside her. "Need help, ma'am? I've got my aid bag."

Samples and Pastorini gave them room, and Pastorini retrieved his M-60. Samples picked up his rifle and left him to circle the chopper and check on his perimeter guards. When he came back around toward the front he met Lieutenant Carr coming the other way with fire in his eyes.

"That son of a bitch!" Carr whispered angrily.

"The colonel?" Samples asked, knowing the answer already.

"He thinks he's in charge, but he doesn't know shit!"

"He outranks you, so what are you going to do?"

Carr grimaced and visibly slowed his breathing. "We'll have to just work around him."

"What do you mean, 'we,' paleface?" Samples joked. "You officers will just have to work it out between yourselves."

"Eat shit, Aaron," Carr responded with a grin. "Remember, the shit rolls downhill, and you're next in line."

"Yes, sir, yes, sir, three bags full, sir."

Carr rolled his eyes. "Come on," he said, "let's find out what Higher wants us to do next."

29

FOUR

"Did you report our situation?" Carr asked Eberhart, who had been hovering near the wounded pilot, observing as the nurse and Allman ministered to him.

"Yes, sir," Eberhart told him. "Told them about the dead copilot, the wounded pilot, and that everyone else is okay, even the girls. Told them about the prisoner, too. They said to wait."

"Of course," Carr said, shaking his head. "So what are we supposed to do while they get their act together?" That question was rhetorical, and Eberhart prudently ignored it. Samples came up and stood beside Carr, and together they looked down at the now-conscious pilot, whose handsome face was stoically grimacing as the red-headed woman and Doc Allman tended to his legs.

"How bad, Doc," Carr asked.

The nurse turned her head and shot Carr a defiant look. "His left tibia is shattered, his right knee is broken, and he's got numerous cuts and abrasions. So it's bad, lieutenant." Her tone was a little angry, and a little officious. Doc Allman kept his head down, and Carr understood why. This woman didn't take shit from anyone. When she turned back to the pilot, Carr looked over at Samples, who just grinned at him. So he turned to look at the helicopter.

The prisoner sat at the tail end of the skid, his body secured to the skid support with some kind of strap Reedy had found on the chopper. The three Japanese girls were huddled together a few feet away, giggling and chattering in their own language, oblivious to the danger they were in. The colonel, whose name was Tarreyton, sat on the edge of the cabin floor, his briefcase sitting on the floor beside him. Tarreyton had his right hand firmly placed on the handle of the briefcase, ensuring no one could take it from him. Carr noted the metal CIB pinned to his chest, and wondered about it.

31

When they had first arrived, the man had announced himself to Carr as "Lieutenant Colonel Tarreyton, Deputy Assistant for Logistics." Carr wasn't sure what that job title really meant, but the man was apparently a highly-placed officer on Division staff. And Tarreyton obviously felt that his rank granted him all sorts of privileges, and made him the man ultimately in charge.

Tarreyton saw Carr looking at him, and swelled his chest. "What's your plan, lieutenant?" he demanded. "I need to get to Cu Chi ASAP."

"I understand, sir," Carr told him as patiently as he could muster. "We're waiting on instructions. My battalion CO is conferring with Brigade and Division."

"Do I need to get on the radio and get this situation unfucked?" Tarreyton snarled.

"The CO, Sir," Eberhart interrupted. The young RTO had just appeared at Carr's side, holding out the radio handset for Carr to take. Gratefully he took the hard plastic device and turned away from Tarreyton, the coiled cord pulling Eberhart with him. He listened to his company commander and made appropriate responses, then handed the mike back to Eberhart.

"Sergeant Samples," he said, beckoning his platoon sergeant. Because of the colonel's presence, he was being more formal than usual. He and Samples moved closer to Tarreyton, who stood up and joined them, his briefcase dangling from one hand.

"We are to hold here for the night," Carr told them. He could see by Tarreyton's expression he was about to object, so he continued before the colonel could say anything. "There's a company of Wolfhounds to our south, moving up to reinforce us. They should be here in about an hour or two. In the morning we'll clear an LZ to evacuate you and the others, colonel."

"In the morning?" Tarreyton yelped. "I need to get back tonight!"

Carr shrugged. "Not my decision, sir. My CO says it came down from Division."

32

Tarreyton sputtered, bringing the briefcase up to clutch to his chest. "How will you clear a landing zone?"

"Not sure, sir. I'm hoping the Wolfhounds are bringing some engineer tools or demolitions, or maybe they'll airlift something in, in the morning."

"You hope, they may. That's pretty weak, lieutenant. You need to come up with a better plan than that."

"I'm open to suggestions, sir," Carr replied, putting the onus on the blustering colonel.

"Do I have to do all the thinking here?" Tarreyton sniffed. "You're the field officer, they're your men, *you* put them to work right now."

"Excuse me, sir," Carr said through gritted teeth, "I'm going to inventory our resources." With that he turned away, tilting his head at Samples to follow him.

"Nice fellow," Samples said with a bland smile when they were far enough away that Tarreyton couldn't hear them.

"He's a fucking asshole!" Carr spat out. "And what is with that damn briefcase?"

"Probably got his dirty underwear in it," Samples suggested. "Or maybe secret plans to win the war."

Carr scoffed, and then took a deep breath to calm himself. "Okay, do we actually have anything that could be used to clear an LZ ourselves?"

Samples reached up and scratched his ear. "Not really. Some grenades, a couple bayonets, maybe something in the chopper. And I doubt the Wolfhounds have much either. Maybe some entrenching tools, a little C-4."

Carr looked at the surrounding forest, growing dimmer by the minute as night closed in. Many of the tree trunks were over two feet thick, difficult to cut down even with axes, and they would have to clear an area at least forty yards in diameter to allow a chopper to land. It would take a couple hours, at least, even if they had the right equipment.

33

Captain Gaither strode up to them. "You didn't tell me your prisoner was wounded," she confronted Carr.

"I, uh," Carr stumbled, caught off guard.

"Do you object if I tend to him?" she asked, clearly not expecting him to do so. Carr saw Samples smiling at her, out of her line of sight.

"Uh, no, ma'am, go ahead. Be careful, though."

She gave him a dismissive look and stomped over to the seated VC. When the man objected to her touching his shoulder, she snarled at him and he quickly relented. He was as intimidated by the woman as Carr was.

"I like her," Samples said quietly. "She gets shit done."

Carr didn't know what to say to that, so he changed the subject. "That door gunner?" he asked, looking over at the big man leaning against a tree.

"Pastorini?" Samples said.

"Pastorini? He doesn't look Italian."

"Southern Italy, I reckon," Samples suggested with a chuckle. "They call him Preacher, for some reason. Good man. Strong."

"And he's got an M-60. We can use the extra firepower. Do you think the gooks will try to attack us tonight?"

Samples shook his head slowly. "Who knows? But if I were a betting man, I'd say the odds are outstanding. The gooks own these woods, especially at night. Got bunkers and tunnels all over the place."

"Well, with a company of Wolfhounds, we can mount a pretty good defense." The Wolfhounds, the official nickname for two battalions of hard-core straight-leg infantry, had the reputation of being fierce warriors. And an entire company, over a hundred men, would certainly improve their defensive posture. "When they get here, I'll talk to their CO about how to set up the perimeter, maybe send out some LPs or even ambush patrols."

"Hope they get here soon," Samples said. "It'll be hard to deploy them in the dark. How far away are they?"

"The CO said they were only a few clicks south. What that means exactly, I don't know."

The two men stood there in the gathering gloom, pondering the possibilities. Carr saw that the nurse had the prisoner's shirt half off and was instructing Doc Allman on how to bandage the man's wounded shoulder. Allman knew his job, but was patiently following the captain's orders. The Girlfriends had been softly singing something about going to the chapel and getting married, but then they stopped. As he watched, one of the singers went over and tapped Captain Gaither on the shoulder. The girl looked a little anxious and pulled Gaither aside, speaking softly and gesturing with her hands in odd motions. At first the nurse seemed confused, and then she raised her head and nodded. She strode over to Carr and Samples, nodding to the sergeant before facing up to Carr.

"The ladies need to use the latrine," she informed him bluntly.

"Uh, we don't have a latrine out here," Carr answered, cursing himself for pointing out the obvious.

Gaither let out an exasperated sigh. "They've got to take a leak, lieutenant."

"Okay. So, uh. . ."

"They need privacy. I've seen how your men have been looking at them."

"Well, but. . ."

Samples jumped in to help him. "I'll have someone dig a cat hole and put a couple ponchos around it," he offered, smiling helpfully at the nurse.

"Good," she replied. "Do that, Sergeant."

"Yes, ma'am." He turned to the door gunner. "Preacher, can you go take over for one of my men on the perimeter and send him to me? Thanks." Pastorini grinned, shouldered the M-60, and took off into the woods. Gaither walked away to explain things to the three girls. Carr saw how Samples watched her walk away with far more attention than necessary.

"Aaron," he said, "don't *even* think about it."

"What, sir?"

Carr started to give him a lecture about fraternization, but the look of innocence on his sergeant's face dissuaded him. Instead he just shook his head and sighed. Samples was the oldest man in the platoon, and certainly the most experienced, so it was probably a waste of time for Carr to lecture him on anything.

*****

Samples surveyed the area around the chopper, looking for a place to set up the impromptu latrine. They were deep in the Boi Loi Woods, and the helicopter had slid down between the trees in an almost miraculous landing. There was no real clearing here, just spaces between the tree trunks that were often filled in by bushes and saplings. He noticed that a relative quiet had settled over the woods, as the last of the helicopters circling overhead had departed. He had finally zeroed in on a space near the tail rotor of the helicopter when PFC Roland Sweet jogged up to him.

"Yeah, Sarge? What do you need?" Sweet was one of the youngest guys in the platoon, which was saying something, since almost all were still in their teens. He was slightly built, and wore glasses, but was always ready to do whatever needed to be done. He also was usually ready to do things that didn't need to be done, especially if he thought they might be fun.

"You got your poncho?" Samples asked, still eyeing the surrounding area.

"Yep," Sweet responded, patting the rolled up plastic sheet that was tied to the back of his pistol belt.

Samples spotted something in the fading light and strolled over with Sweet following close behind. It was one of the tail rotor blades, sheared off when the chopper crashed down through the trees. It was about three feet long, and ragged at one end where it had broken from the rotor. He picked up the light-weight metal blade and handed it to Sweet.

"Use this to dig a cat hole over there by that big bush," he told the boy. "Make it about a foot deep, and a foot wide. Then string your poncho and mine around it to make a latrine for the ladies." Samples pulled his own poncho off his pistol belt and handed it to Sweet.

"Uh," Sweet said, apparently wanting ask a question, but then stopped. "Okay," he finally said, looking a little unsure, but willing to make the attempt.

"Have you got any C-rats toilet paper you can loan them?"

Sweet patted his pockets. "Yeah, I think so, Sarge."

"Good. Rock out."

While Sweet got to work, Samples walked over to where the nurse and Doc Allman were finishing up with the prisoner. As the gook shrugged back into his shirt, Samples noted the red star tattooed on his unwounded shoulder. *Dedicated communist, I guess,* he thought. Out loud he said to Captain Gaither, "The latrine should be ready in just a few, ma'am."

"Thank you, Sergeant," she replied with a warm smile that made Samples feel pretty good.

"Anything else I can do for you?" he asked.

"Besides get us the hell out of here?" she replied, still smiling. "No, I guess not."

"Just let me know," he assured her, wishing he could think of something else to say, just to continue the conversation. He didn't often get the chance to talk to women, especially American women, and he missed that. It looked like she was going to say something else to him, but instead cocked her head to one side to listen. Samples heard it, too. It was the sound of distant gunfire.

It began with a crackle of scattered shots, but quickly grew into a rolling thunder of many guns popping off simultaneously, interspersed with the small explosions of grenades. Samples slowly pivoted with his eyes closed, determining that the sounds came from almost directly south of them, far on the other side of the chopper they were standing next to. The firefight raged on, but from the low volume, Samples estimated it had to be occurring at least a couple miles away.

Carr ran up to where Samples and Gaither were standing. "Our Wolfhounds?" he asked, looking through the open cabin of the chopper into the woods beyond.

"Probably," Samples answered. "Don't know who else it could be."

"Not good," Carr commented.

"No, sir, not very good at all," Samples confirmed.

"You think it's the guys who were coming to our rescue?" Gaither asked. Samples was pleased that her voice carried no sign of panic or worry.

"Afraid so," Samples told her.

"That sucks," she said with a sigh. "So now what?"

"Eberhart!" Carr called out. The RTO was helping Sweet string up the ponchos for the latrine, but he immediately grabbed his rifle and trotted over to his platoon leader. "Check with Higher. See if that is our guys in contact to our south."

Eberhart nodded and began speaking into the handset.

"What is that noise, lieutenant?" Tarreyton demanded, stomping over to join the others.

"Contact, sir," Carr said. Samples could detect the anger hidden in the patient response. Before his lieutenant could say something he would regret, Samples jumped in.

"We think it's the Wolfhounds that were coming to reinforce us, sir," Samples explained to the chubby officer. "They must have run into some gooks."

"So you think they'll be delayed?" the colonel asked, still directing his questions at Carr.

38

"Definitely, sir," Samples told him. Even in the dim light of dusk Samples could see that Carr was about to explode at the colonel's obtuseness. Carr turned away, apparently so the colonel couldn't see the expression on his face, while pretending he was waiting for a report from Eberhart.

"For how long?" the colonel demanded, now turning toward Samples, who at least was listening to him.

"Hard to say, sir. Sounds like a pretty big firefight."

"Sir," Eberhart said, holding out the radio handset, "Battalion." Carr took the handset and stretched out the coiled cord as he moved away from the colonel. Samples could only hear Carr's end of the conversation, but it didn't sound good. Carr signed off and rejoined the colonel, the nurse, and Samples.

"They ran into a bunker complex," Carr told them solemnly. "They're going to pull back and call in arty."

"Are they still coming here?" Tarreyton asked anxiously.

"Not anytime soon," Carr told him. "They've got casualties, and don't know how large a force they're up against. They're guessing it's an NVA battalion, at least."

"They'll have to hunker down for the night," Samples said. He cocked his head to one side to listen to the distant roar, which seemed to be slackening. "Sounds like they're breaking contact. Not much else they can do in that situation."

"They could go around the bunkers," Tarreyton blustered.

"That'll be up to their commander," Carr told him. "In the dark, with casualties, against an unknown force. . .I'd be surprised if they did."

"So where does that leave us?" Captain Gaither asked. "SOL?"

"Higher is working out an alternative plan," Carr told them. "Meanwhile we maintain a defensive posture here. We're not under fire, so we're reasonably safe."

39

"I'll spread the word, sir," Samples told Carr, and walked away to let the rest of the platoon know what was happening. He saw Sweet walk over to the Japanese girls and make a sweeping gesture like a movie usher, showing them the latrine was ready for them. They smiled and giggled at him, and one of them scampered over to duck behind the ponchos.

When Samples approached him, Sweet grinned proudly. "Want me to guard the latrine, Sarge?" he asked, in all seriousness.

"I don't think that'll be necessary," Samples told him. "They look old enough to manage on their own, and no one's going to steal it. You can head back to the perimeter. Come on, I'm going out to check our positions now."

Samples told Sweet about the Wolfhounds as they walked out into the woods. He posted Sweet at a good spot, and then began making his way around the perimeter, whistling and calling ahead to find each of the men guarding the site. He told each of them the situation, and warned them to listen carefully for any movement out there. The last man he came to was Pastorini, who was almost invisible in the dark, crouched behind a tree.

"How you doing, Preacher?" he asked.

"I'd rather be back at the base camp, sleeping in my bunk," the man answered truthfully.

"Yeah, I know what you mean. Look, the infantry guys that were coming to reinforce us, they ran into an NVA bunker complex. Doesn't look like they're going to make it here after all." They both heard the first explosions of an artillery barrage that grew in intensity, somewhere to the south.

"Must be a big bunker complex," Pastorini commented. The barrage had swelled to a constant roar of high explosive. "So, we still staying here?"

"They're working on that," Samples told him. "Looks like I'll have to pull the perimeter in closer and work out some kind of guard roster."

"Maybe those guys down there will keep the gooks busy, and they won't bother us."

"We can hope," Samples said with little conviction. Then he heard the short burst of AK-47 fire to the northeast.

FIVE

Lieutenant Carr dived to the ground and low-crawled closer to a tree trunk. He heard two M-16s open fire, and then a couple bursts from the M-60. Belatedly he looked around at the passengers from the helicopter, and was dismayed to see that most of them were panicked and confused. A few feet away Colonel Tarreyton was squatting down, his head swiveling back and forth, his eyes wild with fear. Over by the chopper Gaither was crouching over the prisoner, helping him maneuver his bindings so he could lie down. Two of the Girlfriends were hugging each other and crying, while the third was screaming from inside the latrine. Doc Allman, who had hit the dirt just like Carr, got up and ran over to the girls, telling them to get down. When they didn't understand, he put his arms around them and pulled them down, just as the third girl, the blonde, came out from behind the hanging ponchos. She was holding the upper part of her unzipped flight suit at her waist, revealing a bright red sparkly top underneath. Seeing her two friends with Allman, she plopped down beside them, still screaming hysterically. Allman kept hushing them and trying to calm them.

Tarreyton finally figured out what he should do, and sprawled forward, his arms around the briefcase and his head lying on top of it. The gunfire quickly petered out, and Carr started to push himself up when there were more shots, this time from the northwest. Another AK, it sounded like, and his men over there responded with their M-16s. Night was closing in, and apparently the VC were doing so as well. Beside him Eberhart was talking into his headset, just loud enough to be heard by whoever was at the other end. "Earnie," Carr said to him, "have you reported this?"

Eberhart gave him a "wait a minute" look as he listened to incoming traffic, said "Roger" into the mike, and nodded at Carr.

"Yes, sir. They were just telling me that we should hold here until morning."

Once again the gunfire sputtered to a halt. Carr figured the gooks were just probing to determine what his defenses were. He had no idea how large a unit the enemy had to his north, but his own forces were stretched thin to defend even this small area. And he now knew there was a large NVA unit to his south, one that, having pushed back on the Wolfhounds, could presumably send troops north toward the downed helicopter. As if to reinforce that concern, the rumbling roar of artillery rounds exploding to his south abruptly ceased. Sergeant Samples suddenly appeared beside him, kneeling down but keeping his head up and swiveling back and forth. Carr rolled over and sat up.

"Need to bring the men in closer," Samples urgently told him. "They need to be in sight of each other."

"Take care of it," Carr told him. Samples nodded and darted away. Carr stood up, but leaned against one of the trees. Eberhart followed and knelt beside him. Carr could hear the colonel breathing heavily, and it almost sounded like he was whimpering. Carr didn't have time to deal with that right now.

Eberhart stretched out his arm with the handset. "Colonel Duran," he said.

Carr took the hard plastic handset and placed it against his ear, pushing the rubber-covered button on the side. "This is Yankee three-three Lima, over."

In response he heard the calm voice of his battalion commander. "How are you holding up, son?"

"We're taking fire from our north. Small arms. Snipers. Over.

"How are the passengers, over?"

"One kilo, one whiskey: the two pilots. The rest are okay. We also have a POW, over."

"Roger. Wait one."

Carr figured the colonel was conferring with his staff, and probably also talking to Brigade and Division. The woods were eerily silent, except for the muffled crying of the Girlfriends, and the rustle of brush as Samples repositioned the platoon closer to the chopper. The last glow of sunset had faded completely, and only starlight gave him any idea of what was around him. He tried to remember when moonrise would be on this date—soon, he hoped. The radio hissed at him.

"Three-three Lima, this is two-niner Tango, we believe your best bet is to maintain your current position. We have your coordinates, and can provide fire support, over."

That was not what Carr wanted to hear. "Is there an alternative?" he asked.

"Negative. We will have air and ground support to you at dawn. How copy?"

"Good copy," Carr replied without enthusiasm. "Out."

Sergeant Samples again appeared out of the darkness and stood there in the open, no longer concerned about sniper fire. "What's the word, sir?" he asked.

Carr shook his head. "We're to stay here, call in arty if we need it."

"Arty?" Samples said with disgust. "The gooks can get within twenty meters of us without us knowing, and we can't call in arty then. I don't trust them gun bunnies to be that accurate."

"I know," Carr sighed. "But those are our orders."

"And what if the NVA come up from the south? If they can kick the Wolfhounds' asses, they can come kick ours, too."

"I completely agree," Carr told him. "But for now, all we've got is a couple snipers. And that's what they're looking at."

"Shit!" Samples said disgustedly. Changing tone, he reported, "I've closed up the perimeter, for what good that will do. We don't have enough men to send out LP's, and in the dark we can't see shit. Probably should have brought the starlight scope." LPs, or listening posts, consisted of two or three men sent out at night a short distance from the main perimeter to listen for any approaching enemy.

"We should have brought a lot of things," Carr said, "but we didn't. Now we'll just have to make do."

*****

Lieutenant Harry Masters stood outside the Alpha Company headquarters, a small wooden building with a pitched tin roof. The Dau Tieng base camp was mostly dark, although a few lanterns shone here and there, in defiance of the black-out regulations. Inside, Spec Four Ford from third platoon was on CQ, sitting at the desk that held the radio and field telephone. Ford was one of several men who were in the rear area recovering from minor wounds or illness, and regularly pulled Charge of Quarters duty at night. The company first sergeant had flown to Cu Chi that morning, supposedly to attend some NCO meeting there. Masters suspected his primary mission involved booze and prostitutes. PFC Chalmers, the company clerk, had just left to pull berm guard somewhere on the east side of the base camp.

Previously Masters had been poring over the maps he had found in the back of the bottom drawer of the company's only file cabinet. Most of them were simply old Army maps of the areas between Dau Tieng and Tay Ninh, ones that had been abused and marked up enough that they were no longer serviceable. Among them, however, he had found some old French maps from the fifties, ones that presumably French forces had needed when operating against the Viet Minh, back before Dien Bien Phu. Masters had taken two years of French in high school, which was just barely enough to help him read the maps. He found them fascinating, and had been comparing them to the American maps, identifying the different way roads were routed and named. Then Chalmers, who at that point was putting on his combat gear before leaving for guard, told him about the situation in the Boi Loi.

When he had first gotten word about the track problems in the Boi Loi, Masters had run to the battalion motor pool to line up

45

mechanics, but by then all the mechanics had taken off for the evening. He eventually tracked a couple of them down at the Enlisted Men's club and dragged them back to the workshop, where they were now on reluctant stand-by. He heard the field phone rattle inside, but couldn't make out what was said by Ford as he answered it. Ford hung up the phone and came to the doorway.

"That was the gate, sir. They said that our tracks just came through."

Harry breathed a sigh of relief. "Thanks," he told Ford. "How long do you think till they get here to the company?"

Ford shrugged. "Normally only takes about five minutes, but that's in the daytime with the tracks all running right. At night, towing one of them, who knows?"

"Call over to the motor pool, tell those two guys they're on the way."

"Roger." Ford went back inside to make the call.

Masters pondered what he should do meanwhile, and then made a hasty decision. "I'm going to go meet them," he yelled through the door to Ford, and then took off at a slow jog. His plan was to intercept the tracks on the road through the base camp and guide them to the battalion motor pool. They probably knew how to get there, and probably knew that was where they needed to go, but he wanted to make sure. A good officer, he had repeatedly been told, never assumed and never left anything to chance.

He had to tread carefully, because the recent rains had turned the road to mud that had been churned up and then dried, creating deep ruts and scattered mounds of dirt. The light from the rising moon, stars overhead, and the illicit lights in the buildings, however, illuminated the road enough to find his way, although he kept stumbling and tripping as he ran. He stopped when he heard the unmistakable sound of armored personnel carriers moving slowly toward him. A minute later they appeared out of the dimness. A soldier was walking ahead of them, acting as the ground guide required while moving big vehicles inside the base camp at night, while the four tracks followed him. The second track in line was

46

being towed, jerking occasionally as the tow cable slackened and then tightened again.

Masters had so far met very few of the Alpha Company personnel, and knew none of the first platoon soldiers by sight. He stood in the road with his legs apart and his hands on his hips, in what he hoped was a commanding posture, and waited as the ground guide got within a few feet of him. The man threw up his fist in the air and yelled "Hold up," over his shoulder.

"I'm Lieutenant Masters, the company XO," Masters announced.

"Sir," the soldier acknowledged.

"And you are?"

"Oh, uh, Sergeant Jamison, first platoon, first squad."

"Okay. Sergeant Jamison, I've got some mechanics ready for you at the battalion motor pool. I'll take you over there."

"Uh, I know where it is, sir," Jamison said politely, but Masters detected a little condescension as well.

"I'm sure you do, Sergeant, but I want to ensure those repairs get done as quickly as possible. You may need me to jack up those mechanics."

"I appreciate that, sir. Go ahead, we'll follow you."

"This way," Masters told him, pointing in the direction of the motor pool. Jamison waved back at the driver of the lead track and began walking as the tracks jerked forward behind him. Masters fell into step beside Jamison. "So exactly what's wrong with it?" he asked, meaning the disabled vehicle.

"Transmission's busted," Jamison replied. "Can only get it into reverse and neutral."

"Think it'll be hard to fix?"

"Beats me, sir. Gunn, my driver, thinks it might just be the linkage. Me, I have trouble just changing a flat tire on my car."

"Well, let's hope it's something simple," Masters said encouragingly.

"Yeah," Jamison agreed wearily. Then he changed his tone and asked, "What about the rest of the platoon? Are they doing okay?"

"I think so," Masters told him as they trudged through the darkness. "Last I heard, they had reached the helicopter, and all the passengers were safe, but the pilot's injured and the copilot is dead."

"Have they made any contact?"

"I heard something about snipers, but I'm not sure about that. Regardless, we need to get your track repaired tonight, so you can go pick them up in the morning."

As he said that, they reached the cleared area and tents that comprised the battalion motor pool, and the two mechanics rose from the crates they had been sitting on and ambled over to meet them. Jamison explained the problem to them, and they showed him where to pull the broken vehicle to so they could work on it. Once the track was in place, next to a wooden shed, the tow cable was unhooked and the tow vehicle rejoined the other two.

"What now, sir?" Jamison asked when he walked over to where the lieutenant was waiting. Masters suspected the young sergeant knew exactly what to do next, but was simply showing military curtesy. Regardless, Masters had been thinking about that problem, and thought he knew the answer.

"Let's get the other tracks over to the headquarters building. You and your men can get something to eat and rest up. Then we can figure out what to do in the morning. By the way, do you need fuel?"

Jamison shook his head. "We tanked up this morning. Oh, and Gunn will be staying with the track. He doesn't really trust the mechanics to do it right. Do you think the mess hall is still open?"

"I doubt it," Master told him, "but I'll find out if they have something for you." Jamison waved to the tracks to follow him, and Masters fell in beside him as they led the three APCs to the company area. Masters knew they were looking at a long night ahead of them, but was energized by the fact that he now had a real mission to accomplish, something other than routine administrative duties.

Along the way to the company headquarters building, Masters peeled off and went to the battalion mess hall. Inside he found a single cook, who was making biscuits for the next day's breakfast meal. When Masters explained the situation, the cook found some breakfast ham and sliced cheese, and added some bread and a jar of mustard, which Masters gathered up and took back to where the first platoon men were securing their tracks and setting up cots. They told him Jamison had gone back to the motor pool to help Gunn. While they gratefully took the food and began making sandwiches, Masters went inside to check with Ford, and was surprised to see four soldiers in brand new uniforms sitting on their duffle bags, their weapons leaning against the wall. When they saw Masters, all four jumped to attention. Ford looked up from the comic book he was reading.

"FNGs," Ford explained. "Battalion sent them over a few minutes ago." FNGs—fucking new guys—were considered a dangerous commodity in Nam. While everyone appreciated the additional manpower, they knew that the inexperienced young soldiers could easily make mistakes that got themselves—and those around them—killed.

"This late in the day?"

Ford shrugged. "Some paperwork screw-up. Sent them to Charlie Company first."

"At ease," Masters told them, and they relaxed, but stayed standing. Turning to Ford, he asked, "Did you get their orders?"

"Yes, sir. Chalmers will have to log them in in the morning, I guess."

Masters turned back to the newbies. "Did you men get dinner?" They all nodded. "Well, I'm Lieutenant Masters, the XO. There're some extra cots in the first barracks building. Why don't you head over there and get some sleep. We'll square you away in the morning."

"Uh, sir?" one of the young men asked tentatively, holding his hand up at shoulder level.

"Yes, PFC. . . Kirk, is it?"

49

"Yes, sir. Do we need ammo for our guns, in case the base camp is attacked?"

"You have no ammo?"

"No, sir," one of the other boys said. "They said you'd give it to us."

Masters sighed. "Let me see what I can do."

*****

For the time being, it was quiet, but Aaron Samples feared it was just the calm before the storm. Dusk had faded to full night, and the only light came from the stars and a rising half-moon. He couldn't see the moon, of course, this deep in the woods, but he knew it was supposed to be up there. Here in the Boi Loi it was almost pitch dark; he could just make out the shape of the Huey and the nearest tree trunks.

The Girlfriends, despite the danger from the snipers, had taken refuge in the cabin of the chopper, apparently concerned more about bugs than bullets. Doc Allman and Captain Gaither sat on the ground over by the injured pilot, giving emotional support to him and whispering together. Samples presumed—hoped, actually—that they were simply discussing medical issues. He wanted to join them, but couldn't find a plausible reason to do so. The prisoner was sitting down, his head lying on his arms folded over his knees, apparently asleep. Colonel Tarreyton was standing in front of Lieutenant Carr, obnoxiously making hushed demands and unwanted suggestions, while Eberhart stood a couple feet away pretending not to hear.

With only ten line soldiers to work with, plus Pastorini, Samples had been hard pressed to come up with a workable defensive plan. Because the scattered sniper fire they had received earlier was from the north, he had posted the door gunner and his M-60 facing that direction, only twenty feet from the chopper. He then paired up the remaining men and stationed them in a circle around the chopper at the same distance as Pastorini. He told each pair that they could take turns sleeping if they got too tired, but he suspected few would take advantage of that opportunity. Samples would pair up with Pastorini when he could, to let the big man snooze a little. If they were attacked, Carr, Eberhart, and Allman would act as a reserve force to reinforce the section of the perimeter most in danger. Each of the chopper pilots had carried pistols, M1911 .45 automatics, and these had been given to Gaither and Tarreyton. The nurse had expertly dropped the magazine, worked the slide, popped the magazine back in, chambered a round, and stuck it in the cargo pocket of her pants. Samples had smiled in admiration of her skill. Tarreyton, however, had handled his pistol like it was a live rattlesnake, and quickly put it in one of the lower pockets of his shirt, buttoning the pocket closed.

Samples made one more round of the perimeter, checking on each of the pairs of men. He had teamed each of his three available squad leaders, Sergeant Montoya, Sergeant Reedy, and Spec Four Reyes, with newer guys, and placed them every other pair. The other two pairs each had an experienced spec four along with a newer PFC. Having assured himself everyone was properly placed and alert, he dropped down alongside Pastorini, who had extended the bipod legs on his machine gun to support it while he relaxed next to it.

"How's it going, Preacher?" Samples quietly asked as he stretched out on the ground.

"On the whole," Pastorini said with a bad W. C. Fields accent, "I'd rather be in Philadelphia."

Samples chuckled. "I guess you're not used to this kind of shit, huh?"

"I was in the infantry before," Pastorini said, "Ninth Division down in the Delta. Volunteered to be a door gunner, to get away from this kind of stuff."

"What goes around, comes around," Samples advised him. "So, how'd you get the name Preacher?"

Pastorini didn't say anything for a minute, and Samples began to worry he had somehow offended the man. Finally he spoke, struggling to keep his deep rumbling bass as quiet as possible.

"Back home I was a lay minister. I made the mistake of telling the guys at my last unit."

"Where's home?"

"Nashville. Wish I was back there now."

"What church?" Samples didn't know much about churches, and wasn't really curious, but just wanted to continue the conversation.

"Holy Ghost Tabernacle. Little bitty church. Good choir, though."

"So, uh, you're pretty religious?"

"Not so much anymore. Kind of hard to be pious and forgiving under these conditions, seeing what I've seen. You know?"

"Yeah, I think I do."

They both fell silent, listening to the sounds of the forest. They heard leaves rustling and limbs creaking in the slight breeze that never reached the ground, the clicking and chirping of insects, and occasional clunks and ticks from the chopper as metal cooled and settled. They also heard human sounds: a soft cough or throat clearing from the men on perimeter guard, a muttered angry phrase from Colonel Tarreyton, a frightened high whisper from one of the singers. And then Samples heard the unmistakable sound of a twig breaking somewhere out in front of him. He reached over and nudged Pastorini, who immediately hissed, "Yep, I heard it."

SIX

Lieutenant Colonel Tarreyton was still complaining, and Carr was getting really sick of it. The chubby little man with the ever-present briefcase kept harping on unimportant details and demanding something—he didn't know what—should be done. Carr, for his part, was struggling to be patient while increasingly less politely repeating his request to keep it down. He had a lot more vital tasks at hand than worrying about one of his soldiers having written the name of his home town on his helmet cover, or providing culturally appropriate meals for the Japanese singers. Tarreyton finally shut up when they both heard the single rifle shot.

The colonel dropped to the ground like a sack of potatoes, but Carr, having recognized the sound of an M-16, simply turned to the north and peered through the trees, hoping to see something, anything. After a couple seconds there was another shot, and then a burst of M-60 machine gun rounds, followed by a shriek of pain.

"Got him!" he heard Samples call triumphantly, but immediately there was another rifle shot, one that sounded like an AK-47 or SKS carbine, this one from the northeast. An M-16 to Carr's right front responded with three evenly spaced shots, and then Carr barely heard a thunk and a hiss, followed by the sound of something crashing through the leaves and bouncing off a tree trunk. "Grenade!" someone yelled, and Carr hit the dirt, joining Tarreyton and Eberhart. The flash of the explosion momentarily lit up the forest, and the concussion assaulted his ears, but Carr could tell the device had gone off beyond their lines and probably not caused any casualties.

Multiple M-16s opened fire, along with the M-60, and soon almost everyone on the perimeter was firing away. Carr felt helpless and out of control, since he didn't know if the men actually had targets or were just reacting to the noise. His platoon's gunfire drowned out any possible sounds of enemy fire, and the heavy woods preventing him from seeing any muzzle flashes that might indicate where the enemy was. Carr rose to a squatting position and listened for the supersonic crack of bullets lying over his head, but heard none.

"Cease fire!" he hollered. "Cease fire!" Other men echoed the command, and quickly the gunfire petered out. Rising to his feet, he waited and listened, hearing only the sound of his men putting in new magazines. "Who's got movement?" he demanded. No one answered.

"Aaron, how many are out there?" Carr knew that using Samples' first name would annoy Tarreyton, and didn't care. In fact, he hoped it did.

"Two or three," Samples called back. "Pretty sure I got one of them."

"All right, listen up, people! Conserve your ammo. Don't shoot unless you have a definite target. Aaron, to me."

Tarreyton was still prone, but when he started to get up, Carr told him, "Better stay down, sir. We don't know how many are out there." Tarreyton didn't protest, but just sank back down, hooking one arm around the briefcase. "Everybody, stay down," Carr called out, primarily for Tarreyton's benefit. He was pretty sure everyone else had sense enough to figure that out on their own.

Samples ran up and halted in front of Carr, while Eberhart, now kneeling, called in a sitrep to battalion. "What do you think?" Carr asked his platoon sergeant.

"So far just these probes. If they had more men, they would have used them."

Carr nodded. "Think we can hold them off?"

Carr sensed Samples' shrug more than saw it. "For now, sir, but what if they've got more men coming? Like those NVA to our south."

"I know. I know." Carr mulled it over, considering all the possibilities. If more VC showed up, and/or NVA arrived from the south, they would be surrounded. His men had never been issued bayonets, much less entrenching tools, so they had no way to dig in. This position was damn near indefensible, and artillery support would be either extremely dangerous or uselessly distant.

"I think we need to book it," Samples suggested, echoing what Carr himself had been thinking.

"You're right," Carr told him. "We can't go back the way we came, though. If more VC are coming, that's probably where they'll come from, and we already know some are there. Can't go east, because that takes us to the Saigon River. South's out, obviously. So I guess we'll have to do a Horace Greely, and 'Go West, young man.'"

Eberhart, who had overheard the conversation, reminded Carr, "Battalion says to stay put."

"Yeah, but they aren't here, are they? If we don't tell them we're leaving, they can't tell us to stay."

Tarreyton jumped to his feet and confronted Carr. "Lieutenant, you have direct orders to remain in place. As your senior officer, I must insist you do that."

Carr took a deep breath and tightened his jaw. "With all due respect, sir, you are not in my chain of command, and my mission is to rescue the people on the chopper. I cannot do that by staying here and being massacred like General Custer. You are welcome to stay here with the chopper if you so desire, but the rest of us are getting the hell out of Dodge." Carr abruptly turned away, leaving Tarreyton to sputter at his back.

"We've got to slip away quietly," he told Samples, "so the gooks don't know we're gone. You pass the word to the men, while I get these passengers organized."

"What about the pilots?" Samples asked. Carr cursed. He hadn't thought about them. They couldn't leave the dead copilot's body for the VC to desecrate, and the pilot couldn't walk.

"Are there any stretchers in the Huey? I know it's not a dust-off, but maybe?"

"I'll check with Preacher," Samples said, and scurried off.

Eberhart tapped his shoulder. "Battalion wants to know if you want some H&I." H&I was harassment and interdiction fire, artillery rounds dropped along suspected infiltration routes or on possible troop concentrations, without any specific targets in mind.

"That might be a good idea," Carr said, thinking it would help mask their departure. "Tell them to drop it to our north and south, at least three hundred meters out."

Pastorini emerged from the trees, set his machine gun down near the front of the chopper, and politely scooted the Girlfriends aside as he rooted around in the cabin of the Huey. A moment later he emerged with two folded up stretchers, and began opening them up. "Just happened to have," he remarked as he locked the aluminum poles apart, stretching the canvas taut.

"Can you and Doc get them loaded up?" he asked Pastorini. "I'll get my men to carry them. We need you on that M-60."

"Roger that, sir." Pastorini dropped one stretcher beside the dead man, and then carried the other over to the pilot, where Doc Allman and the nurse helped roll the injured man onto it.

The men from the perimeter began to appear out of the woods as Samples made the rounds and filled them in on what was happening. The first two men he saw were Johnson and Hicks, so he told them they would be carrying the pilot. Then he went to the three singers and told them in pidgin English and broad gestures that they were moving out. He noticed that all three were wearing brightly colored tennis shoes, and hoped they would hold up to walking in the forest.

As the girls climbed down from the chopper and quietly chattered among themselves, Samples reappeared. "I left Reyes, Montoya, and Reedy out there for now," Samples reported. "They'll maintain a lookout, and once we're on the move, they'll fire a few rounds and then catch up." Samples looked over at Johnson and Hicks, who were experimentally lifting the stretcher to see what the best way to carry it would be. They had laid their rifles alongside the pilot. "What about the dead guy?" Samples asked.

"We're taking him with us. The prisoner can be one of the stretcher bearers, and you choose the other one."

"Greenberg," Samples called, and the young man trotted over. "You and the gook are going to carry the dead guy out. Load him on the stretcher, put the gook in front, and keep your rifle handy in case he tries anything. Got it?" Greenberg nodded, and Eberhart offered to help him untie the prisoner and load up the body.

Captain Gaither came over and accosted Carr. "He really shouldn't be moved," she told him crossly. He assumed she meant the pilot.

"We can't stay here, Ma'am," he told her. "It's too dangerous."

"I thought we were supposed to stay here all night. Can't you make up your mind?"

Samples gently took her elbow and led her away, saying "Ma'am, let me explain it to you." Carr was glad that Samples had relieved him of one of the many problems he was facing. He turned to Tarreyton.

"Are you coming with us, sir?" he asked.

"Of course, lieutenant," Tarreyton angrily barked. "Do you take me for a fool?"

Carr withstood the desire to answer the question truthfully.

He waited while Greenberg, Allman, and the POW had loaded the body and lifted the stretcher off the ground. The man in black pajamas winced at the pain in his shoulder, but otherwise cooperated. He saw that Samples had somehow mollified the nurse. "Okay," he announced, here's the march order. I'll be on point with Earnie, Vasquez and Lenny behind us. Sergeant Pastorini, if you'll fall in behind them. Then Johnson and Hicks with the pilot, Doc and Captain Gaither, Colonel Tarreyton, and the Girlfriends. Behind them will be Greenberg and the gook with the copilot's stretcher, then Sweet and Crosby, the three squad leaders, and Sergeant Samples bringing up the rear. Questions?"

No one said anything, they just shuffled around getting into line as directed. Carr finally heard the sound he had been waiting for—the whistle of artillery shells and the crunching explosions that followed, both to their north and south. The Japanese girls crouched and cowered at the unexpected noise, and even Tarreyton jerked in surprise, but the rest were unmoved.

"That's the signal," Carr announced. "Let's move out."

*****

Samples watched the line of men and women snake away through the trees, and his eyes lingered on Captain Gaither, who showed no signs of fear or nervousness, unlike the colonel and the singers. He admired her composure and strength under what were certainly unusual and trying circumstances for her. And although it was too dark now to make out any details, he remembered from earlier how well she had worn the baggy jungle fatigues. She was carrying two cans of M-60 ammo for Pastorini, who carried a third can in addition to the big machine gun. Behind her was Lieutenant Colonel Tarreyton, one of the least inspiring officers Samples had ever met, clutching his bulging briefcase and trying to mask his anxiety with bluster.

He was worried about the Girlfriends; they were totally out of their element, with the wrong footwear, and potentially endangered by the language barrier. They kept ahold of each other's flight suits, as if ensuring that they didn't get separated was the most important thing in their lives right now. Samples was even more worried about the prisoner. There was something not quite right about the guy, but Samples couldn't pin it down. The most concerning problem was his attitude: quietly defiant, undefeated, and appearing to know something that no one else did. Samples wished they had that interpreter, what's-his-name, who had been with them in Ba Nha, so they could interrogate the little bastard.

Over the roar of the artillery rounds he heard the scattered shots of M-16 fire, and hoped Reedy, Montoya, and Reyes were simply following the plan, and hadn't really seen anything. Just as

58

Sweet and Crosby followed the stretcher bearing the dead copilot into the trees, Reyes came running up, followed closely by Montoya and Reedy from other directions.

"Follow them," he told the three squad leaders, pointing at the barely visible Crosby's back. "Watch the gook." He waited until they joined the column, and then fell in behind them. In just seconds they were out of sight of the downed helicopter, immersed in the spooky Boi Loi Woods as artillery continued to rain down in the distance. Samples was impatient with the slowness of the march, but knew it was inevitable, considering the civilians and the stretchers. He also didn't like how they were all bunched up together, but that was unavoidable as well. They couldn't afford for anyone to get lost or left behind, and to avoid that, they had to stay close. In this dense forest, in the dead of night, you could be only a few steps away and already unable to see anyone else.

While the artillery explosions continued unabated, Samples followed Reyes as the column wound its way between the trees and bushes. He kept turning around and walking backwards for a few steps, to see if anyone were following them, even though he could only see a few feet before the darkness enveloped the woods. He stifled his annoyance as the line ahead of him would halt unexpectedly, pause, and resume the march, creating an accordion effect. He assumed that these stops were caused by things like the lieutenant pausing to shoot an azimuth, or the stretcher bearers needing to maneuver between tree trunks, but he wished they could move faster. The sooner they were away from the crash site, the better.

During one of those halts Samples tried to see his watch, but couldn't make out the hands. Judging by the sound of the artillery explosions, they had gone perhaps half a mile, but it seemed to have taken over an hour. No, he though, it can't be more than twenty minutes; it just seems longer. The line started moving again, and then Samples found himself entering a small clearing, where the rest of the people had already dispersed around the edges. The stretchers were being set down, the Girlfriends were squatting, and Captain Gaither was over checking on the pilot. He immediately began doing a headcount and directing the men to form a defensive perimeter, and only then noticed that the artillery barrage had ended.

"Aaron, over here," Lieutenant Carr quietly called to him. Samples finished designating positions for Dave Vasquez and Lenny Sorenson, and then joined Carr and Eberhart in the center of the clearing. Here he could look up and actually see some stars through the opening in the forest canopy.

"All present and accounted for," he reported to Carr, who nodded distractedly as if he was expecting nothing less.

"There's a stream up ahead," Carr told him. "Pretty sure it's the same one we crossed this afternoon."

"Gonna be a bitch crossing it with the stretchers," Samples commented, thinking of how soft and unstable the ground had been earlier.

"Agreed," Carr said. "I had them stop the arty just now. Think the gooks know we're gone yet?"

They heard the rattle of AK-47 fire far behind them. It sounded like short bursts from two or three different weapons.

"Guess not," Samples said. "When we don't shoot back, though, they'll know."

"Let's give them a minute," Carr said, and Samples wondered what he meant. The AK fire stopped, and Samples could just imagine the VC cautiously approaching the downed chopper, wary of it being a trap. The woods were silent, both here in the clearing and back at the crash site. Carr spoke quietly to Eberhart. "Tell them, fire for effect." Eberhart passed the message along on the radio, and Samples looked at Carr. Although Carr certainly couldn't see Samples' expression, they knew each other well enough that Carr recognized the unspoken question.

"They're going to fire on the chopper itself," Carr told him. "And anyone near it." Samples could hear the distant thump of 105mm howitzers firing, and shortly after that he heard the sound of those rounds impacting back where the helicopter was, raining explosives down on the aircraft and the surrounding forest. The clear patch of sky overhead lit up as the fuel on board the chopper erupted, and there were the firecracker sounds of machine gun ammo popping off in the flames.

"That ought to slow 'em down," Samples noted. "But doesn't that constitute destruction of government property? That's a UCMJ violation, I'm pretty sure."

"They can take it out of my pay," Carr responded, unconcerned. "Okay, let's get across that creek."

Samples nodded. "Break's over," he announced. "On your feet!"

SEVEN

With one last check of his compass, Carr led off again, shoving his way through some low bushes as the trees became smaller and farther apart. They were approaching the open area that marked the course of the invisible stream, and already the ground was feeling squishy. When he broke out of the last of the trees, he could see the majestic sweep of stars above, and a half moon just rising in the east, bathing the meandering clearing in a silver light. Just like the area where they had crossed the stream earlier, the clearing was thick with waist-high plants that hid the actual flow of water. In the pale moonlight he scanned up and down stream to see if there was perhaps a better place to cross, but it all looked just the same. Seeing no alternative, Carr waded out into the bushes, holding his rifle high to keep it from being caught in the foliage.

Although he couldn't see it, he felt the dirt beneath his feet turn to mud and start to accumulate on his boots, slowing his pace considerably. Behind him he heard Eberhart quietly curse as he slipped and nearly fell. Carr realized that the long line of people would be churning up a muddy path that got worse with the passing of each person. As the first person in the formation, he would have it the easiest, and it was already difficult for him. His boots made sucking sounds as each step pulled one foot free from the muck, only to sink in on the next step. Then he felt the water running over the tops of his toes, and knew he had reached the creek itself. At first he was glad, for that meant that for the rest of the crossing it would be getting better, but then he heard the message being passed forward from man to man.

"It's the Girlfriends," Eberhart told him, relaying what he had heard form Vasquez. "Their shoes are coming off."

"What?" Carr stopped in the middle of the stream, feeling his feet getting soaked by the cool water. "Holy shit! Okay, keep going, wait for me in the tree line."

Dodging around Eberhart, Carr headed back along the line, angrily pushing the broad leaves and thin branches out of his way. "Keep going," he repeated to each person as he passed. He noted that Johnson and Hicks were struggling with the stretcher carrying the pilot, but were managing to keep up. Allman and the nurse seemed to be doing okay, and even the colonel was keeping up, holding his briefcase high like he needed to keep it dry. Nonetheless, the man took the opportunity to again criticize Carr. "Are you deliberately going the worst way, Lieutenant?"

Carr just ignored him. Behind the colonel, he discovered, there was a significant gap.

Twenty feet behind Tarreyton he found all three of the little singers clustered together, two of them supporting the third, who was holding one bare foot in the air. Sweet and Crosby were squatting down probing the wet ground with their free hands. The girls chattered at Carr in a mixture of Japanese and broken English, pointing at the one girl's foot.

"Found it!" Sweet announced proudly, holding up a mud-caked shoe. The girls all said "T'ank you!" as they worked together to put it back on her bare foot. Sweet and Crosby stood up, brushing back the branches and leaves that engulfed them. Behind them Carr could see the prisoner waiting patiently, holding the front of the dead man's stretcher with no apparent pain or fatigue.

"Those tennis shoes ain't gonna make it in this mud, sir," Crosby told Carr.

"They're going to have to," Carr said. What options did they have?

There was some rustling as Samples, Montoya, and Reyes detoured around the stretcher to see what the holdup was.

"Girl lost her shoe in the mud," Carr explained to Samples.

"But I found it," Sweet beamed. "She's got it back on now."

"This mud really sucks," Reyes said, well aware of the double meaning. "Why don't we carry them across?"

"Yeah," Sweet agreed enthusiastically. "We can carry them piggy-back. I'll take Crystal."

The blonde girl perked up, having heard her name mentioned.

Carr wanted to object, but had to admit it was the best solution available on short notice. The other men watched him, waiting for him to give them permission. "Okay," he said, intending to add a warning, but Crosby and Reyes cut him off.

"I'll take Rhonda," Crosby announced, reaching out toward the taller girl.

"And I'll take Sherry," Reyes crowed, moving closer to her. Carr hadn't remembered the girls' names, but wasn't surprised that his men had learned them already. Sherry, he now knew, was the one who had lost her shoe.

Crosby handed his M-79 grenade launcher to Samples, and Montoya took Sweet's and Reyes' M-16s. With broad gestures and pidgin English the three soldiers showed the girls how to climb up on their backs. The soldiers hooked their arms around the girls' legs, bounced a little to get them settled, and nodded to Carr that they were ready. The girls were all giggling, and the guys seemed a little too pleased to be carrying the extra weight, but Carr accepted it because they didn't have time to waste.

"All right, let's go," he said, moving out to catch up with the rest of the column, who had disappeared in the darkness.

Once everyone was across the swampy open area and had congregated in the trees on the other side, Carr and Samples tried to get the column reorganized. The three guys carrying the singers reluctantly let the girls climb down off their backs, and Carr noted with concern that the girls each gave their bearer a hug of thanks before clustering together to giggle and whisper with each other. Specialist Reyes was brought up to follow behind Eberhart, giving Carr a squad leader close enough to pass commands through. Sergeant Montoya was inserted between the Girlfriends and the POW carrying the copilot. Sergeant Reedy was kept just in front of

Samples. When the line was finally reformed and ready to continue, Carr reached for his compass to ensure they were headed the right direction, and felt a sharp sinking feeling when he couldn't find it. It had been in his right lower shirt pocket, but when he put his hand in there, his fingers found only the large hole that had been ripped in it.

"Shit!" he cursed. He patted all his pockets, just in case he had put the compass somewhere else and forgotten about it, but it was nowhere to be found. Most likely it was somewhere in that stream clearing, buried in the mud. Turning to Eberhart, he asked, "You don't happen to have a compass on you, do you?"

"Sir?" Eberhart replied with a mixture of worry and puzzlement.

"Wait here," Carr told him. Trying to remain calm and exude an attitude of confidence and competence, he walked back along the column asking if anyone had a compass, knowing it was probably a futile gesture. He made a point of not asking Tarreyton, not wanting to get into another pissing match with the obnoxious colonel. His last and best hope, Sergeant Samples, just shook his head.

"Should we go back and look for it?" Samples asked.

"A waste of time," Carr admitted. "It's long gone now."

"We can always look for moss on the north side of trees," Samples suggested facetiously.

"Oh, sure," Carr scoffed. "We could steer by the stars, if we could see them."

"Well, the moon's up in the east," Samples pointed out. "You can see it occasionally through the leaves. If we keep it at our backs, we'll at least know we're generally headed in the right direction."

Carr sighed. Samples was right. "I guess it's all we can do. We'll go another mile or two west, and then turn north to see if we can find the road."

"Works for me," Samples reassured him.

Carr nodded and said, "Shit," again. Angered at his own failure, he began plodding back up toward the head of the line, only to be stopped by Colonel Tarreyton.

"Is there a problem, Lieutenant?" the man demanded. "I hear you lost your compass. Is that right?"

"It's all under control, sir," Carr replied with more confidence than he felt.

Tarreyton scoffed. "You are a sorry excuse for an officer," he commented maliciously. "This will all be in my report."

"Fine, sir. Now, if you'll excuse me, I need to lead us all out of here." Carr pushed around the man and hustled back up to the front of the column. With a glance over his shoulder to see if he could see the moon, he started out again, winding his way through the forest in what he hoped was a westerly direction, repeatedly checking behind him to make sure the rest of the line was following.

*****

Samples nudged Reedy in the back and whispered, "Pass the word up the line to keep the noise down. No talking." Reedy nodded and punched Crosby on the shoulder, who had been joking with Sweet about the girl singers. While the command was passed forward, Samples dropped back about twenty feet, listening intently to the sounds of the forest. Even after the conversations ahead dribbled to a halt, he could still hear the footsteps, the jangle of equipment, and the swishing of leaves and branches being brushed aside, but he could also begin to hear the sound of insects, the distant drone of a high-flying airplane, and something else.

He stopped and waited until the column was almost out of hearing range, slowly turning in a circle and closing his eyes to get a better sense of what he was hearing. For several minutes he thought he had detected the sounds of someone following, but he wasn't sure. Now, as soon as he stopped, those ephemeral noises also ceased. Were they being followed, and had the follower noticed that Samples had stopped, and followed suit? Samples hated being out in the woods at night like this, and worried that his own paranoia was finding danger that wasn't really there. He listened for another thirty

66

seconds, heard nothing, and hustled to catch up with the column. It wouldn't pay to get separated. In the forest, at night, he would be unable to follow any trail, and getting lost out here could be death sentence. It was with a great sense of relief that he finally glimpsed the shadowy movements ahead of him that soon resolved into Reedy's back. He fell into step behind him.

"Where'd you go, Sarge?" Reedy whispered over his shoulder.

"Just checking," Samples responded. He heard a high-pitched muted squeal up ahead, followed by intense giggling. "Don't those girls ever shut up?"

"Not for long," Reedy said.

Samples rolled his eyes, although no one was there to see it. This was one situation that he had never trained for at Fort Polk, or ever seen in a training manual. He could just imagine it: TM-257-43, Section 8, Paragraph b, Escorting USO singers in the woods at night in a combat zone. Step 1: Refer to FM-495-12 on incidental contacts with civilians. Step 2: Consult with your unit's Civil Affairs officer. Step 3: just shoot yourself.

At the very edge of his hearing Samples thought he detected the snap of a twig breaking. He jerked his head around and froze, letting Reedy continue away from him. He heard the helicopter pilot moan in pain, and Allman say something in a reassuring tone, but nothing else. He held that pose for almost a minute before relaxing. Shaking his head, Samples moved out again, quickly catching up to Reedy, who apparently had not noticed his brief absence. Samples' back was tingling, and the hairs on his neck were standing. His gut told him there was someone behind them, but he couldn't pin down any real evidence of it. And even if there were, what could he do about it? He couldn't risk starting a firefight, not with all those non-combatants in the column, and he didn't know how many people might be back there. If any. At least the follower, or followers, if they existed, hadn't fired on them. Yet.

And as if that weren't enough to keep him uneasy, he also worried about the loss of their only compass. He didn't blame Lieutenant Carr, who couldn't know that a thorn had ripped his pocket open while pushing through the thick undergrowth, but he did blame himself for not bringing his own compass. They so rarely needed compasses when their primary mission was protecting the convoys that he had put his away in his ammo can to keep it safe, and hadn't thought to retrieve it during the turmoil of having a track stuck in the mud. And that was his fault. He was the platoon sergeant, and it was his job to think of all these possibilities and prepare for them.

Thinking of the missing compass made him look up and back, trying to spot the moon through the thick canopy of leaves. He finally managed to spot a brief glimmer of blue light, and was relieved to see that it was directly behind them, where it should be. Then he tripped on a tree root, stumbled, and bounced off a tree trunk as he regained his balance.

"You okay?" Reedy asked.

"Yeah," Samples told him, "just tripped." That's what you get for not looking where you're going, he told himself, and concentrated on his footing. Part of the problem was the excruciating slowness of their progress. He knew it was unavoidable, due to the darkness, the closeness of the forest, the two stretchers, and the Japanese girls, but it was hard for him to walk this slowly. He longed to stretch his legs out and make better time, get far away from the crash site, and find the main road. Only then would he feel relatively safe. As it was, they had probably gone only a mile or so since leaving the chopper. Samples tried to picture the map of this area in his mind, but what he remembered was mostly just vast stretches of light green, unbroken by roads or buildings or rice paddies. It might as well have an illustration that says, "Here there be dragons."

Samples was caught by surprise when Reedy slowed down and stepped to one side. Looking around, Samples realized the column had entered some sort of a clearing, and Carr was spreading the personnel out and calling for a rest break. Samples took charge of the defensive perimeter, and began posting his men at the edges of the clearing. The two stretchers had been put down, and Captain Gaither and Doc Allman were fussing over the pilot. Colonel Tarreyton was sitting on the ground with his briefcase in his lap, ignoring everyone else. Greenberg was guarding the prisoner, and the Girlfriends were close by, subtly flirting with Greenberg. It wasn't until he was satisfied with the disposition that he joined Carr, who was muttering on the radio. He could tell from the few words he could hear and the defensive tone of Carr's voice that the lieutenant was catching hell for leaving the crash site against orders and destroying the downed chopper with artillery. Samples guessed that senior officers had all gone to bed before that happened, and had just now been awakened and made aware of the fact. *Fuck 'em if they can't take a joke.*

While he waited for Carr to finish with his ass being chewed, he peered through the darkness, surveying the clearing. It seemed to be a long narrow clearing, running roughly north and south. The gap in the trees was just enough for him to see the half-moon—and see the dark clouds moving in from the west. He couldn't help wondering why this clearing even existed. Usually a clearing was roughly oval in shape, or indicated the course of a stream, but this one was different. There was a distinct line of trees on either side, with smaller saplings and bushes filling in between them. Samples began walking around in ever widening circles, feeling the ground underneath the weeds and bushes with his boots. The earth in the center of the clearing was more compacted than at the edges, and seemed to be ever so slightly higher. Convinced of what he had found, he strode over to Carr, who was just giving the handset back to Eberhart.

"Well," Carr told him with a sigh, "Colonel Duran is not happy, because the brigade commander is pissed, and the division commander is even more pissed. I explained the situation, but they didn't want to hear it. They all think we should have stayed with the chopper."

"Yeah," Samples said, "but they aren't here, and we are. You made the right decision, Eltee. We'll back you up."

"I doubt that Tarreyton will."

"Want me to frag him?" Samples asked with mock seriousness. Fragging was a growing problem in Viet Nam, with disgruntled enlisted men using fragmentation grenades to eliminate officers they didn't like.

"Don't even joke about it," Carr warned him. Then he added, "If you do, don't tell me ahead of time." They both chuckled.

"Hey," Samples said, changing the subject, "this clearing? I think it used to be a road."

"A road? Out here? To where?"

"Beats the shit out of me, but I can feel the crown when I walk around. It used to go somewhere. I figure if we follow it north, it's bound to connect with the highway."

In the dim light of the moon Samples could see Carr turning his head back and forth, looking first one way and then the other as he gazed at the vague outline of the clearing. Then Carr nodded. "I think your right, Aaron. Let's check the map again." Carr withdrew the plastic-covered map from his cargo pocket and opened it. They both squatted down facing each other, and Samples pulled his flashlight from his pistol belt. Shielding the light with his hand, he pointed the beam at the map as Carr turned the map until it was oriented to his liking.

"The chopper was here," Carr said quietly, pointing to a grease pencil mark on the plastic. "So we should be somewhere around here." Samples waited as Carr bent down farther to study the map closely, tilting it to reduce the reflections off the clear plastic, and touching the map with his index finger. Then he began moving the map in a slow circle, widening his search. Finally he stopped. "Nope, no roads anywhere near here, as best as I can see. At least not on this map."

"This is a pretty old road," Samples noted. "Probably abandoned before this map was made."

"Could be," Carr admitted.

Samples clicked off the flashlight, and noted that the clearing seemed darker than before. At first he thought it was because his eyes hadn't adjusted from flashlight, but then he looked up and saw that the moon had gone behind the clouds. He also felt the first raindrops on his upturned face. "Well, shit," he said. "Now it's raining."

70

A single rifle shot echoed through the forest, and as Samples dived to the ground, he heard Sergeant Reedy yell, "'Fuck me!" Several of the men opened fire with their M-16s. It sounded like the first shot had come from the southeast. He heard Pastorini's M-60 fire a couple bursts, and then the gunfire subsided. Everyone had sprawled on the ground, making them virtually invisible in the waist-high grass and foliage. Samples raised his head just enough to see over the bushes, and beside him Carr called out, "Hold your fire!" Everyone waited. "Anyone hit?"

There was a low-key chorus of no's.

"I meant to tell you," Samples said conversationally. "I think someone's been following us."

"You think so?" Carr asked scathingly. "Thanks."

"Any time," Samples offered helpfully. "Seriously, though, it was just a feeling. Nothing concrete."

"Don't mean nothin'," Carr said, repeating one of the common catch phrases of the men. "How many, do you think?"

"Just one or two," Samples guessed. "Any more than that, they would have jumped us on the trail." He listened for sounds of movement in the forest, but all he could hear was the patter of raindrops on his helmet. The rain was starting to come down harder.

"Well, we can't stay here," Carr said. "If there're any other gooks out there somewhere, they undoubtedly heard the gunfire and will be heading this way."

"Keep heading west, or follow this road north?" Samples asked, trying to indicate his preference by his tone of voice. He and Carr were well attuned to each other's thoughts, and Carr picked up on it immediately.

"We'll go north. The road should be faster going, and it should get us to the highway sooner. And without the moon, we have no other way to stay on course."

"Roger that," Samples agreed. He scrambled up into a crouching position and called out to the others. "We're moving out. Follow the lieutenant. Stay low."

71

EIGHT

The radio on the desk in front of him hissed and crackled with static. Lieutenant Masters had turned off the squelch, afraid he might miss a weak call. The dial light gave him just enough illumination to write into the company log what was happening out in the Boi Loi Woods, or as much as he could figure out from the traffic between Lieutenant Carr and Battalion. He felt sorry for Carr, who had just taken a load of crap from the battalion commander that Masters felt was undeserved. He was a little ashamed that he was glad it was Carr and not him that was taking the heat. Spec Four Ford, the CQ, was sitting at the other desk trying to stay awake, his head occasionally tilting forward slowly only to jerk upright a moment later. PFC Delaney, the CQ runner, was standing in the door watching the rain.

The four new guys had all crashed on cots in the barracks building. Masters had scrounged some extra magazines, enough for each of the newbies to have four, and the first platoon guys had supplied a can of M-16 ammo from their tracks. The recently arrived soldiers had nervously filled each magazine, one of them reminding the others to only put nineteen rounds in each twenty-round magazine, to avoid stretching the spring. Otherwise they had been issued the typical minimum amount of combat gear: helmet, pistol belt, canteen, two ammo pounces, and a gas mask. They would just have to "acquire" whatever additional equipment they wanted or needed.

"A track's coming," Delaney announced. Masters leaned back from the radio and picked up the growl of a diesel engine slowly approaching. Grabbing his poncho, he slipped it over his head and pushed past Delaney out into the rain. With only its blackout lights showing, silhouetting a soldier walking ahead of it as a ground guide, a single M-113 was approaching the other three APCs that were clustered just outside the headquarters building. At a signal from the man walking ahead of it, the vehicle jerked to a stop alongside the others. The narrow dim lights went out, and the engine was cut off. Masters ran over to the man on the ground, who he knew had to be Sergeant Jamison. Wearing his boonie hat and no poncho, Jamison was soaked to the skin, but seemed oblivious to the rain.

"All fixed?" Masters asked anxiously.

Jamison wiped the rain from his eyes and peered closely to see who was addressing him. When he finally recognized Masters he nodded. "Yep. Turned out it was just the linkage. We're good to go now."

"Oh, that's terrific," Masters enthused. This wasn't his platoon, but it was a part of the company that he was the XO for, so he had taken a proprietary interest in the situation. He may have been disgraced, but he was still gung ho.

"What's happening with the rest of the platoon?" Jamison asked. Behind him the driver called out, "I'm going to rack out," disappeared down inside the driver's compartment and slammed the hatch shut over him.

"They're okay," Master reassured him, "but Higher is pissed at them."

"That's normal," Jamison chuckled. "I heard some of it on the radio on the way in, but lost comms when we got here. Fuckin' antenna's for shit."

"Come on inside," Masters invited him. ""Get out of the rain, and I'll tell you what I know." He turned back toward the headquarters.

"You got anything more to eat or drink in there, sir?" Jamison asked, following him.

"As a matter of fact," Masters told him, pulling open the screen door and letting Jamison enter ahead of him. "There's still stuff for ham and cheese sandwiches there on the desk, and we've got a few warm sodas, if you like RC."

While Jamison shook off the excess rainwater and used a church key to open a can of soda, Masters began filling him in on the recent events in the Boi Loi, or at least what he knew of them. Jamison listened to the story with alternating smiles and frowns as he fixed himself a sandwich and began eating it.

"So they're still just wandering around in the woods?" Jamison asked after Masters had finished.

"More or less," Masters admitted. "Lieutenant Carr said they were heading west, and were going to try to go north to the highway as soon as they could."

"And no one's helping them?"

Masters shrugged. "The rest of the company is supposed to leave the fire support base at dawn, and choppers will be back up then, but for now they're on their own. They've been taking some sniper fire, I heard, but so far no one's been hit."

"Shit!" Jamison put the remainder of his sandwich down. "And we can't do anything, either. We'd just get stuck in the mud again, even if we could find them in the dark. Where are they, anyway?"

Masters snatched one of the Army-issue topo maps off his desk and spread it out in front of the Jamison, then shone a flashlight on it. "The chopper went down here." Masters put his finger on the X he had previously marked on the map. "If they headed west, they should be somewhere about here."

Jamison squinted his eyes and leaned closer. "So they could be back on this side of the creek, right?"

"Should be. But they're still at least four clicks from the road. And you've been in the Boi Loi. Isn't that pretty thick woods there?"

Jamison nodded. "Yeah. Too thick for tracks in the dark. We'd get lost, or stuck, or both. Fuck!"

Jamison studied the map some more, sipping the warm soda. "Where was that bunker complex the leg unit ran into?"

75

Masters circled his finger on the map. "Somewhere around here. I didn't get the exact coordinates."

"So if those gooks decided to go after our guys, too, they could be there almost any time."

Masters sighed. "That's possible."

"And with those women, and a guy on a stretcher, the platoon's not going to be moving all that fast." Jamison pounded the desk with his fist. "Talk about FUBAR."

Masters silently agreed. Without a doubt, the situation was fucked up beyond all recognition.

*****

Thorny bushes and wait-a-minute vines clutched at his clothing, and the branches of small trees kept slapping him in the face, but Lieutenant Carr plowed through the thick undergrowth with determination. The ground-level vegetation on this long-abandoned road was far denser than was the case deeper in the woods, but the old crowning of the roadway gave him more solid footing, and, more importantly, it gave him a definite path to follow. In terms of progress, he guessed it was a trade-off—they were slowed by the thick foliage, but saved time by not wandering off course. The trees here were smaller than in the woods, but still big enough to mostly block out the dark sky. Not that seeing the sky would help, what with the continuing rain, which had left Carr totally wet from head to toe. He had donated his poncho to one of the singers, since he didn't want to wear it anyway. The poncho hindered his movements too much, and made it harder to hear what was around him. He had intended to give it to Captain Gaither, but Samples had beat him to the punch in that regard. Shoving aside the dripping leaves of yet another sapling, he wished he had a machete.

There had been no further gunfire since they started down the road, but Carr was certain there were gooks still shadowing them, somewhere out there. He worried that there were a lot of them, and that they might be scurrying through the woods to their east trying to get ahead of the rescue column to ambush them. So far they had only run into Viet Cong, and only a few of them at that, but the existence of the bunker complex to their south that had stymied the Wolfhounds, one housing at least a company of North Vietnamese regulars, and maybe a battalion, was far more concerning. According to intelligence, VC units in this area of operations were small and scattered, but the NVA had infiltrated in force, with at least a regiment of troops. If the NVA, with their larger numbers, better weapons, and better organization, came after them, they would be in deep shit.

"Eltee!" Eberhart whispered urgently behind him. Carr stopped and turned to see what the matter was, fearing something terrible had happened. Instead he saw his radioman pointing off to his left. Carr wiped the rain from his eyes and peered through the sodden darkness, at first seeing only more bushes and trees. Behind Eberhart the column accordioned to a stop, with whispered questions passing up and down the line. Then he saw it: a slight flicker of light and the rectangular shape of a small building shrouded by trees.

"Everybody down," Carr ordered quietly, patting the air with his hand even though no one could really see it. He crouched down, and sensed the others doing the same. There weren't supposed to be any buildings out here. If it was some peasant's hut, it could only be there with the permission of the VC, which meant that the occupants were VC sympathizers, if not actually VC themselves.

"What's up?" Sergeant Samples whispered, having appeared just behind him. Carr had no idea how the platoon sergeant had come up the line so quickly, but was glad he had. He needed a second opinion on what to do now.

"There's a building over there," Carr explained quietly, pointing. "We saw a light inside." The light had since been extinguished.

"I'll go check it out," Samples offered.

"I don't know," Carr said doubtfully. "Maybe we should just pass it by and hope they don't know we were here."

"We need to stop anyway," Samples told him. "Those Jap girls are worn out, and the guys with the stretchers need a rest. Captain Gaither wants to check on the pilot, too. I'll take Reyes and see what we've got."

Before Carr could think of a good reason to object, Samples tapped Reyes on the shoulder and the two slipped away into the brush.

"Want me to tell Battalion?" Eberhart asked, still holding the handset to his face.

"Not yet," Carr said. "Let's wait until we know more." Carr's motive for not reporting was more than just a need for more information; he didn't want Battalion or anyone else telling him what to do, especially when they weren't here to accurately assess the situation. "Stay here," he told Eberhart. "I'm going to check on the others." With that he rose to a half-crouch and began working his way down the line of people he was responsible for, patting them on the shoulders, asking how they were doing, and giving them a brief explanation for the halt. Johnson and Hicks had set down the stretcher with the wounded pilot and were stretching and wiggling their arms to restore circulation and ease the muscle pain, while Gaither and Doc Allman knelt on either side of the stretcher checking the man's legs and asking how he was doing. Instead of criticizing Carr, the nurse simply ignored him. Carr wasn't sure if that was an improvement or not.

Tarreyton, however, was another story. In a whining whisper the colonel demanded to know everything. "Why are we stopping? Why aren't we out of these damn woods yet? Do you have any fucking idea what you're doing, Lieutenant? This is ridiculous!"

"There's a building over there," Carr said as patiently as he could muster. "We're checking it out."

"A building? Why aren't we inside yet, out of this damn rain? What are you waiting for?"

"It might be Viet Cong, sir. Sergeant Samples is investigating."

Tarreyton took a breath in preparation for another tirade, but Carr didn't wait for it. Montoya had heard the conversation with the colonel, so Carr moved over to the girl singers, who were huddled together for warmth. He spoke to them in reassuring tones, cognizant of the fact that they probably didn't understand half of what he said, and then moved on to the second stretcher, which was lying on the ground with its inert cargo, while the prisoner squatted beside it. Greenberg was a couple feet away, holding his M-16 pointed at the gook. Sweet, Crosby, and Reedy had moved up and gathered around Greenberg to help him keep an eye on the prisoner. Carr had just given them his little pep talk and sitrep when Montoya hissed at him.

"Free is back," Montoya said, referring to Sergeant Samples by his behind-the-back nickname.

Carr nodded and rushed back up the line to Eberhart, where he found Samples and Reyes waiting for him.

"What have we got?" Carr asked, kneeling down on the damp earth.

"A temple," Carr said succinctly. "A very small temple. Maybe you would call it a chapel. Looks Cao Dai."

"Yeah," Reyes chimed in, "I saw the big eye on the front." Cao Dai, a local religion that was a combination of several other religions, was familiar to all the soldiers in this area. The Cao Dai temples, ornate buildings with minarets and columns, always featured a picture of a giant human eye over the front door, the "All-seeing Eye."

"In the middle of the woods?" Carr asked rhetorically.

"There used to be a road here," Samples pointed out. "Maybe it was a stop for travelers or something."

"Abandoned?"

"Actually seems like it's been kept up, or cleaned up recently."

"Anyone inside?" Carr asked. "We saw a light earlier."

"I didn't go in," Samples said. "The windows are dark. It's hard to hear anything over the rain, but I think there might be one or two people inside."

"Armed?"

Samples shrugged. "Only one way to find out."

*****

The area closest to the building had been cleared of undergrowth, some of which had been piled to one side. Trees grew as near as ten feet, their limbs arcing over the building and hiding it from the sky. Samples approached the chapel from the southeast, with Reyes, Vasquez, and Lenny Sorenson trailing behind. The front of the building had a single opening, a narrow doorway between two ornate pillars. In the dripping darkness it was hard to see details, but it looked like the doorway was open to the inside, with no actual door. He motioned for Reyes to take a position where he could watch the door, while Samples stealthily led the other two men around to the south side, which featured a single small window high in the middle of the wall. Samples tugged at Sorenson's arm and motioned for him to take a position beside the window.

He hadn't seen a rear entrance on his first recon, but Samples checked again, closer in this time. The back wall was featureless, with not even a window. He led Vasquez on around to the north side, where there was another high window, identical to the south side. He stationed Vasquez there while he continued on around to the northwest corner. Stepping around the corner, keeping his back to the wall, his eyes strained to see through the blackness. Although he was only twenty feet away, Reyes was almost invisible. With broad gestures Samples conveyed his intentions, and Reyes gave exaggerated nods to show he understood.

Reyes came closer, and both men crept along the front wall until they were positioned on either side of the doorway. Reyes was left-handed, so it was natural for him to hold his M-16 in his left, and a flashlight in his right. Stretching his arm out until it cleared the door frame, he waited a second while Samples crouched down and edged around the opposite side, and then clicked on the light. Samples sprawled forward, his rifle sweeping the space inside while he took in the dimly lighted scene. There was no reaction from inside, and at first he detected no movement. Reyes continued to play the yellow flashlight beam around the room, stepping forward so he could shine it into the nearer corners.

The room was about fifteen feet square, with bare walls and a raised platform at the back. Samples saw what looked like a bed made of bamboo, a small table of the same material, a wooden crate and some metal ammo cans, and a wooden folding chair. A heavy wood cabinet sat in the middle of the raised wooden floor at the back with candles on it; Samples figured it was an altar of some sort. Some clothing was hanging from a peg on the north wall, and a pile of fabric sat on the bare dirt floor in the northeast corner, just to Samples' right. Samples was puzzled, because he was sure he had heard someone moving around on his earlier approach, and wondered if the occupant had slipped away into the forest in the meantime.

"Knock, knock," Reyes said, still sweeping the room with the flashlight.

"Doesn't look like anyone's home," Samples said, pushing himself to his feet. He nearly jumped out of his skin when the pile of fabric in the corner suddenly moved, and a small hooded man rose and yelled "No shoot!" in a strange accent. Fortunately for the man, Samples hadn't fully arisen at that moment and didn't have his rifle ready, for otherwise he would have instinctively fired at the movement. The man wore a long hooded robe, but had his hands raised as he repeatedly pleaded for them not to shoot. Reyes came in behind Samples and pointed the flashlight directly at the man, who quickly turned away, keeping his face in shadow. Samples had caught a brief glimpse of glasses with thick black plastic rims.

"Who the fuck are you?" Samples asked angrily, mad that he had been so startled and caught off guard.

"Monk," the man replied in a squeaky voice. "Cao Dai monk." He edged over and knelt down in the middle of the room,

81

facing the far end of the room. "You go. You not Cao Dai." The robe he was wearing was brown and looked amateurishly made, the hood attached crookedly. The monk kept his head down, bowing in the direction of the presumed altar in the middle of the raised wooden floor at the back of the room.

"Any weapons here?" Samples demanded.

"You go," the monk repeated. "Temple here. You no Cao Dai."

Samples signaled to Reyes to search the room, then called out, "Vasquez, Sorenson, come on in." Samples watched the robed man, wondering just what in the hell was going on here. A monk in an old chapel out in the woods, miles from civilization: did that make any sense? He knew that some religions had monks who became hermits, and maybe that was the case here. He also knew that soldiers were expected to respect religious buildings and personnel, but something just didn't feel right about this one.

No sooner had Sorenson and Vasquez come in out of the rain than Samples heard the shots. It sounded like two different guns, from two different locations, probably AK-47s or SKS's. There was an immediate response from the Americans waiting out along the abandoned road, with M-16s barking and Pastorini's M-60 chattering. "Stay here!" Samples ordered the others as he darted out the door into the rain. He had to be careful approaching the column, to avoid being shot by his own men. Dodging from tree to tree, he carefully hurried toward the action, only to hear Lieutenant Carr call for a cease fire.

The gunfire subsided quickly, and quiet reigned again, at least for a few seconds. "I'm coming in," Samples warned, and darted forward in a crouch to find Carr and the others prone on the wet ground. He knelt down next to Carr. "It's a temple or something," he explained in a rush, "and there's a monk inside. He's says we've got to leave."

Another burst of AK-47 fire ripped through the air, and it was coming from the north, right where they had intended to go. Samples stood up and fired five rounds toward where he thought the shots had come from, then ducked back down. "It's a brick building," he told Carr. "It's better than out here in the open."

"Definitely," Carr agreed. "Get them moving, I'll cover you." Carr rose to a kneeling position and fired three shots toward the north. Samples duck-walked down the column, telling each person to make their way to the temple as quickly as they could.

"Preacher," he said to Pastorini, "can you stay here with the lieutenant until the rest are inside the temple? Provide some additional cover fire?"

"No sweat," the big man said, and stood up to fire a burst of machine gun fire from the hip.

Samples had to herd the Girlfriends like sheep, urging them to run toward the temple. The others sought the shelter of the building without delay, and even the prisoner hustled to get the stretcher carrying the dead copilot through the trees. Samples figured he wasn't anxious to be killed by his own side. When they had all crowded inside, Samples ran back to where Carr and Pastorini were popping off rounds sporadically. "Let's go," he called to them, and as they passed him he stood and fired a few more rounds into the surrounding darkness. An AK fired from somewhere to the east, the bullets snapping over his head. Samples fired a couple more rounds in that direction then turned and ran in a crouch back to the building.

Crowding in behind Pastorini, Samples yelled, "Everybody against the walls! Leave the middle of the room empty! And get down!" The doorway was an open invitation to a sniper, and he didn't want anyone directly in the line of fire. With so many people stuffed into the single room, there was no way they could all avoid any incoming, but he needed to reduce the possibilities. The room was pitch black, but he could hear the scuffling and mutterings as everyone found some place to sit near a wall. Unclipping his flashlight from his pistol belt, Samples put his back against the wall next to the door and clicked it on, pointing it at the vaulted ceiling so the reflected beam threw a diffused light over the entire room.

For some reason the light didn't draw any fire, for which he was very thankful. In the dim illumination he did a rapid head count, letting his gaze linger on Captain Gaither for perhaps a second longer than the others. The Cao Dai monk was at the back of the room, on the raised section of the floor, squatting with his hood pulled forward over his face. Colonel Tarreyton sat on the bamboo bed near the north wall, his ubiquitous briefcase on his lap. The Girlfriends were clustered opposite Samples in the southeast corner of the room, pulling off their ponchos, running their fingers through their wet hair, and quietly chattering. Everyone was accounted for. He snapped off the light just as Lieutenant Carr came up beside him.

"What do you think?" Carr asked, keeping his voice low.

"We're out of the rain," Samples commented, feeling that was about the only improvement in their situation.

"What is this thing made of? Feels like stone."

"Cinder block, probably. It'll stop rifle rounds, but won't stand up to RPGs."

Carr grunted. "Let's hope they don't have any of those."

"Are we going to hold out here until morning?" Samples asked.

"Still deciding. It gives us some protection, but also kind of traps us."

"Like the Alamo," Samples suggested.

"Where everybody died," Carr replied. "Let's think of a better analogy."

"Custer's Last Stand?"

"Aaron, you're not helping."

"How about Bastogne, the Battle of the Bulge?"

"That's better."

"Yeah, we can be the Battlin' Bastards of the Boi Loi."

"Whatever." Carr was quiet for a minute. Now that his eyes had adjusted to the darkness again, Samples saw the small triangle of grey at the peak of the ceiling in the back. A ventilation opening, he guessed.

"If we keep going," Carr surmised thoughtfully, "those snipers can pick us off from the woods. But if we stay here they might get reinforced by those NVA."

"So," Samples summed up, "we're fucked either way."

"Yeah, but I think we're less fucked staying here. The NVA might not be coming, and the building will give us some protection even if they do. I just wish I knew where we are. Then we could call in arty."

"This place isn't on the map?" Samples asked, surprised by the revelation.

"I don't think so. I'll look at the map again, but last time I couldn't see any roads or buildings in this area. And with this rain, and the thick canopy, asking arty for marking rounds isn't going to be useful."

"Okay," Samples told him helpfully, "at least in the morning we can pop smoke. Assuming we make it till morning."

NINE

Using the mental image of what he had seen with the flashlight as a map, Samples moved around the room, giving assignments to his men and checking on the others. Carr and Eberhart were managing on their own, using the radio in the northeast corner. Montoya and Vasquez were by the north window, and Samples told them to keep a sharp eye out for anyone approaching from that direction. Colonel Tarreyton had stretched out on the bamboo bunk, using his briefcase as a pillow. Samples thought of some subtly cutting remarks he could make to the officer, but held his tongue. Beyond the bed, on the raised part of the floor, was the stretcher carrying the injured pilot, and though he couldn't really see them, Samples sensed that Allman and Captain Gaither were kneeling beside it.

"How's he doing?" Samples asked gently.

"I've been better," the pilot answered, obviously awake and aware.

"Thank you for finding this shelter, Sergeant," Gaither said with a sincere tone, and Samples was pleased at her words.

"Sorry, sir," Samples said to the pilot, "but I didn't get your name."

"CWO Whitmore, Roger."

So he was a Chief Warrant Officer, Samples thought. Not really an officer, but not really an enlisted man.

"We'll get you out of here as soon as possible, Chief," Samples told him.

"Appreciate it," Whitmore said. "I've got a hot date later." Although Whitmore said it with a chuckle, Samples sourly suspected the handsome and dashing pilot really did have a date with some good-looking nurse or donut dolly. Maybe even with Captain Gaither, which gave Samples a little twinge.

"Where do you want me, Sarge?" Pastorini asked, shifting his grip on the M-60. The big man was standing at the foot of Tarreyton's bunk, patiently awaiting orders. His question took Samples' mind off the red-headed nurse.

"We need to block the door," Samples replied. "Think we can move that altar or whatever it is? Put the M-60 on it?"

"No sweat," Pastorini said, putting the gun down on the bunk, pushing aside Tarreyton's legs to do so.

"Hicks, help him," Samples ordered. "And after you do that, get that crate and put it under that ventilation hole near the roof. See if you can stand on it and look out the hole, watch for anything coming from that direction."

Hicks gave an exaggerated sigh of self-pity, but grabbed the side of the altar. With Pastorini on the other side, they began maneuvering it across the crowded room toward the door. The monk got out of their way without protest, which surprised Samples. He had assumed the religious man would object to moving the altar, decrying it as some sort of sacrilege. Instead he just let them pass and then crouched over by the wall, his back to the room.

Johnson and Greenberg were in the southeast corner, keeping their rifles trained on the prisoner, who was sitting on the edge of the raised floor, apparently unperturbed by his situation. "Better tie him up again," Samples told them.

Crosby was sitting at the small table, rocking back and forth on the rickety wooden chair. "What do you want me to do, Sarge?" the young man asked.

"There's some clothes or something hanging over on that wall," Samples informed him. "Get some of those and cover the body."

"Roger." Crosby got up and stumbled on the edge of the raised floor as he went to find the clothing.

Lenny Sorenson and Sergeant Reedy were on either side of the south window, peeking around the edges of the window to observe the rain dripping through the trees outside. "Seen anything?" Samples asked.

"Nothin'," Reedy replied.

Sweet was standing close to the Girlfriends, acting very protective. Samples rolled his eyes in the dark, but didn't reprimand him. Instead he just patted the boy on the shoulder and stepped around him to talk to Reyes, who was helping Hicks and Pastorini position the heavy wooden alter in the doorway. "How about you?" he asked Reyes when he stood back from the altar and picked his rifle up again. "Any movement?"

"Not so far," Reyes replied. "Not that I can see shit in the dark anyway. Wish we'd brought the starlight." The starlight scope electronically amplified existing light to allow soldiers to virtually see in the dark. The scope was heavy and bulky, however, so Samples had left it in the track.

"Yeah, me, too. Can't think of everything." Here in the doorway there was just enough light for Samples to tell that Pastorini had pulled down the bipods on the M-60 and laid it across the altar. Crosby came up behind them carrying the two cans of M-60 ammo.

"That nurse said you might need this," Crosby told them.

"Thanks," Pastorini rumbled, sitting down on the muddy floor behind the altar. Crosby moved away to pick up the clothing and spread it over the dead copilot. Samples finished his circuit of the room and stood next to Carr, waiting for the platoon leader to finish his radio conversation. He kept thinking of how the men were deployed, and wondering what he had forgotten or not considered.

"They don't know where we are, either," Carr told him as he passed the handset back to Eberhart. "This temple, or chapel, or whatever, isn't on any of the maps they have. They're going to check with the District Chief in the morning, but that won't do us any good now." The District Chief was the local Vietnamese government official in charge of this area, kind of like a county supervisor, but with a military rank.

"They can't wake him up tonight?"

"Apparently not," Carr groused. "He only works nine to five."

"Typical," Samples grumbled. Changing the subject, he reported, "I've got all the windows covered, and the sixty in the door. Everyone's accounted for. The pilot's awake—CWO Whitmore."

"What about that monk?" Carr asked.

"What about him?"

"Maybe he can show us on a map where we are."

"I don't think he speaks much English, and he isn't happy we're even here, but I guess it's worth a shot. Want me to get him?"

"Yeah. We can huddle here in the corner, so the flashlight doesn't show."

Samples walked carefully to the back of the room, dodging around the copilot's stretcher and the end of the bamboo bed. He nearly tripped on the edge of the raised floor, and made the prisoner yelp when he grabbed the man's wounded shoulder to steady himself. "*Xin loi*," he said to the man with no sincerity, not caring if he had correctly pronounced the Vietnamese phrase for "sorry about that." In the extremely dim light filtering in through the doorway, he could tell that Hicks was standing on a wooden crate peering out the ventilation opening. Touching his leg, he asked, "See anything yet?"

"Huh-uh," Hicks replied without moving.

"Good."

Samples reached down and tapped the monk on the shoulder. The man shook his head violently under his hood and grunted negatively. "You go!" he said. "You number ten."

Samples grabbed the man's upper arm and pulled him to his feet. "The lieutenant wants to see you."

"No!" the man squealed, trying to pull away.

"He's not going to hurt you," Samples assured him. "He just wants to ask you some questions."

"No speak English," the man countered.

"You don't have to," Samples said, pulling the man toward the front of the room. "Just look at a map." The man tripped on the end of the stretcher, but Samples' iron grip on his arm kept him upright. "Watch your step." Limping and stumbling, the monk finally allowed Samples to guide him over to the corner where Carr was waiting. Carr knelt down and flicked on the flashlight, pointing it at the map that Eberhart had spread across a box he had found.

"Where are we?" Carr asked, using broad gestures to indicate the building around them and then placing his finger on the map. The monk knelt down across from Carr and bent closer to study the plastic-covered paper, pulling the hood forward even more as he did so. Carr put his finger on some of the landmarks. "Dau Tieng is here, the Saigon River, and here's Ben Cui." He made a circle over the Boi Loi Woods and again asked, "Where are we?"

"*Khong biet*," the man said, "*khong biet*." Samples knew that meant "I don't know."

"How can you not know where you are?" Samples demanded. He poked the man in the back to encourage him, but it had the unintended effect of making the man lose his balance and fall over on his side. The monk clutched at his robe and pulled the hood over his face as he sprawled on the dirt floor, but in the flashlight's scattered illumination Samples saw the man's feet clearly for the first time, and they were covered by Army-issue jungle boots.

"What the fuck!" Samples exclaimed angrily. "Look at his boots!" He grabbed the man's arm and pulled him up to a sitting position, then wrestled with the man to pull back his hood. Finally ripping it out of the man's hands, Samples jerked the hood back so Carr could point the flashlight at the man's face. Closing his eyes against the bright light, the man grimaced and tried to pull away.

"He's not Vietnamese," Eberhart observed. The man had stringy brown hair, pale skin, and a pair of Army-issued glasses with fairly thick lenses.

"You're American!" Carr accused.

Tears were now oozing from his tightly closed eyes as the man nodded.

"What's your name, son?" Carr asked, taking on a more gentle tone.

"Bolling, sir," the young man whimpered. "PFC Alex Bolling. Twenty-Fifth Supply and Transportation."

"A truck driver?" Samples asked disbelievingly. "What are you doing out here in the woods?"

Before the man could answer, there was a simultaneous bang outside and a bullet slamming into the wall just above Carr's head. Samples, Carr, Eberhart, and Bolling all fought for space on the floor as they dived for cover, and Carr switched off the flashlight. Over at the south window Sergeant Reedy fired off a few single shots into the dark woods. Obviously a gook had seen the light through that window and found a position, possibly up a tree, that allowed him to take the shot. That confirmed for Samples what he had already suspected: the gooks were still out there, and had surrounded the building.

Thinking the incident was already over, Samples started to get up when he heard something heavy hit the door frame and clatter on the wooden altar. Pastorini yelled "Oh, crap!" and grunted with some urgent physical effort. A moment later there was a burst of light like a flash bulb going off just outside, accompanied by a sharp explosion.

"Hand grenade!" Pastorini yelled, louder than really necessary, and began firing his M-60. He was firing in one long burst, spraying the area in front of the building in a wide arc from left to right.

"Easy, easy!" Samples warned him. "You'll burn out the barrel."

Pastorini lifted his finger from the trigger and gulped in air, his breathing very noticeable in the ensuring silence.

"What happened?" Carr asked from behind Samples.

"Potato masher," Pastorini explained as he caught his breath. "Hit the door, then landed on top of this cabinet. I threw it back." The Communist soldiers, both VC and NVA, generally used Chinese-made hand grenades similar to those used by the Germans in World War II. They looked like a can of beans with a wooden handle stuck in one end, and back in the day they had resembled the old-style kitchen potato masher.

"Good work," Samples praised him.

"But how did he get close enough to throw it?" Carr asked.

"We were ducking the sniper's rounds," Samples pointed out reasonably. "Plus, it's dark and wet out there."

"Think you got him?" Carr asked Pastorini.

"Damned if I know," Pastorini replied, calmer now. "Sure hope so."

"And we know there's at least two of them now," Samples remarked. "Unless Preacher got the guy out front."

Samples heard the rising murmur of the other people in the chapel as they recovered from fright of the incident. "Keep it down! We need to be able to hear what's happening outside." The muttering diminished, but didn't go away completely. "Anybody get hurt?" There were a few scattered "no's" and no "yes's". Samples was relieved when one of the negative replies came from Captain Gaither.

*****

"Bolling!" Carr said sharply, transferring the residual fright and anger of the brief attack to the young truck driver. "What the hell are you doing here?"

"Uh," the soldier stammered, "uh, just hiding out, sir. From the gooks."

"But why here, out in the middle of the Boi Loi Woods?"

"Um," Bolling hesitated, apparently trying to come up with a good answer. "Well, you see, sir, my truck broke down, and, uh, I had to go to the bathroom, and I went into the woods, and next thing you know I was lost. Yeah, I was lost in the woods, and I could hear gooks, and then I found this place."

"How long have you been here?"

"Uh, not long. A few days."

"Bullshit!" Samples said.

"No, really," Bolling protested. "I figured I was safer here than trying to find the road again."

So what have you been doing for food?" Carr asked.

"Uh, you know, whatever I could find."

"There's a couple cases of C-rations under the bunk," Vasquez said from over by the north window.

"Yeah, I don't know how those got there. They were here when I got here."

Samples scoffed loudly. Carr reached out and put a warning hand on Samples' shoulder.

"So why did you pretend to be a monk when we showed up?" Carr asked quietly.

"Well, you see, I figured you would think I was a deserter or something at first. I was going to tell you after everything calmed down. Honest."

"PFC Bolling, you are not a good liar. It's all going to come out eventually, so why don't you start over and tell us the truth."

Bolling sniffed a couple times, and then began sobbing. His crying was pitiful, but Carr had little sympathy for the young man. He waited patiently until Bolling was able to tell his story.

"My truck did break down. My sergeant said he was going to have me court-martialed when we got back to Cu Chi, because I hadn't checked the oil. I mean, he didn't check the oil either, so it was just as much his fault as mine. He told me to stay with the truck while he went for help. I grabbed some C's and went to hide in the woods. I don't know what I was thinking. I just didn't want to be court-martialed. And then I did get lost. It was really hard. Lugging those cases of C's around in the woods, no weapon, worried about being shot. Then I stumbled across this place. It was all overgrown, looked like no one had been here for years, so I thought it was a good place to hide out until I figured out what to do next. I cleaned it up a little, found that old robe, and pretended to be a monk. The VC leave me alone, I guess because they think I'm a real monk."

"So how long have you really been here?" Carr was amazed at the story, but found it credible. He had heard of other soldiers who had deserted and hidden out in the countryside.

"About a month," Bolling confessed.

"And you've survived on a couple cases of C-rats?"

"Well, sometimes I go back out to the highway and buy stuff from the Coke kids. I had just been paid, so I have some money. And sometimes I'd find stuff."

"So you know where the road is?" Samples demanded. "How far is it?"

"About two miles," Bolling said. "Straight north. I can show you."

Carr dismissed that idea. With the hidden road easy enough to follow, finding their way wasn't the problem. It was the threat of the gooks hiding in the woods outside that kept them trapped in this building.

"Go over and sit by that gook we captured," Carr told Bolling. "We'll have to take you back with us, and then you can explain what happened to the MPs."

Bolling sniffed loudly and choked back a sob, but obediently stood up and made his way to the back of the room.

"Fuckin' deserter," Samples muttered.

"Yep," Carr agreed, "but keep in mind that he doesn't seem like the brightest guy in the world, and he's probably a draftee that didn't want to be here in the first place. He's more scared of spending time at Ft. Leavenworth than he is about hiding in the woods from the VC. I've heard of guys trying to get arrested and sent to Leavenworth, saying it's better than Nam."

"Yeah, well," Samples grumbled.

"And we've got more important things to worry about right now."

"Want me to report this guy to Battalion?" Eberhart asked.

"Not right now," Carr told him. "I want them to concentrate on getting us out of here. Have they had any luck with their maps?"

"Haven't said anything," Eberhart replied. "I told them about the sniper and the grenade. They didn't seem impressed. Said to keep our heads down."

"Never would have thought of that," Samples growled.

"So what do you think, Aaron?" Carr asked, wondering, as always, if he was making the right decision. "Should we try for the highway?"

Samples took a deep breath while he considered the question. "I don't think so, Eltee. With the stretchers, the girls, the prisoners, Captain Gaither, it'd be too complicated and too slow. The gooks could pick us off pretty easily. If it was just our platoon, I'd say maybe, but not with these other people."

"I notice you didn't mention Colonel Tarreyton," Carr said with a chuckle.

"He's a colonel; he can take care of himself. Supposedly. And if he can't, well, that's no skin off my nose."

"While I tend to agree with you, he is our responsibility."

"Him and his damn briefcase," Samples complained. "What do suppose he's got in there that's so damn important?"

"Don't know, don't care. As long as he stays out of my way. But back to my original question. There's probably only two VC out there right now, don't you think?"

"Probably. If there was more, we would have heard from them by now."

"And for all we know, one or both of them might have been shot just now, or that one blown up with his own grenade."

"I haven't heard any moaning or yells or anything," Samples cautioned. "I guess it's possible. But how would we know?"

"They say the best defense is a good offense. Maybe we ought to send out a patrol to hunt those guys down."

"That's a thought," Samples grudgingly agreed. "How many guys are you thinking?"

"Four, five?"

"Naw, they'd just get in each other's way. I'll take one guy, Reyes maybe."

"I didn't mean you, Aaron," Carr said quickly.

"I don't trust anybody else," Samples said. "They're good, but I've had more experience in night fighting than they have. Reyes has good night vision. I've got my bayonet, and Reyes has a wicked hunting knife. SBD—silent but deadly."

Carr didn't like the idea of the platoon sergeant he depended on—and was close to—going out into the rainy dark woods, but conceded that he was the best person to send.

"When are you going to go?" Carr asked.

"Sooner the better. Hey, Carlos, come here."

TEN

There was a small underground bunker next to the company headquarters, and Lieutenant Harry Masters had gone down there so he could turn on the lights and study the maps he had brought with him. Sitting on a wobbly cot, he spread the maps across his knees and hunched over with a flashlight to examiner them more closely. He had listened to all the radio traffic between Lieutenant Carr and Battalion, and knew that the headquarters staff had been unable to precisely locate the platoon out in the Boi Loi. Masters was hoping that the old French maps he had found might have forgotten details that would point him in the right direction. On a current Army map of the Boi Loi Woods he had used a grease pencil to circle the general area where the patrol was suspected to be, somewhere west of the helicopter crash site. The French map for that area looked significantly different, and he spent a lot of time doing back-and-forth comparisons. The French map was drawn to a different scale, used different symbols for landmarks, and had the names of locations and descriptions all in French, naturally. Masters' high school French was barely adequate to even guess at some of the notations.

There! In tiny grey letters next to a small black square was the word *chapelle*. In the bad light, on the faded map, it was easily missed, but he had found it at last. It was located next to a faint dotted line running north and south that Masters was certain indicted the abandoned road Carr had described on the radio. Now all he had to do was pin down the coordinates, and that wouldn't be easy. The French map showed degrees and seconds of latitude and longitude, while Army maps were graphed in UTM coordinate grids, a decimal system easier to use than the older lat/long method. Converting from one to the other was complex and difficult, and Masters had never really understood the process. Instead, he used a pencil and a ruler to draw lines on the French map connecting the chapel with definite landmarks like the right-angle turn of the highway at Ben Cui, a prominent bend in the Saigon River, and a road intersection at Bao Donh. Using the acetate protractor he had been issued back in Officer Basic at Ft. Benning, he then measured the angle of each line and jotted it down in his pocket notebook.

Next he picked up the Army map and did the same process in reverse, drawing lines from the reference points at the proper angles until they all intersected. Assuming he had done it correctly, that point where the lines all crossed was where Carr and his men were sheltering the people rescued from the helicopter. On the Army map, there was no indication of a building or a road—just the light green background that indicated a forest, with no discernable landmarks. Masters was pretty sure he had their location pinpointed, but self-doubt began to creep in. Just to be sure, he re-measured all the angles on the French map, and then double-checked the lines he had drawn on the Army map. Everything checked out. Masters leaned back and took a breath, smiling to himself.

"Incoming!" The shout came from up above, and immediately he saw legs on the ladder as first Delaney and then Ford scrambled and slid down into the bunker with him.

"Rockets," Ford told him in a matter-of-fact tone. The rocket attacks on the base camp were a common occurrence, though they rarely occurred when it was raining. In the glare of the bare bulb hanging from the low ceiling of the bunker, Masters could see the dark speckles on Ford's shirt from his hurried run through the rain from the headquarters building to the bunker. He both felt and heard the crunch as a rocket exploded somewhere nearby. The 122 millimeter rockets were launched from makeshift wooden troughs out in the Michelin rubber plantation, and weren't very accurate, but they could do a lot of damage. He heard another rocket explode, this one some distance away.

"What about the new guys?" Masters asked, just remembering them himself.

"There's sandbags around the barracks," Ford replied, perhaps a little defensively. The sandbags only covered the lower portion of the building, about two feet up from the floor.

Without a word Masters climbed up the ladder, hesitated a moment at the entrance to listen for the whoosh of a rocket, and then darted over to the barracks building. It was too dark to really see anything, but he could hear—and smell—the young men lying on the wooden floor. "Follow me to the bunker," he told them. "Now!"

He heard the scuffling and grunting as the guys got to their feet and crowded toward him. "Come on," he encouraged them, hustling through the rain back to the bunker entrance. Masters stood aside as they filed down the ladder, letting the rain soak his uniform while he listened for more incoming. The last of the new guys had just dropped down the hole when he heard it—the whistling swoosh rising in volume as a rocket headed his way, arcing though the low rain-soaked clouds. Masters jumped in and slid down the ladder like a fireman's pole, hitting the floor just as the rocket exploded somewhere very close, near enough for the flash to briefly illuminate the bunker's opening.

The bunker was never meant to hold seven people, and Masters could barely turn around in the cramped space. The bulb hanging from the ceiling was still lit, but it was swinging back and forth after someone had bumped into it with their head. Ford and one of the new guys were sitting on the cot, and the others just stood around looking bewildered. The new guy on the cot was in full uniform—apparently he had chosen to sleep that way, or had been too exhausted to get undressed. Two of the other newbies had only their pants on, their boots unlaced and caked with mud. The fourth new arrival was wearing only his boxer shorts, his feet bare and dirty. He would learn, Masters thought. Delaney was leaning against the wall with an air of assumed nonchalance.

"Does this happen a lot, sir?" the guy in his boxer shorts asked nervously.

"Pretty much," Masters told him. "It's best to keep your boots handy. As well as your pants."

"Yes, sir," the young man said, abashed.

99

"Will there be a ground attack?" the new guy on the cot asked. He just seemed curious, not worried.

"Probably not," Masters answered. "They fire the rockets, and sometimes mortars, just to keep us on our toes."

"They got my attention," one of the other guys said.

Masters pushed his way between the standing men to the cot. "Where are my maps?" he asked Ford, reaching down between Ford and the new guy.

"Maps, sir?" Ford jumped up, and so did the new guy, trying to get out of Masters' way, and only partially succeeding. At that point the light went out, plunging the tiny room into pitch darkness.

"Damn it!" Masters cursed. "Where's a flashlight?" He began feeling around in the dark, and could tell that others were doing the same. He also felt paper under his feet, and heard it rip as he tried to lift his feet off of it.

"I got it," somebody said, and a weak flashlight beam came on and pointed right at Masters, temporarily blinding him.

With his eyes almost all the way closed to block out the glare, Masters reached out and said, "Give it here." He felt it placed in his hand, and then pointed it down at his feet, pushing back against the crowd of men behind him. As he had feared, the French map was on the floor, torn and muddy. The floor of the bunker was made of shipping pallets with narrow gaps between the boards, and the map had been half caught between the slats and then shredded by muddy feet jostling for position. Masters squatted down and retrieved the ragged remains. He tried to smooth it out, but the decades-old paper, thin and wet, just fell apart.

"Where's the other map?" he asked, anxiously shining the flashlight beam in ever widening circles.

"This one?" Ford asked, holding up an Army map that was crumpled but otherwise undamaged.

"Thank God," Masters breathed, snatching the map away from him. Spreading it out on the cot, he sighed with relief when he found the pencil lines intersecting in the middle of the Boi Loi. At least he still knew where Carr and the others were. As soon as the rocket attack ended, he would take it over to Battalion.

*****

Carr had mixed feelings about the proposed search and destroy mission. He didn't like the fact that Samples and Reyes would be putting themselves in such danger, especially since Carr so heavily depended on Samples for advice and support. And Reyes wouldn't have been Carr's first choice to accompany the platoon sergeant. A Texan with a rebellious streak, Reyes had been designated a squad leader only because they had no sergeants available, and he was the most senior of the E-4s. Worse, in Carr's opinion, was the fact that Reyes was getting short. He had less than two months left in country until he DEROSed, and that often led to soldiers being overly cautious. A soldier's Date Estimated for Return from Overseas Service was something every man knew intimately, and they all counted down the days. Samples, however, had faith that the young man would develop into a leader given the opportunity, and Carr knew better than to go against him.

If the two men were able to track down and neutralize the Viet Cong that were skulking through the woods, that would allow Carr to lead the platoon and their charges out of the Boi Loi to the relative safety of the highway, where they could be picked up by American vehicles as soon as it got light, or maybe even sooner. The problem, of course, was that they weren't sure how many VC were out there, or where they were located. If Samples and Reyes managed to find and kill or capture two VC, which is the number they were currently assuming to be out there, how certain could Carr be that there were no others? If he led the group out into the woods and there were others, he risked getting additional people killed or wounded. There were too many uncertainties, and Carr was frustrated.

"All right, we're ready," Samples announced quietly. Despite the intense darkness, Carr could tell that Samples and Reyes had shed their helmets, pistol belts, and other gear, and were carrying only their rifles, a few extra magazines in their pockets, and their knives. "We're going to go out the ventilation hole in back," Samples told him.

"Is that big enough?" Carr asked doubtfully.

"Yeah, I think so. Somebody will have to boost us up. There's a beam sticking out we can hold onto before dropping to the ground."

"How will you get back in?"

Carr detected some movement that made him believe Samples had shrugged. "Hopefully that won't be a problem. If we get the gooks, we can walk in through the door."

"And if you don't?"

"*Xin loi*, I guess. I'll figure something out."

"What if they're watching the back when you go out?" Carr kept quizzing Samples, hoping to perhaps cause him to rethink this operation.

"Why don't you have the guys at the door and windows open up for a minute or two. The noise and muzzle flashes will distract the gooks until we get clear."

"Okay," Carr grudgingly agreed. "You're sure about this, Aaron?"

"I can't stand just sitting here waiting," Samples told him. "I gotta do something."

Carr nodded his understanding. "Whistle when you're ready back there."

While Samples and Reyes went to the back and got someone to help them reach the triangular ventilation hole near the rook's peak, Carr walked around and quietly told the soldiers at the other openings what they were to do. Then he stood in the middle of the room and waited for the signal.

There were some scuffling noises at the back, and then Carr saw the dim opening get darker as someone blocked it with their head. There was a low whistle.

"Commence firing," Carr ordered loudly, and the room reverberated with the sudden onslaught of noise from M-16s and the M-60 firing into the dripping night. With the guns creating a deafening cacophony that bounced around the walls of the chapel, and the flickering muzzle flashes creating a strobe effect, Carr kept his attention focused on the opening at the back. He was pretty sure he saw first one body, and then another, squeeze through the narrow hole and drop away. The aperture became clear for a few seconds, and then Carr saw a helmeted head rise up and a rifle poked out, presumably Hicks resuming his guard position.

"Okay!" Hicks yelled over the noise.

"Cease fire!" Carr commanded, and the noise abated as quickly as it had begun. His ears still ringing, Carr listened for any response. There was no return fire. Samples and Reyes had made it into the woods safely, at least for now.

"What the hell was that all about, Lieutenant?" Colonel Tarreyton demanded, not bothering to rise from his seat on the narrow bed.

Carr took a couple steps over and stood in front of the colonel, intentionally taking the metaphorical high ground. "I sent out a patrol to find and neutralize the VC," Carr told him calmly. "The firing was to distract the enemy."

"Why didn't you keep me informed?"

"I'm sorry, sir, but I just didn't have time," Carr lied. "We had a narrow window of opportunity."

"So, your patrol takes out the gooks, and then we continue our trek, is that it?"

"Possibly."

"I don't like it," Tarreyton grumbled. "Too dangerous. We need to stay here until the cavalry comes."

"My concern, sir, is that there's a large NVA unit to our south, and they may be sending troops to assist the Charlies."

Tarreyton scoffed. "Not likely. Aren't they engaged with some Wolfhounds?"

103

"Not anymore. The Wolfhounds had to pull back."

"Nonetheless. I can't see any reason they'd be sending troops here."

"Why not?" Carr decided to appeal to the man's vanity a little. "They might think the chopper had important people aboard, like you, sir."

"Yes, well," Tarreyton huffed. "I see your point."

"And I assume you're carrying important papers or something that they might want."

Tarreyton clutched the briefcase closer to his chest. "That's true. We can't let this briefcase fall into enemy hands."

"May I know what's in it?" Carr asked casually.

"You don't have a need to know," Tarreyton replied haughtily. "In fact, it's better that you don't."

Carr suppressed a guffaw at the man's self-importance. "I'm sure you're right, sir."

"Lieutenant!" Nurse Gaither's strident tone pierced the short distance to the raised floor just on the other side of the make-shift bunk. "Why did you send Sergeant Samples out like that? It is way too dangerous out there."

Carr could barely make out her form in the darkened room, but he sensed her imperious stance. "It was his idea, ma'am."

"Bullshit! Well, you should have stopped him."

"Ma'am, when Aaron Samples gets an idea in his head, I've learned not to interfere."

"That's his first name, Aaron?"

"Yes, ma'am. Why?"

"No reason," Gaither replied, but with a strange tone of satisfaction.

"How's Warrant Officer Whitmore doing?" Carr asked to change the subject.

104

"Better," the man answered for himself. "Your medic has given me some good drugs."

"Under my supervision," the nurse clarified unnecessarily.

"Yeah, Doc knows what he's doing," Carr said. Allman himself stayed silent, probably not wanting to get involved with officer conversations. And wisely so.

"How long are we going to be here?" Whitmore asked from the stretcher.

"Not sure," Carr told them. "If my two guys can find the VC and take care of them, we might try for the highway tonight. If not, we'll have to stay here until the cavalry comes in the morning."

"Didn't I hear something about some NVA in the area?" Whitmore asked.

"It's possible," Carr admitted. "We don't know for sure."

"And if they show up?" Gaither asked. She sounded more curious than concerned.

"Let's hope they don't." Carr didn't want to get into what-ifs with these people. That would only increase their anxiety—and his own. To avoid further questions, Carr turned and said, "Hicks, you see or hear anything out there?"

From up near the roof Hicks answered without turning around from the opening. "Nope. Free and Carlos got away clean. Haven't heard anything since."

"Good."

"Sir?" It was Bolling, the deserter, speaking from his seat to Carr's left. "Is there anything I can do to help?"

"For instance," Carr replied with a tinge of disgust.

"I don't know. If I had a weapon, I could help guard or something."

"And why don't you already have a weapon?" Carr knew the answer, but wanted to hear it from Bolling.

"I left it behind," Bolling answered, the shame evident in his voice.

"Uh-huh. Well, we don't have any spare weapons right now, even if I were so inclined. I tell you what; you keep an eye on that gook next to you, and let us know if he tries anything."

"Yes, sir, I can do that."

Carr moved toward the south window, edging his feet forward slowly until he felt the handles of the other stretcher bang into his ankles. He wondered about the advisability of keeping the dead copilot there in the middle of the room, but what were the other options? If they had left him outside, the body could have been further damaged by enemy fire, and that wasn't acceptable. Inside, the least safe place for a living person was the center of the room, open to incoming from either window or the front door, so that was the logical place for someone that was already dead. Not very respectful, perhaps, but logical. Shuffling his feet to avoid tripping on the stretcher, Carr moved over to the window, behind Sorenson and Sergeant Reedy who were on either side of the opening, watching the outside.

"Anything?" Carr asked Reedy. Outside all Carr could see was rain and the dark columns of nearby tree trunks.

"Not lately," Reedy answered softly. "Been really quiet."

"Did you see Sergeant Samples and Reyes when they took off?"

"No, and that's a good thing. If we didn't see them, then the gooks probably didn't either."

"Well, be careful. Don't shoot unless you're sure it's not them. Don't want any friendly fire incidents."

"Roger that, sir."

Carr felt the side of the dead man's stretcher pressing against the back of his combat books, and carefully stepped around the end of the stretcher where Robert Crosby and Roland Sweet were entertaining the three Japanese girls. While most of the men in the platoon were still teenagers, Crosby and Sweet were undoubtedly the least mature of the bunch. They were just out of high school, and they acted like it. Crosby even looked young; slender, sandy-haired, soft features, he was what Carr imagined teen-aged girls would call "cute," but boyish. From his behavior and his conversations, Car figured Crosby was probably still a virgin—he got very shy when the boom-boom girls came around, although he liked to talk to the young girls who just sold sodas. Sweet, with dark hair a little longer than regs allowed and Army glasses, struck Carr as one of the guys in high school who hung out with the hoods, hoping to get some bad-guy aura rubbing off on him. He was actually a very nice and polite kid, even when he tried to act tough.

Carr was about to gently reprimand them for not helping with the guard duties when the girls began singing softly. "Wait, mister postman, rook and see, is there a retter in your bag for me."

"Yeah, cool!" Sweet said. Carr put his hand on the boy's shoulder.

"What are you two doing?" he demanded. The girls stopped singing abruptly.

"We were just telling them how much the mail means to us," Crosby explained. "You know, letters from home and stuff."

"We didn't know they were going to sing," Sweet said defensively.

"And you two don't have anything better to do than talk to these girls?"

"Do you have something for us to do, sir?" Crosby asked, trying to ingratiate himself.

"Why don't you two help Sergeant Pastorini at the door?" Carr suggested strongly. "One of you can be his loader, and the other one be a spotter. Okay?"

"Yes, sir," Sweet said contritely.

Gentling his tone, Carr told them, "You'll be right there, not far from the girls, so you can still keep them safe. Or something." He heard Pastorini chuckling, and it sounded like a diesel truck at idle. He walked behind the machine gunner and rejoined Eberhart in the northeast corner.

"Anything new from Battalion?" he asked.

"Same-same bullshit, sir."

ELEVEN

Samples stopped and went down on one knee. Behind him Reyes did the same. The forest surrounded them with dripping leaves and unseen thorns. Here in the woods it was so dark he could barely make out anything at all—just vertical irregular columns that represented trees—so he had to depend on his other senses. The patter of rain on the canopy was a constant murmur up above, which had its good points and its bad. While the noise covered the sounds he and Reyes made as they slipped through the underbrush, it also drowned out any tell-tale sounds the enemy soldiers might be making. And while they could see almost nothing in the gloom, the distinctive snare-drum beat of the raindrops on the tin roof of the chapel provided an aural compass that helped them stay oriented as they sneaked through the trees. At one point Samples even thought he heard singing, which puzzled him until he remembered the Girlfriends, and the fact that Sweet was "guarding" them.

Another advantage of the rain was the way it disguised their body odor. It was an article of faith among the GIs that the gooks could detect the distinctive smell of Americans at great distances. Samples wasn't sure how true that was, but acknowledged that he had occasionally detected the odor of Vietnamese people when they were several feet away. Here and now, however, all he could smell was rain and wet earth.

"Anything?" Reyes whispered in his ear.

Samples shook his head, and then said, "Negative," when he remembered that Reyes couldn't see him in the dark. After they had scooted away from the back of the chapel, he had led them about fifty feet into the forest going straight west, and had then begun circling the building counter-clockwise, keeping the sound of the rain on the roof, and the muted conversations inside, to his left. They moved very slowly, stepping carefully to avoid breaking twigs on the ground and feeling with their hands in front of them to avoid unseen branches or prickly bushes, and they stopped every few feet to listen for any unexpected sounds. When he had felt the ground under his feet start to rise a few inches, he figured they had reached the old roadway, and he had halted there to decide what to do next.

Although he couldn't see anything in the damp darkness, couldn't smell anything other than dank forest, or hear anything other than rain and unthreatening sounds from the building, Samples still could sense something. It was like the feeling you get when you're in a crowd and you can tell someone is staring at you. He didn't believe in ESP or other paranormal activities, but he knew that his mind could sometimes pick up on subtle sensory cues that he couldn't consciously perceive. And that was what he was trying to tap into now. He blanked his mind and just waited for something, anything, to trigger an alert. He could feel Reyes behind him, perhaps because he could hear him breathing, and he opened his mind to the sounds of the rain, imagining he could pick out the plop of individual raindrops. He peered through the darkness, striving to enhance his night vision by concentrating on his peripheral vision, picturing the forest around him in his mind as if it were daylight. He sniffed at faint odors, filtering out the natural vegetative smells of the woods in the hope of detecting something human, anything besides Reyes' and his own sweat. He couldn't identify anything out of place, but something was niggling at the back of his mind.

Crouched at the edge of the abandoned road, Samples knew that the foliage was less dense along the route, and tried to put himself in the position of the Viet Cong. Would they take positions on the road, where there was more room to maneuver and the ground was firmer, or melt back into the heavy woods across the road, where there was more cover and concealment? For him there was no doubt: the deep woods would feel safer. Even though they almost certainly didn't know they were being hunted, they would shelter in the dense trees, far enough away that they could talk and plan their next moves without fear of being heard. Samples turned and leaned back to whisper into Reyes' ear. "We're going across the road, about thirty feet into the woods, and then hang a left." Reyes nodded and patted Samples' back to show he understood.

Samples rose up and began carefully weaving his way through the saplings and bushes that masked the former road. He felt the edge of the road drop away almost imperceptibly as the foliage became thicker, and knew they were now plunging deeper into the woods on the other side. Behind him Reyes followed closely, his nervous breathing barely audible above the gentle drumming of the rain. Samples was trying to estimate how far they had gone when suddenly he stopped, and was almost knocked off balance when Reyes bumped into his back.

"What?" Reyes urgently whispered. Samples half turned and put his hand on Reyes' lips. The both stood there frozen for a couple seconds, and then together they slowly lowered their bodies to a squatting position. Something was out of place. He held his breath and listened intently. There it was again: a murmur, a quiet muttering, in the peculiar cadence of Vietnamese. Someone was close by, ahead and to the left. Shifting his position as slowly and quietly as he could, Samples turned to face the sounds, and reached back with his left hand to find Reyes' right arm. With tugs and taps he signaled Reyes to shift slightly to the left and take a position beside Samples, a couple feet away. Now on line, they rose to a crouch and began inching forward, their rifles pointing the way.

They came to a huge tree trunk, and Samples pressed his left shoulder to the bark, while Reyes mirrored him on the other side. There was an open space ahead of them, a small clearing in the woods, that Samples could feel more than actually see. In the middle of the glade he could hear the low sound of two men conferring, and against the charcoal gray of the woods his eyes detected the black shape of two figures close together. He hoped that Reyes had noticed as well. Wondering if these were the only two VC in the area, Samples paused and put out his mental feelers for anyone else that might be close by. At first he sensed nothing, and as he raised his M-16 to his shoulder he began tightening his finger on the trigger, knowing that Reyes would be doing the same, waiting for Samples to give the signal. Then he heard a twig snap behind him.

The two men in the clearing went silent and squatted. A few feet behind him Samples heard someone call out softly in Vietnamese, apparently announcing his approach. The two men in the clearing rose up and answered. Samples and Reyes were caught between the new arrival and the men in the clearing. He had only a second to react.

"Behind us!" he barked at Reyes, and opened fire on the men in the clearing. Reyes reacted as he had hoped, and spun around to spray the woods behind them with his own rifle, firing semi-automatic as fast as he could pull the trigger. Despite Samples' rapid fire, which had surely caught the men in the clearing by surprise, one of them returned fire with an AK-47 on full auto, bullets slamming into the tree and then one punching Samples in the right thigh, feeling like someone had hit him with a baseball bat. His leg went numb, but the tree trunk provided the support he needed to stay upright, and he kept firing, the rifle jerking against his shoulder as he swept the darkness in front of him with bullets, aiming for where he had seen the muzzle flashes.

Although he couldn't take time to analyze the situation, he was vaguely aware of the rifle shots coming from behind him, and Reyes' continued rapid fire, followed by a yelp from the woods. In front of him the AK had gone silent, and someone was moaning. The bolt of Samples' rifle locked to the rear, meaning the magazine was empty. He pressed the release to let the magazine drop to the ground, and pulled a full magazine from the cargo pocket on his right leg. His pants were wet, but the moisture was warm and sticky—not rain, he realized. He slipped the magazine into the well, slapped it home, and punched the bolt release.

"They're down," Reyes said from the other side of the tree. Samples could hear the clicks and clacks as Reyes also replaced his magazine. Only then did Samples accept the silence for what it was. The moaning had ended in a gurgle, and the enemy was no longer firing at them. "I'll check this one," Reyes said, moving back the way they had come.

Samples hobbled forward into the clearing and fell to his knees, twisting around to a sitting position on his left buttock to relieve the pressure on his right leg. Reaching out, he touched the two bodies that had crumpled to the ground. Both were deadly still, and clearly no longer a threat. He felt the silky fabric of the black pajamas on one of the fallen men, but the other had on a rougher cotton fabric. Convinced the men were dead, Samples laid his rifle down and gently probed his right thigh, searching out the wound. As yet there was no bright pain, just a dull throbbing, but the hot wetness of blood was unmistakable. He found a hole in his jungle fatigues, and put a finger through it to find the hole in his leg. It stung when he touched it, but he was relieved that the blood was flowing, but not spurting, so the bullet had not pierced his femoral artery. He kept searching, and found the exit wound on the back of his thigh. That was good, too, relatively speaking. A through-and-through wound that didn't cut a major artery was usually not fatal, and something he could recover from.

"He's dead," Reyes said as he came into the clearing. "SKS. What about these two?"

"Both dead," Samples replied, surprised by the weakness in his voice. "One AK for sure."

Reyes knelt down beside him. "You hit, Sarge?" His voice was full of surprise and anxiety.

"Yeah," Samples said, gritting his teeth as a sharp pain suddenly coursed up his body. "Leg wound. Right thigh. Not too bad."

"Oh, shit, man. And no field dressings." They had both left their pistol belts behind, and their belts carried the field dressings.

"See what these guys have," Samples instructed, leaning back on his left elbow. He could feel the fatigue and shakiness building up in his body. Reyes was duck-walking around the bodies, searching for anything to use for Samples' wound.

"This guy's wearing a uniform," Reyes blurted. "He's got a pith helmet, too. Fuckin' NVA!"

"Fuck," Samples cursed. "I was afraid of that."

"No field dressing, though. But he's got a scarf around his neck."

"Use that," Samples said, trying to keep his voice from quivering. Hold it on with my pants belt." While Reyes untied the scarf from the body, Samples lifted his shirt and found the narrow web belt that held up his pants. Releasing the buckle, he tugged on it to pull it around his body. Reyes came over and helped him pull it free, then folded the scarf as best he could and handed it to Samples.

"You put it over the wound, and I'll strap the belt on," Reyes said. Samples refolded the scarf until it was about a foot long and three inches wide, and then pressed it to his leg so that each end covered one of the holes. He held it in place, feeling slightly dizzy, while Reyes ran the belt around his leg, threaded the end through the buckle, and pulled it tight around the make-shift bandage. Samples gasped in pain.

"Sorry," Reyes apologized.

"It's okay. Gotta stop the bleeding."

They both heard the shout. It was in Vietnamese, and it wasn't that far away. It was clearly someone calling to the now-dead soldiers.

"Shit!" Reyes spat. "We gotta go."

"Help me up." Samples picked up his rifle in his right hand while Reyes pulled on his left arm, lifting him up to stand on one leg. Samples gingerly put some weight on his right leg, winced in pain, and leaned against Reyes, wrapping his left arm around the man's shoulder.

"You gonna make it?" Reyes asked worriedly.

Samples took a deep breath. "Yeah. Head for the building." Leaning to his left, Samples hopped on his left foot, dragging Reyes along with him. Samples flashed back to summer camp when he was a kid, and he had entered a three-legged race with one of his buddies. They had lost the race back then, falling down several times; he couldn't let that happen now.

*****

114

Lieutenant Carr took a long drink from his canteen, idly wondering why he was so thirsty, with all this rain. He slid the canteen back into the metal cup and snapped the cover shut, and was about to ask Eberhart a question when he heard the shots. It was a rapid mix of M-16 and AK-47 fire, and came from somewhere in front of the chapel, and not too far away. The scattered low conversations inside the chapel immediately halted, and the men at the door and windows came to high alert. Carr could hear the clicks of selector switches going off SAFE.

The exchange of gunfire ended almost as quickly as it had started, and Carr tried to analyze the sequence of sounds to determine what had happened. It seemed like the last shots fired had been the 5.56mm of M-16s, but he wasn't sure that really meant anything. Countless scenarios jumped in and out of his consciousness, and he contemplated sending out some sort of reaction force, but worried he would just risk more lives in the process. Amidst the total silence inside the room, Carr edged over and stood behind Pastorini, staring out the doorway into the inky night in the vain hope he would see something that brought clarity to the situation.

"What's happening?" Crosby whispered, his voice quivering.

"Sh!" Carr reprimanded him. He was straining to hear something besides the constant drum roll of rain on the roof. Over in the corner the Japanese girls were totally silent, for what seemed like the first time since he'd met them. In the back of the room he heard a feminine voice start to speak, only to be shushed by someone else. Everyone waited. A minute, two minutes, the time dragged by, and then Carr heard the shout in Vietnamese. It sounded like someone calling out, seeking information. There was no response, and Carr chose to take comfort in that. If no one answered, then either the other gooks were dead, or they were afraid to reveal themselves, which, in either case, meant Samples and Reyes were probably still alive. He hoped.

More waiting, and Carr was as tense as a rubber band stretched to its limit. Then he heard the thrashing out in the woods, and a muttered curse. He sensed Pastorini, kneeling at his feet behind the M-60, take a deep breath and prepare to fire. He reached down and

115

put his hand gently on the big man's shoulder. "Not yet," he cautioned quietly.

"Make a hole!" It was Reyes' voice, and Carr made out the vague shape of two men, very close together, approaching the front of the chapel in a controlled stumble. Pastorini had seen them, too, and lifted the machine gun up as he rose to step aside. There wasn't time to move the heavy cabinet, because suddenly Reyes and Samples were right there, with Reyes pushing Samples onto the top of the cabinet. "Pull him in," Reyes shouted.

Carr and Pastorini both grabbed Samples' arms and pulled him over the cabinet and laid him down on the floor inside. Reyes jumped on the cabinet, banged his head on the low door frame, and scrambled inside. "Motherfuck!" Reyes cursed, and then urgently called out, "Doc, Free's wounded. Right leg." There was a flurry of activity in the back and then Allman and Captain Gaither rushed forward and knelt beside the sergeant, who was struggling to get up.

"Stay down, Sergeant," Gaither ordered. "We need light."

"Move him to the corner," Carr said, trying to drag Samples by himself. Pastorini and Allman quickly came to his aid, and the three men soon had the protesting sergeant stretched out in the northeast corner after Eberhart moved out of the way.

"I'm okay," Samples insisted weakly. "Just a flesh wound."

"Are you a medic, Aaron?" Gaither asked.

"Uh, no, ma'am."

"Then shut up," she said gently. "Please."

While Pastorini picked up his M-60 and resumed his position in the doorway, Carr called out, "Get me a couple ponchos." Several of the rubberized sheets were passed to him, and he and Eberhart held them up like curtains around the group on the floor. "Okay, go ahead and use the flashlight."

A dim yellow glow lit up the makeshift operating room, and Carr looked over the edge of the poncho to see how bad it was. Samples had a blood-soaked pad of cloth on his thigh, held there with a belt, and the entire pants leg seemed red with blood. Then

116

Gaither moved around and blocked his view as she began removing the bandage.

"Take his pants down," Gaither told Allman, putting the belt and bloody rag aside.

"What?" Samples yelped.

"It's okay, Aaron, I'm a nurse. Nothing I haven't seen before."

"But. . ." Samples started to object, but grunted and grimaced with pain as Allman tugged his pants down to his knees. Like most of the men, he didn't wear underpants, to reduce the likelihood of getting crotch-rot.

"How bad is it?" Carr asked. He was directing his question at Samples, but Gaither answered.

""I don't know yet, Lieutenant," she said curtly. "Now let me work."

"Let me hold that, sir," Reyes said, taking the corners of the poncho without letting it drop.

Carr let Reyes take it and retrieved his rifle. "So what happened out there?" he asked Reyes.

Talking over his shoulder, his arms spread wide with the poncho, Reyes described the brief firefight. "One of the guys was NVA," he told Carr. "Full uniform. And then we heard some other gook calling for them, so we got the fuck out of there."

"NVA? Oh, shit. I was afraid of that." Carr knew if there was one NVA in the area, there were soon to be more, if they hadn't already arrived.

"We need water," Gaither demanded from behind the poncho curtain. Carr reached for his canteen, and Crosby scampered over and handed Carr his own canteen. Carr passed the two canteens through the gap between the two ponchos, and then took the radio handset clipped to Eberhart's backpack strap.

"Set to Battalion?" he asked the RTO, who, like Reyes, was holding a poncho outstretched like Dracula's cape.

117

"Yep."

He called and spoke with the S-3 operations officer, who took down the details but offered little encouragement. He offered random artillery rounds to disrupt the enemy, but they would have to be targeted far enough away to not endanger the Americans, which meant they probably wouldn't bother the gooks either. Carr declined.

"We'll be there at first light, over," the major told him.

Carr lifted his arm high enough that he could catch a little light from behind the ponchos, and finally made out the time on his watch. Dawn was still hours away. He signed off.

"Ow!" Samples bleated.

"Oh, don't be a baby, Aaron," Gaither admonished him. "It's just a couple stitches."

"Easy for you to say," Samples grumbled.

"Can I ask how he is yet?" Carr said tentatively.

Gaither heaved a heavy sigh. "He got a bullet through his upper thigh, in and out. There's some muscle damage, but no major veins or arteries were hit. I've pretty much stopped the bleeding, but he'll need X-rays and a doctor as soon as possible. It's probably a million-dollar wound."

That was what soldiers called a wound that was serious enough to get you sent back to the States, but not permanently disabling. Knowing Samples like he did, Carr doubted the dedicated sergeant would accept the trip.

TWELVE

Trudging back to the company headquarters, Lieutenant Masters was frustrated and angry, angry as much at himself as at the battalion staff. When the rocket attack on Dau Tieng base camp had ended, he had rushed over to the battalion headquarters with the map he had marked up, showing the location of Lieutenant Carr's group. The battalion's TOC—Tactical Operations Center—was out at the fire support base, where the commander and most of his staff were located. The men here at the base camp were mostly rear area support staff. The Staff Duty Officer this night was a Warrant Officer from Supply, a lumpy, swarthy, embittered man nearing retirement. He had listened and scowled as Masters had shown him the map and explained how he had arrived at his conclusions, but the massive doubt was evident in the tone of his questions.

"So where is this French map? Sir." Technically Masters, even as a lowly second lieutenant with only a few weeks experience in Nam, outranked Warrant Officer Cottom, who probably had over twenty-five years in the Army. But the way Cottom said "sir" made it clear he had no real respect for the earnest young man. He had obviously heard about Masters' problems in Bravo Company, and figured that gave him a license to dismiss anything the green lieutenant said. The Staff Duty NCO, an E-5 that Masters knew as the battalion's finance clerk, was at a nearby table writing a letter and studiously ignoring the officers' conversation.

"It got damaged during the rocket attack," Masters explained, not for the first time. "But I had transferred the location to this map before that happened."

"Uh-huh." Cottom was clearly humoring Masters, and only because Army protocol demanded it. "So, uh, what do you want me to do?"

"I'd like you to forward this information to the battalion TOC, Chief." Masters called him "Chief" hoping to ingratiate himself with the grumpy man. Cottom was not a chief warrant officer, just a WO1, and his official title was "Mister," but Masters hoped that by using the higher ranking form of address, he would convince the supply officer to pay a little more attention to him. The look of disdain on Cottom's face showed he was used to that trick and was not impressed.

Cottom heaved a theatrical sigh. "Okay, sir. Leave the map with me and I'll pass it on."

Masters knew what that meant—nothing would happen. And he wasn't about to give up the map he had so assiduously worked on.

"I need to keep this map," Masters told him. "Have you got another one of this area somewhere? I'll mark the location on yours."

Cottom had the SDNCO find a map, and while Masters marked the new map with the location and wrote up an explanation on a piece of typing paper, Cottom went back to studying the pictures in a well-worn copy of *Playboy*. The warrant officer barely looked up from the magazine when Masters handed him the map and notes, mumbling a vague promise to get right on it. Disgusted, Masters left the bunker and emerged into the rainy night.

Masters just knew he was correct about the location of the temple, and was convinced someone had to do something. The question was, what? He walked past the four angular dark lumps that were the armored personnel carriers of first platoon, and over the patter of raindrops he could hear gentle snoring coming from the open ramp of one of them. The crews were taking advantage of the rare opportunity to sleep straight through the night without having to get up to stand guard. Masters, however, was wide awake, and was actually surprised at the energy coursing through his body. He knew he should try to get some sleep, but the thought of what might be occurring out in the Boi Loi right now had him totally jazzed.

When he entered the headquarters building, he found Ford scribbling furiously in the log book, and Delaney

120

uncharacteristically alert, fine-tuning the radio. Ford looked up as Masters entered, quickly finished his entry, and said, "Sergeant Samples is wounded."

"What? What happened?"

Ford swiveled in his chair to face Masters. "Samples and another guy went out in the woods to hunt down the snipers. They killed three gooks, but Samples got a round in the leg. Looks like he'll be all right, but he says one of the gooks was NVA."

"Oh, shit!" Masters, despite his recent arrival in country, knew what that implied.

"Yeah, and they heard someone else out there, too. So that wasn't all of them."

"So what's battalion say about it?"

Ford shook his head slowly. "They said they'd be there at dawn. Otherwise, not much."

"Man," Masters grumbled, "if the NVA arrives in force, Carr's guys are going to be fucked."

"Maybe they won't," Ford said hopefully. "Maybe it was just that one guy. A liaison, or whatever. And it's only a few hours till the guys from the FSB can roll out."

"Yes, but that's then, not now, and they don't know where they're going."

"You showed them your map, didn't you?"

Masters shrugged. "The SDO didn't believe me. Hell, no one believes me."

"For what it's worth, sir," Ford consoled him, "I believe you. I saw the map, and how you figured it out. I think you're right."

"Thanks, I appreciate that. But it doesn't help Lieutenant Carr."

Delaney spoke up for the first time since Masters had returned from Battalion. "Maybe *we* should do something, sir."

That started Masters thinking. He was already on the shit list, so he had nowhere to go but up. He looked over at Ford. "Get me a list of everyone that's here in the base camp. The guys out in the tracks, the new guys, everyone. Delaney, go find Chalmers. Get him off berm guard and back here ASAP." A plan was developing in Masters' mind; it would almost certainly get him in more trouble, but he just didn't care anymore.

＊＊＊＊＊

The pain was constant, a throbbing ache in his thigh like someone was hitting him with a small ballpeen hammer in a metronomic rhythm. Samples had refused any morphine, out of concern it would cloud his judgment during this night of danger, and a deeper worry that he might become addicted. After Anne Gaither had neatly bandaged the wound and finally let him pull his pants back up, she had ordered Colonel Tarreyton to get up and had made Carr and Allman carry Samples over to the bamboo bed and lay him on it. Samples had tried to sit up, but Gaither had gently but firmly forced him back down, leaving her hand on his chest perhaps longer than necessary. He was grateful for her care and concern, but he was obligated to perform his duties no matter what. So he rolled onto his left side, propped himself up on one elbow, and took stock of the situation.

Lieutenant Carr brought his rifle over to him and leaned it against the side where Samples could reach it. Reyes brought him his web gear, ammo, and helmet, sliding them under the cot. Carr tested the strength of the makeshift bed with one hand, and then slowly sat down at Samples' feet, making sure the bed wouldn't collapse under the weight.

"NVA, huh?" Carr said.

Samples shifted a little to make room for Carr, and then stifled a groan from the pain. "Yeah. Had to be."

Gaither, who was sitting cross-legged on the raised floor between Samples and the stretcher carrying Whitmore, said, "He needs to rest, Lieutenant."

"I'm okay, ma'am," Samples said over his shoulder.

She put her hand on his right hip, tugging gently to show he should lay flat, but he refused to roll back. She left her hand on his hip anyway.

"We heard someone else. Know who that was?" Carr asked.

"Not for sure. Sounded like he was calling to the guys we had just zapped."

"Just one, or more, do you think?"

"Just heard the one. Doesn't mean there wasn't more out there, though." Samples found himself extremely aware of the touch of Captain Gaither's hand on his hip. It gave him a suffused glow of pleasure, and somehow eased the pain in his thigh. He forced himself to concentrate instead on the precarious situation the people in the temple faced.

"Think the NVA guy was an advanced scout for the main group?" Carr asked.

"Probably," Samples admitted. "I hope not, but, shit, why else would he be here?"

"Some kind of liaison?" Carr mused.

"Maybe."

"Sir?" Bolling, the deserter, was sitting just a few feet away on the edge of the raised floor, close enough to listen in or the conversation. "Can I speak to you a minute?"

"What is it?" Carr asked in a peremptory tone.

Bolling stood up and came round to the head of the bed and knelt down beside it, close to Samples' face. In a conspiratorial whisper that caused Carr to lean in, he said, "That gook prisoner? I don't think he's Vietnamese."

"What?" Samples and Carr blurted simultaneously.

"When we heard that shooting just now, he said something in Russian. He was just talking to himself, but I heard it."

"How do you know it was Russian?" Samples asked him, keeping his voice down.

"I speak Russian," Bolling explained. "My mom is Russian. My dad met her in France at the end of World War II."

"Your dad was in the Army?" Carr asked, with a hint of disbelief.

"Yeah, he was a colonel in Army Air Force. He died a couple years ago. So my mom was a war bride."

"If she's Russian, what was she doing in France?" Samples asked.

"Her folks were White Russians that emigrated during the Russian Revolution. It's a long story."

"Okay, okay," Carr whispered, "so what did this guy say?"

"I, uh, something about Americans. I couldn't make it all out. I wasn't expecting him to speak Russian."

Samples shook his head. "So it *might* have been Russian, is what you're saying."

"No, honest, it was Russian. I'm sure. I can prove it."

"How?" Carr sounded even more dubious than Samples felt.

"I'll go say something to him in Russian, and you can watch his reaction."

"In the dark?" Samples said sarcastically.

"Well, you'd have to use the flashlight."

"There are gooks out there," Carr pointed out, "just hoping for us to give them a target."

"But," Samples noted, "the target would be the prisoner. Don't know that I care if they shoot him."

"Well, all right," Carr said grudgingly. Samples felt the bed move as Carr stood up, pulled his flashlight from his belt, and stepped over in front of the seated prisoner. Samples winced as he twisted around to see beyond his feet. Bolling stood up, but remained at the head of the bed. "Ready?" Carr said, and then switched on the light, shining it right in the prisoner's face. The man squeezed his eyes shut against the unexpected illumination and half-turned his head away.

Bolling said something loudly, something that sounded like "Yobe tvo-you maht."

Samples saw the prisoner's reaction, which was immediate. His eyebrows shot up, his eyes opened in furious glare, and he bared his teeth. Then, just as quickly, he took on an obviously fake look of confusion. Carr switched off the flashlight. "What did you just say?" Samples asked Bolling.

"I said I fucked his mother."

"He didn't seem to care for that," Carr observed with a chuckle.

The tattoo Samples had seen earlier jumped into his mind. "He's got a red star tattooed on his shoulder," Samples said. "I saw it when Doc and Captain Gaither were patching him up."

"Let me see," Carr said, stepping forward and tugging at the man's black shirt. Greenberg came forward and helped pull the shirt off his shoulders until it was gathered around the man's bound wrists. Carr flicked on the flashlight again and played it over the prisoner's body. The white bandage on his shoulder was now tinged with red, but on the other shoulder was red star with a black border. It occurred to Samples that the Viet Cong flag had a gold or yellow star, not a red one.

"There's something back here, too," Greenberg announced, pointing at the man's back.

Carr grabbed the man's bicep and spun him half around so he could illuminate his back. Across his shoulder blades was something written in ornate Gothic letters.

"Spetznaz," Bolling read it aloud.

"What's that?" Samples asked, never having heard the word before.

"It's like our Green Berets," Bolling explained.

"He doesn't look Russian," Carr said.

"He's probably not," Bolling replied. "The Soviet Union has all sorts of nationalities in it. He's probably from the far east, along the border with Mongolia or Manchuria. Those people are Oriental. But they can join the Soviet Army, and they speak Russian."

"Then what the fuck is he doing here?" Samples demanded. The man was now glaring at his captors with unbridled hatred.

"My guess is he's some kind of advisor," Carr suggested. "They probably sent him because he could pass for a gook. The Russians aren't supposed to be involved here."

"That's all we fuckin' need," Samples complained. "A Russian disguised as a gook, a deserter, and three little girls. Bring in the damn clowns."

"Now, Aaron," Carr chided him. "That's why we get the big bucks."

A gun barked outside somewhere, and a bullet smacked into the back wall of the temple just to the left of where Hicks stood on the crate. Carr immediately doused the light he had been absent-mindedly playing on the prisoner and ducked down, while Samples grabbed his rifle and trained it on the front doorway. The prisoner snickered at their fright, until Greenberg kicked him from where he lay on the floor. The room went silent as everyone waited for the next shot, but none came.

"Well," Samples drawled, "I guess there's at least one still out there."

No sooner had he said that than another shot rang out from the north side of the building, shattering the edge of the window there and spraying Samples with small pieces of brick and mortar.

"Shit!" Vasquez yelled from the floor where he had dropped. "Motherfucker almost got me!" He jumped up, poked his rifle out the window, and began firing wildly.

Samples let him empty his magazine, and then said, "That's enough, Vasquez. Cool it." With a growl Vasquez removed the empty magazine and slapped a fresh one home, but didn't resume firing.

After two minutes of no further incoming, people began to relax a little. At Captain Gaither's gentle urging, Samples lay back on the bunk and tried to ignore the pounding in his thigh. Carr went over to call Battalion on the radio, and Greenberg prodded the prisoner with his gun barrel, just to let him know he was being closely watched. Samples closed his eyes and tried to think, but the pain in his leg crowded out all other considerations. He wished he could go to sleep, but that seemed impossible.

A few minutes later he woke up with a start from a dream about his ex-wife. In the dream she was berating him for not washing the car. Now that he was reminded of her, he kept thinking about how his marriage had crumbled when he caught her in bed with a dipshit lieutenant. After that he had sort of sworn off women in general, immersing himself in his military duties, and volunteering to go back to Viet Nam. It had been a long time since he had enjoyed the touch of a woman, and he realized that was probably why he was so appreciative of the comfort Captain Gaither was giving him. He thought about the first time he had seen Anne's face, and realized she wasn't a spectacular fashion model beauty, but somehow her features were still very appealing, at least to him. He smiled to himself as he thought of her, and fell back asleep.

THIRTEEN

"What did they say, Lieutenant?" Colonel Tarreyton demanded. Carr had just given the handset back to Eberhart, and Tarreyton, who had been sitting on the floor with his back to the wall, had risen up and now crowded close to Carr, his heavy briefcase dangling from his left hand.

Carr paused to phrase his answer diplomatically. "We are to keep the prisoner safe and secure so he can be interrogated by someone from the State Department. I don't know why. We are to maintain our defensive posture here until help arrives in the morning. And they said the Division Commander wants you to be preparing a full report on your activities here."

"Me?" Tarreyton was flustered. "I haven't really been involved in the decision-making here. Why me?"

"Can't say, sir," Carr told him unsympathetically.

"Well, that's ridiculous. But, maybe, because I'm the senior officer here, I would be the logical person to report on the mistakes that have been made." With this rationalization, his voice got stronger. "Indeed, I will begin making mental notes and start composing an exhaustive review of the circumstances and occurrences that have led to this fiasco. Lieutenant, I understand that you have been doing what you think best, but I will have to let the chips fall where they may. You understand, of course. I certainly hope it will not be too damaging to your career."

Carr resisted the urge to strangle the arrogant prick. "Thank you, sir," he said through gritted teeth. The only saving grace was that what Battalion had said about Tarreyton and his report had the subtle undertones of a reprimand for the colonel, not a vindication. It sounded to Carr like division commander wanted to know what

128

Tarreyton was doing there in the first place, and why he had gone to Dau Tieng. It sounded like office politics at division level, something Carr absolutely did not want to get involved with.

Over in the corner the Girlfriends hummed, and then began softly singing. "I will forrow him, forrow him wherever he may go." Carr had to laugh. When the situation is this screwed up, all you could do is laugh or go crazy.

Carr went back over to the bamboo bed and sat down at Samples' feet. Gaither was tenderly wiping his forehead with a damp cloth. "Did you hear?" Carr asked Samples, referring to his conversation with Tarreyton. Samples had slept for nearly half an hour, and Carr really envied him, but now he was awake again.

"Yeah," Samples replied. "Same ol' same ol'."

Outside the rain continued to drizzle down, and the constant patter on the roof had faded from his consciousness and now became just background noise that he filtered out. The humidity inside the temple, however, had become oppressive. With so many people crowded together in a room with so few openings, their breath and perspiration added to the rain-soaked atmosphere so much that Carr suspected he would see a cloud in here, if there were enough light. And there was the heat, but that was something you just came to accept as normal in Viet Nam. Just like the smell. Carr remembered stepping off the plane when he first arrived in country. The first thing he noticed was the heat, and the next was the odor. The country smelled of human waste, rotting vegetation, diesel fuel, and God knows what else. He had gotten used to both the heat and the smell, but both were intensified here in the temple.

"What time is it?" Samples asked.

"About oh-two-forty-five," Carr answered without trying to check his watch.

"Another two or three hours then, huh."

"Maybe more," Carr said quietly, to limit who all could hear him. "They have to roll out, come down the road, and then try to find us by busting jungle. If the rain keeps up, they probably won't use choppers."

"But at least we've got entertainment," Samples chuckled, nodding toward the girls in the corner, who were apparently in a medley of songs about young love. Their singing was cut short by another burst of gunfire, this time from Hicks. Standing on the crate at the back of the room so he could reach the triangular opening at the peak of the roof, Hicks fired off five quick rounds from his M-16, then ducked as an AK-47 spat rounds back at him. Most of the incoming thudded into the outside of the back wall, but one came through the gap and slammed into a roof beam.

"I guess I missed him," Hicks said blandly. "The son of a bitch." He popped back up to the hole and fired three more shots into the rainy night, before again crouching down out of the line of fire. Two more pops from the AK that apparently didn't even hit the building, and then it was quiet again. "Damn gook was trying to sneak up on us," Hicks explained mildly. Cautiously he straightened up and peeked out the hole. After a moment he sniffed and said, "Gone now. Sorry rat bastard."

"Just the one?" Carr called over to him.

"That's all I saw," Hicks replied.

"VC or NVA?"

"Didn't see him real good. Wasn't wearing a helmet, though." Which meant he was probably VC, but it wasn't conclusive evidence.

"Just one guy, moving around a lot?" Samples suggested.

"Could be," Carr said. "Or there's just a couple of them. Not a lot, anyway."

"That's good," Samples said. "We can deal with a couple of them."

"I'm afraid they're just out there keeping us pinned down until the others arrive."

"Maybe," Samples agreed, "but whatcha gonna do?" It was a rhetorical question, but Carr knew he had to come up with an answer, and soon. If a bunch of NVA showed up, the Americans would be besieged, and he wasn't sure how long they could hold out. He had to think of the wounded and the women; should he risk their lives by resisting the enemy attack, or surrender in the possibly vain hope they would be treated properly. Theoretically that decision should be made by the senior officer present, but Carr didn't trust Tarreyton to make the right choice. Besides, the colonel seemed to prefer the role of umpire and judge to actually being in charge. So it was all on Carr. He got up from his seat and walked over to stand behind Pastorini, exposing himself to stare out into the dripping woods. He almost wished some gook would take a shot at him. If he were dead or wounded, he wouldn't have to be making these life-and-death decisions any more.

*****

The orderly room was packed with soldiers, most standing, but some sitting on the desks. None had their battle gear on; some had no shirts, and others had unlaced boots. Only the new guy who had shown up in the bunker in his boxer shorts was now in full uniform. Their hair was mussed and their eyes still looked sleepy. Lieutenant Masters and Spec Four Ford had roused the crews from the APCs, the four new guys, a guy named Smith from Second Platoon who was supposed to start processing out to go home, and two guys getting medical treatment for VD. Masters looked them over and saw the doubt and disgruntlement on their faces. They didn't know why he had called them together, but they were sure it wasn't good news. The lights were on in the room, against regulations, but Masters needed to observe the men closely when he made his announcement.

The door creaked open and Delaney came in, followed by PFC Chalmers, the company clerk, who was still dressed in full combat gear and carrying his weapon.

"I'm supposed to be on guard, sir," Chalmers protested. "The sergeant's going to be pissed."

"I'll deal with the sergeant," Masters assured him. "I need you here. Get ready to take notes." Chalmers made a face, but took off his helmet and motioned one of the others to get out of his chair so he could sit behind his desk.

Masters moved to the end of the room so he could see everyone and took a deep breath. "Men," he started, but it came out squeaky and high-pitched. He cleared his throat and began again, forcing a deeper, manlier tone. "Men, as many of you already know, First Platoon is out in the Boi Loi Woods, after rescuing some folks from a chopper crash. They have taken shelter in an old Cao Dai temple, but the gooks have them surrounded, and they are expecting the arrival of a large NVA unit in the area at any time. Now I have determined the location of the temple, but Battalion doesn't consider the coordinates definite enough to fire arty, and doesn't plan to send out a search party until dawn. We are the closest Alpha Company element, so I propose we go out and get them right now."

Masters paused to gauge the reaction on the men's faces. Some looked confused, some looked doubtful, and some were nodding. He took that as a good sign. Then Sergeant Jamison spoke up. "Does Captain Raymond know?" Raymond was the company commander, and Jamison was obviously questioning Masters' authority to make such a decision.

"Yes, I have spoken to the commander." Which was true, up to a point. He had called Raymond on the company radio net and outlined his plan. The captain had plainly been dubious, but hadn't specifically said he couldn't do it. Instead he had said that while he could not approve the plan, he would leave it up to the Masters' judgment. In other words, it was Masters' ass if it went wrong. On the good side, however, Raymond said he would wait until Masters was actually on the road before he informed Battalion of the operation, "in case you change your mind."

Jamison still looked dubious. "So, uh, what's the plan, sir?"

"Well, we'll mount up on your tracks, take off, find that old road, and RIF down it to the temple." Masters hoped he had used the RIF term correctly. It stood for Reconnaissance In Force, and was used when the unit did a mounted sweep at moderate to high speed.

132

"When, sir?" someone else asked. Masters still didn't know most of their names.

"Right now."

"In the dark?"

"This is an urgent mission," Masters insisted. "The tracks have headlights, don't they?"

Aiello, one of the track drivers, said, "Yeah, but we never use them. I'm not sure if they all work."

"Mine do," one of the other drivers offered proudly.

"So we're going to just charge down the road with our lights on?" Ford sounded very skeptical. Masters suspected Ford was bolder in his questioning than the others due to his being more familiar with Masters, having worked with him for several days.

"It's the only way we can get there in time," Masters asserted. "And the gooks won't be expecting us to do it, so we should be safe from ambush."

There were some whispered conversations between the men, but no further questions for a minute. Then one of the new guys raised his hand and asked, "Are we all going?"

This was the moment Masters had been dreading. He knew he was going to sound like a character in a movie or TV show. "I'm asking for volunteers. I know this is a very risky mission, and there will be no shame or repercussions if you choose to stay back. Can I see the hands of those who want to participate." He winced at that last remark, knowing it sounded more like an invitation to play volley ball than a request to risk their lives.

There was a brief pause as no one moved, and Masters started to get worried. Then Sergeant Jamison's hand shot up, and others followed. Within thirty seconds every man had his hand in the air, including Chalmers, the clerk. Masters felt a glow of pride and satisfaction.

"Thank you, men," Masters said in a voice choked with emotion. "PFC Chalmers," he said, turning to the clerk, "I appreciate your volunteering, but you'll have to stay here and man

133

the radio. And Smith, you're too short. You should stay here with Chalmers, be his runner. Next, I want to get a list of everyone that's going out." He didn't say why he wanted the list, and nobody needed to ask. With a mixed group like this, someone had to keep track of the personnel, in case someone got killed, wounded, or went missing. While Chalmers started taking down names, Masters tried to match them to the faces and commit them to memory, knowing he would probably forget most of them within fifteen minutes.

There were the eight men who had come in with the tracks: Sergeant Jamison, his driver, PFC Gunn, Specialist Tenkiller, PFC Pratt, Specialist Aiello, PFC Merrill, PFC Knox, and PFC Rancy. He of course knew Specialist Ford, a radio repairman from headquarters platoon who was recovering from a bout of some intestinal flu, and PFC Delaney, from third platoon, who had been in base camp for three days trying to get his pay problems straightened out. From second platoon were the two guys with venereal disease, PFC Purdey and Specialist Karper. They had already gotten their penicillin shots, or whatever it was, and were due to return to the field anyway.

Masters was a concerned about the four new guys. They were being thrown into combat their first day in the field, before they had time to even be assigned to a squad and get some initial orientation. PFC Wilson was a tall thin blond who sounded like he was from the upper Midwest somewhere, maybe Wisconsin or Minnesota. PFC Kirk was a short pudgy kid with black hair and a Boston accent. PFC Dubois was a light-skinned soul brother whose speech patterns tagged him as coming from somewhere in the deep South, and PFC Handleman was a small guy with frizzy hair who was clearly from New York City. Handleman was the guy who had shown up in the bunker during the rocket attack wearing only his boxer shorts, but now was fully dressed. Masters would have to keep an eye on him.

After each man gave his name to Chalmers, Masters sent him out to get all his gear and weapon, and come back for a final briefing. As soon as everyone was back, now decked out with helmet, web gear, and weapon, Masters had each of the four track crews move to separate corners of the room. Then he assigned one new guy to each crew, along with one of the base camp people.

Chalmers took notes on the assignments. Masters thought about giving them a pep talk, or telling the more experienced men to help the new guys, but decided that wasn't really necessary. These men knew what they were doing. So he got to it.

"Sergeant Jamison, I'll ride with you. Let's mount up."

FOURTEEN

Lieutenant Carr stood in the middle of the room and fretted, about anything, everything, and nothing. Here he was, lost somewhere in the middle of the Boi Loi Woods, possibly surrounded by enemy soldiers. Or was there only one or two? Inside this small building he had a reduced platoon of soldiers, a worthless colonel, two wounded men, a dead man, a nurse, a deserter, a VC prisoner that was apparently a Russian spy or something, and three Japanese female vocalists. A mixed bag, for sure, with almost as many liabilities as assets. Here inside the abandoned temple they were relatively safe, and they were sheltered from the unrelenting rain, but for how much longer? If, as he suspected, a larger North Vietnamese Army unit was approaching, the temple would rapidly transform from a safe haven to a slaughterhouse. Making a run for it, however, posed more problems than it might solve. Herding this motley group through the woods on a rainy night would be a daunting task, and it would make them easy pickings for any enemy soldiers who were out there. Carr shook his head wearily.

Soothed by Captain Gaither's gentle touch, Samples had somehow managed to fall asleep again, as had Chief Whitmore, the wounded pilot. There had been no more potshots from the gooks outside for nearly an hour, which was a good thing, he hoped. Carr was exhausted, and wished he could take a nap, but didn't dare. Instead he kept moving around the room, talking to his men, making sure they stayed awake as well. Colonel Tarreyton was sitting against the north wall, his head on his knees, snoring. The noise was grating and annoying, but Carr would rather have the man asleep than awake and complaining. The prisoner also appeared to be asleep, but Carr suspected the man was just pretending.

"How're you doing, Preacher?" Carr asked Pastorini, kneeling down next to him.

"Hanging in there, sir," he replied, his deep voice rumbling despite his trying to keep the volume down.

"How well did you know the copilot?"

"We've been flying together for a couple months. Good guy."

"Sorry about what happened," Carr said sympathetically.

"Yeah, me, too. How's the Chief doing?"

"Whitmore? Okay, I guess. He's sleeping right now. That nurse and Doc Allman are taking good care of him."

"And your sergeant?"

"Sleeping, too. Wish I could."

"Bet that, sir."

They both stared out into the rainy night for a minute. Carr clapped Pastorini on the shoulder. "I really appreciate you lugging that sixty around. It's nice to have a little extra firepower."

"No sweat, sir. It's my primary weapon, after all. And thanks to Captain Gaither, we got plenty of ammo for it."

"Yeah, well, let's hope we don't have to use it."

"Roger that."

Carr stood up and wandered a few steps over to the corner where the Girlfriends huddled together. They were all sitting on the floor, and PFC Roland Sweet was squatting in front of them, ready to defend them from any attack. Carr knelt down, leaning on his rifle for support.

"You girls okay?" Carr asked them. One of them jerked a little at the question; apparently she had been asleep.

"Okay," one of the other two replied succinctly. Carr couldn't tell which one was which here in the dark, and wasn't sure he could distinguish them even in the daylight.

"Crystal is from Osaka," Sweet announced, out of the blue. "Rhonda and Sherry are from Tokyo."

"So you've been talking to them?" Carr asked him. "They speak English?"

"Not a lot," Sweet conceded, "but I can figure out what they're saying pretty well."

"Rorand nice," one of the girls said. "He our boyfriend." Another girl giggled.

"Sweet," Carr admonished him, "what have you been telling these girls?"

"Nothin', Eltee. Just talking. You know."

"Well, don't get too involved here. We might get contact, and I'll need you to do your part."

"I know, sir. But somebody's got to take care of these lovely ladies. They don't know anything about combat."

"And you do. Sort of. I suppose you've told them about how you're a hero and all?"

"Not exactly. I just wanted to reassure them that I could take care of them."

"Yeah, right." Carr turned to the girls. "Do you all need anything? Water, food?"

"I gave 'em my C's," Sweet said. "They really liked the John Wayne bar. Didn't care for the ham and lima beans, though."

"I'm not surprised," Carr said. "No one likes the ham and lima beans. Did you give them water, too?"

"Rorand give canteen," one of the girls said. Apparently she knew enough English to follow the gist of the conversation.

"Good," Carr told her. "Now you know we will get you out of here soon, don't you?"

"*Hai*," the girls said in Japanese, and then added, "Yes. US Army number one."

Carr was used to hearing that from Vietnamese girls, but surprised to hear it from these Japanese women. He wondered if that phrase had originated in Japan during the occupation and migrated here to Nam, or whether the girls had picked it up while touring here. Not that it mattered.

"Okay," Carr said, standing up. "You ladies just stay in the corner here, where 'Rorand' can protect you. Sweet, you just keep it in your pants."

"Yes, sir," Sweet answered, sounding a little offended by Carr's suggestion.

A burst of AK fire outside gave everyone a start, the bullets thumping into the south side of the building. Reedy and Sorenson returned fire through the window, their shots echoing loudly inside the room. After five or six shots they paused, waiting for more gunfire from the woods. Carr knew they were watching for any muzzle flashes that would reveal the enemy's location and give them a solid target.

"See anything?" Carr asked.

"Nope," Reedy answered, his eye still glued to the sight of his rifle. "Sounded pretty close, though."

A single shot rang out from the north side, coinciding with the thunk of a bullet hitting the lintel of the window on the south side, just above Reedy's and Sorenson's heads. Vasquez and Montoya opened fire through the north window, firing evenly spaced semi-automatic shots into the dripping trees.

"Shoot low," Carr called to them. He had figured out the trajectory the bullet must have followed to hit the top of the south window, and knew the gook must be firing from a prone position, fairly close by. He started across the room to direct their fire, just as a bullet whizzed by his head a microsecond before he heard the shot from somewhere outside the front door. Dropping to the floor, he yelled, "Get down!" to the rest of the people in the room. A moment later Pastorini pulled the trigger on the M-60, the clattering rhythmic bangs virtually drowning out all other sounds. But Carr could tell that other guns were firing, M-16s at each of the windows and up high at the ventilation opening at the back. It was the natural tendency of soldiers in Nam to open fire when others had done so, whether they had a target or not.

"Cease fire!" Carr yelled from the floor, pushing himself up to his hands and knees. "Cease fire!" The phrase echoed around the room, and the firing tapered off quickly. In the ensuing silence, Carr stood up and waited for more shots from outside. None came.

"At least three of them now," Samples remarked from the bed.

"Just testing us," Carr replied.

"Yeah, well, we're still here," Hicks said from his perch on the crate. "Motherfuckers!" he yelled defiantly out through the opening.

"Lieutenant!" Colonel Tarreyton demanded from his prone position. "You've got to do something!"

He's right, Carr thought, *but what?*

*****

"Hold up," Masters told Sergeant Jamison, tapping him on the shoulder and talking loudly to be heard over the rumble of the engine and treads. Jamison had his CVC helmet on, and used the intercom to relay the order to Gunn, the driver, and the radio to inform the three tracks trailing behind them. The column of APCs ground to a halt in the middle of the wide 'highway,' a dirt road now churned to mud, as water dripped off Master's helmet. Their headlights glittered off the raindrops but only barely illuminated the road ahead, and did nothing to reveal the forest on either side. Masters hadn't fully realized how difficult it would be to find the abandoned roadway to the temple. No one had noticed it during the day, he reminded himself, so how did he think he would see it on a dark and stormy night? Trees and brush had grown up quickly in this environment, filling in the gap and shrouding it from view.

It had not started out well, either. When the four tracks roared up to the main gate of the base camp, MPs had halted them.

"We don't open the gate until daylight," the MP sergeant had told him.

"We're on an urgent mission," Masters had shouted down at the man.

"Let me check with HQ," the sergeant told him, gesturing toward the guard house. He walked away, and Masters felt a sinking feeling in his stomach. If senior officers found out about this, they would squash him like a bug. He briefly toyed with the idea of bribing the sergeant, or even wrestling him to the ground and tying him up, but knew that would only make things worse. Then, just as the sergeant entered the small guard house to make a call, one of the other MPs began unlatching the gate and swinging it open. Maybe he had misunderstood the sergeant's gesture. Regardless, Masters saw the opportunity and jumped at it.

"Move out!" he told Jamison. When Jamison hesitated, he said, "Now, sergeant. While we can." Jamison nodded his understanding, and spoke into the mike on his helmet. Immediately the four tracks roared and surged forward, passing through the gate before the sergeant could come out and stop them. Masters felt a great sense of exhilaration and freedom as they sped through the dark and silent streets of Dau Tieng City and out onto the highway. A few minutes later they crossed the bridge over the Saigon River, waving to the South Vietnamese soldiers who guarded it, and continued south along the Ben Cui rubber plantation until turning the corner and heading west along the southern edge of the rubber. Now here they were, and he didn't know where to go next.

"I need to look at the map again," he told Jamison, and climbed down into the open cargo hatch. At the back of the interior, sheltered by the roof, he fumbled around until he found the switch for the overhead light. Clicking it on, he withdrew the map from his cargo pocket, and opened it up. It was now in a clear plastic sleeve, so it had remained dry, but it was hard to read through the reflections. Holding it up close to the light, he studied the pencil lines he had drawn on it earlier. If he had transferred the markings over from the French map correctly, and if other landmarks hadn't changed significantly, the old road should meet the highway about 300 meters to the west of the Ben Cui rubber plantation. Even in the dark, he had been able to tell when they were passing the rubber; the orderly rows of trees stood out against the jumble of the Boi Loi Woods on the opposite side of the highway. Masters shook his head ruefully. Even if the map were 100 percent accurate, estimating the distance from the edge of the rubber plantation introduced a huge margin of error. Parts of the plantation had been cut back to remove cover used by the communists, but he wasn't sure how much.

The old road was probably only twenty feet wide, at best. They didn't have time to just probe the forest every few feet until they found it, and that was assuming they could even tell when they had found it. Jamison, minus his helmet, jumped down and sat beside him on the bench. "What's the deal, sir?" he asked. There was no malice or accusation in his tone, for which Masters was very grateful.

"That road should be right around here," Masters explained, "but it just isn't visible from the highway. I was hoping we would see something that helped us, but not so far."

"Do you think we passed it?" Jamison leaned over and looked at the map.

"Probably. Don't you think we're more than three hundred meters past the Ben Cui?"

"Oh, at least. Maybe a half klick past."

"That's what I think, too. I guess we'll have to backtrack and look again."

"How about this, sir?" Jamison reached out and traced a finger across the map. "We go into the woods and bust jungle at an angle. Inside the trees the road should be more obvious."

Masters considered the idea. It made more sense than going up and down the highway hoping they would see something, or sending out dismounted patrols that could get lost in the dark. But pushing the tracks through the woods was slow going, and it would be hard to maintain a course in the dark. There didn't seem to be a better option, though. "Okay, we can try that. But where do we start?"

"I don't know, sir. Are you sure we've passed the road?"

Masters looked at his map, and tried to remember the way this area had looked on the French map. "There used to be a village called Ben Cui," he said. "It was at the southwest corner of the plantation. The road must have intersected the highway near the village, I would think. So we must have passed it."

"Then we start here, work our way southeast. If we hit the river, then we know we've gone too far."

"Good point," Masters acknowledged the feeble joke.

Purdey, up in the 50-cal turret, shouted, "Did you hear that? Sounded like a firefight."

Jamison scrambled up over the stacks of ammo cans and grabbed his CVC helmet. Masters climbed up behind the turret and listened intently, but heard nothing.

"Where?" he asked Purdey.

"Sounded like over there," Purdey said, waving his arm in a generally southern direction.

"I heard it, too," Handleman chirped from his seat to the right of the turret. "Lots of shots."

"Do you still hear anything?" Masters asked, concerned at his own inability to hear the gunfire.

"Naw," Purdey said. "It was just a few shots, like maybe, I don't know, somebody popping an ambush."

"And you're sure it was from the Boi Loi?" Masters wondered if maybe the shots were from nervous berm guards back at the base camp, or from one of the ruff-puff compounds. The ruff-puffs were the Regional Forces/Popular Forces, local farmers who had been armed by the government as a militia, roughly equivalent to US Army Reserves and National Guard.

"It was over there, sir," Handleman insisted, standing up to point south-southeast in a more definite manner than Purdey. Masters knew that there were no troops in that direction other than Lieutenant Carr's men.

"How far?" Jamison asked urgently.

143

"Hard to say," Purdey replied. "Five, six klicks?"

"I'd say a couple miles," Handleman offered unconfidently.

Jamison listened to something on the headphones within his CVC helmet and then said, "Merrill says Ford heard it, too. And so did Rancy."

"Then we need to move out smartly," Masters told them, taking his seat.

PFC Gunn locked the left lateral and gunned the engine. The right tread began spinning and spewing mud, and the vehicle slewed around to the left until it was pointed southeast. Gunn released the pivot steer lock and allowed the track to jerk forward, angling across the edge of the road into the cleared area, heading toward the tree line. Jamison was on the radio, explaining to the other track crews what they were doing. Masters glanced back over his left shoulder to watch as the other three tracks did the same and fell in line behind him, the headlights bouncing up and down as the APCs bounded over the ditch and berm that paralleled the highway. When they reached the edge of the forest, they had to slow down while Gunn tried to pick his way between the bigger trees as he smashed down the smaller ones. Masters and Jamison had to keep their arms up to ward off the slashing branches of the trees they were weaving their way between.

"Ow!" Handleman yelped as a thicker branch whacked him on the shoulder and nearly knocked him off the track.

"Hang on!" Masters called to him. "Keep your head low so the branches hit your helmet."

Under him the track rose and fell as it rolled over fallen trees, the engine roaring and spewing diesel smoke that was trapped around them by the trees and the rain failed to dissipate. Masters kept trying to watch where they were going, but the constant onslaught of flying branches forced him to keep his head down, and the flickering of the swerving headlight beams on the wet leaves had a strobe effect that gave him a headache and made it hard to distinguish anything. He had no idea how Gunn was finding his way through the thick woods, but he was extremely grateful for the young man's driving skills. He looked back, squinting against the blinding headlight beams of the track close behind them. The other three had only to follow in Gunn's trail after this lead vehicle crushed the vegetation and showed the way.

Masters was pretty sure he was violating all sorts of policies and regulations by careening off through the woods at night with the lights on, without actual orders or permission to do so. On the other hand, he was already in trouble with his superiors, his career was mostly over, and frankly, he just didn't care. His fellow soldiers were in trouble, and no one else seemed to be coming to their aid, so it was up to him. Who was it that said, "I'd rather be right than President"? That was how Masters felt—he would rather rush to save his buddies than get a promotion by complying with pig-headed orders. *Let the chips fall where they may,* he thought, *and all those other clichés.*

When the track halted, Masters at first though Gunn had run into some kind of blockage, perhaps trees too close together to maneuver through, but Jamison turned his head and said, "We may have just crossed the road. Pratt says he thinks he's sees it. I'll go check it out."

"I'll come with you," Masters told him. Jamison removed the CVC helmet and jumped down, and Masters followed him, brushing aside the small tree limbs and bushes that crowded the side of the track. Behind the vehicle it was easier going, since the treads had crushed the foliage, but many of the saplings and larger bushes had sprung back up partially, so the two men still had to pick their along the trail. The one-two track had backed up a few yards, and Masters saw PFC Pratt scramble down the sloped front of the track and walk forward to meet them.

"Doesn't the ground rise right here?" Pratt asked when they were close enough. He swept his hand left to right, pointing at the ground.

Masters walked forward, avoiding the bent branches and broken bushes, sensing the ground with each step. It might just be his imagination, but he could almost feel the ground come up a little here, and then slope back down a few feet closer to Pratt's APC. He walked back and forth, trying to judge whether there was really a

145

rise in the earth. Shielding his eyes from the headlights, he studied the trees to the north and south of where he was standing, comparing them to those to the east and west. It did seem like the forest was thinner roughly perpendicular to the way they had been traveling. Sergeant Jamison, holding his rifle with both hands, moved south, probing with his feet as he left the opening created by his track and entered the undisturbed woods to the side.

"Might be," he said loud enough to be heard over the idling diesel engines. "Trees are smaller here." Masters headed in the same direction, watching Jamison kick at some leaves on the ground. "Looks like an old ditch here," Jamison told Masters when he caught up. Masters pushed the leaves with his boot, and felt the narrow depression under them.

"Hey, check this out," Pratt said excitedly. He had been exploring a little to their west, along what would have been the other side of the road, if this indeed was the road. Masters and Pratt hurried over to where Pratt was kicking at something half buried in the leaf debris that littered the forest floor. "Looks like a scooter tire," Pratt told them when they arrived. Masters knelt down and felt the object with his hand. It was round, and it was rubber, for sure. Although severely deteriorated, it was almost certainly a small tire, about the size of the ones on the ubiquitous Lambretta three-wheeled scooters that served as taxis here in Viet Nam.

"This must be it," Jamison asserted. "Why else would an old tire be way out here in the woods?"

Masters stood up and took another look around. In the dark, outside the brilliance of the tracks' headlights, he couldn't really see much. He reached out and touched one of the small tree trunks that had sprung up in this area. When he pushed against it, it gave a little, showing how young it must be. All the trees along here were thin and springy. This had to be the road. A clock was ticking in his head, and he knew he had to make a decision. He inhaled and prepared to order the tracks to turn and head south along this strip of slightly thinner forest, but the distinct sound of sudden gunfire made his order unnecessary. Even in the forest the direction the shots were coming from was obvious, and it was directly down this lane.

146

"Mount up!" Masters yelled. "Let's go!"

FIFTEEN

Sergeant First Class Aaron Samples was awakened by the sound of snoring right by his head. At first he thought it must have been his own snoring, but now that he was awake, the sound continued. Clearing the cobwebs from his mind, he realized the grating sound was coming from Lieutenant Colonel Tarreyton, who was sitting on the floor beside the bamboo bed. Samples was annoyed by the colonel's nasal groaning, and he was also annoyed at himself for falling asleep yet again. He didn't even bother to rationalize about his wound and loss of blood; he was a platoon sergeant, and it was his duty to remain awake and ensure the safety and alertness of his men. He wondered how long it had been since the last burst of gunfire.

With a slight start Samples realized the darkness wasn't as thick as it had been before. The doorway and the windows were now charcoal grey rectangles interrupted by the round helmets of the men stationed at those openings. Samples couldn't see his watch, but was sure this was the false dawn, and real sunrise was still an hour away, but any additional visibility was welcome. He also noted that the rain on the tin roof had slackened appreciably, and was now just a gentle murmur overhead. As he looked around, he could almost make out the forms of the individuals within the small building. Vasquez still maintained a watch out the north window, just beyond the sleeping colonel, and Sergeant Montoya stood next to him. Lieutenant Carr and Eberhart stood in the northeast corner, once again studying the map with a shielded flashlight. Reyes had moved around to Pastorini's left side and squatted next to the machine gunner, ready to feed more ammo belts into the gun perched on the cabinet blocking the doorway.

It looked like the three Japanese girls were sitting down against the wall just to the right of the doorway, and Sweet stood guard over them. Sergeant Reedy and Sorenson were at the south window, crowded a little by the stretcher bearing the copilot's body. Crosby was again sitting at the little table, his head bobbing as he fought the urge to sleep. Greenberg and Johnson stood in the southwest corner, guarding the prisoner and Bolling, who were seated together on the edge of the raised floor. Rolling onto his back, Samples was able to pick out Hicks up at the ceiling vent. Doc Allman was back in the northwest corner, kneeling at the head of Chief Whitmore, the wounded pilot, and Captain Gaither was kneeling directly beside Samples. Detecting his movement, Gaither reached out and grasped his right forearm. "How are you doing?" she asked quietly.

"I'm okay, ma'am," Samples replied. "Thanks. Any idea what time it is?"

"Afraid not," she said. "But it seems lighter."

He was about to offer his opinion about false dawn when he heard the shout from out in the woods to the east. Someone was yelling something in Vietnamese, apparently directed toward the temple.

The prisoner yelled something in reply, and even Samples, with his poor language skills, could tell the man was speaking Vietnamese with a foreign accent.

"Shut him up!" Samples screamed. He had no idea what the prisoner was saying, but anything he said would benefit the enemy. There was a scuffling noise and grunts as Greenberg and Johnson grabbed the prisoner, wrestling with him and putting a hand over his mouth.

"Keep him quiet!" Carr ordered.

"Americans!" the voice out in the woods called imperiously. "You release prisoner now."

"Fuck you!" Reyes shouted out the doorway.

148

"Knock it off, Reyes," Samples said. He wanted to hear the offer.

"You release prisoner," the man hidden in the trees yelled, "we let you alive."

While his grammar was poor, his meaning was clear, but Samples doubted the offer was genuine. Samples now understood why the gooks had followed them through the woods and kept them pinned down all night, rather than just wiping them out or melting away in the dark. Maybe Bolling was right, and the prisoner was some sort of Russian advisor. If so, the NVA had to get him back, both to satisfy their Russian masters and to avoid the negative publicity that the capture would generate on the world stage. If the Russians were actively assisting the North Vietnamese war effort, it would drastically change the dynamic at the Paris peace talks.

"We can't do that," Carr shouted back at the man.

"Then you die!" the Vietnamese man threatened.

"The prisoner will die first," Carr countered. Samples liked the way Carr was handling the situation. He tried to sit up, but his leg and hip were so stiff and painful that he collapsed back on the bed.

"Let him go, Lieutenant," Colonel Tarreyton said from right next to Samples' head. He was still sitting on the floor, which significantly reduced his command presence. Belatedly realizing this, Tarreyton pushed himself erect, holding his briefcase in his left hand and the copilot's .45 pistol in his right.

"We can't do that, sir," Carr told him forcibly.

"I'm your superior officer," Tarreyton sneered, "and you'll do what I say."

"We surround you," the man in the woods warned. "I show you!" Then he shouted some long command in Vietnamese, and there was a crackle of gunfire all around the building, single shots from numerous rifles fired in the air at the same time. Samples felt his heart sink. There must have been forty different weapons fired; they were truly surrounded by a superior force.

"See," Tarreyton said smugly when the gunfire ended. "We don't have a choice." He crossed the room to stand in front of the prisoner, who was struggling to break the holds that Greenberg and Johnson held him down with. "Let him up," Tarreyton commanded the two Americans.

"Don't!" Carr countermanded.

"Listen to the lieutenant," Samples hollered at them.

Tarreyton leaned forward and put the pistol to Johnson's head. "Let. Him. Go."

Even in the dark Samples could see the defiance in the Johnson's eyes. "You really gonna shoot me, colonel?" he snarled.

"Colonel!" Carr screamed. "You're out of control! Put your weapon down!"

"Not until this black bastard releases the prisoner!" Tarreyton angrily replied, turning his head to glare at Carr. Johnson took the offered opportunity and let the prisoner go only to reach up and grab Tarreyton's wrist, pushing the gun up and away from his head. Tarreyton pulled the trigger and the blast filled the room with noise, but the bullet harmlessly punctured the tin roof.

Freed from Johnson's restraint, and having somehow untied his own hands, the prisoner wrenched away and slammed an elbow into Greenberg's face, sending the young man sprawling. With incredible quickness the man demonstrated the training he had received in the Russian special forces and pulled the pistol out of Tarreyton's hand, grasping the barrel and twisting it free. Faster than Samples or anyone else could react, the man flipped the pistol around and gripped it for firing, while simultaneously jumping up and hopping around the copilot's stretcher to crowd in amongst the Girlfriends, who had all stood up when the first shout had been heard. Grabbing the blond girl by the neck, he threw himself into the corner and pulled her in front of him. The other two girls scampered away, taking refuge at the back of the room.

"Crystal!" Sweet cried plaintively. "Let her go!" he demanded of the Russian.

Samples was feeling around on the bed, searching for his M-16, but someone must have moved it. Then he felt Captain Gaither take his hand and place the other .45 pistol in it. He released the safety with his thumb, and hoped the weapon already had a round in the chamber. But with the girl in front of the Russian, there was no way to take a shot.

The man shouted something in another language. It wasn't Vietnamese; it was more guttural and full of consonants. Apparently it was Russian, because Bolling was able to translate.

"I think he wants us to surrender," Bolling said. He had stood up when the prisoner was wrestling with Greenberg, and now he began moving slowly toward the front of the room. He asked the gook something in Russian as he approached the man. The man shouted at Bolling, who stopped a few feet away, right in the middle of the room. Bolling spoke again in a calm voice, raising his hands in front of him with his palms out in a gesture of conciliation.

"Tell him that's not going to happen," Carr said to Bolling.

Bolling spoke again in Russian, and Samples wondered what the young deserter was up to. The Russian soldier sidestepped toward the doorway, keeping Crystal in front of him. She was whimpering and crying, but too frightened to resist. "He says to move the cabinet," Bolling translated. "I'll do it." Bolling moved forward, explaining his actions in Russian, and pulled at one corner of the cabinet.

"Bolling, no!" Samples shouted at him. Pastorini resisted, pushing the cabinet back in place. Bolling whispered something to Pastorini that Samples couldn't hear, and Pastorini shook his head. Bolling kept tugging on the cabinet and pleading with Pastorini. Meanwhile the man outside asked something in Vietnamese, and the Russian answered him. It sounded like he was telling the gooks outside what was going to happen inside, and perhaps giving them instructions.

A rifle shot rang out, and Pastorini jerked backwards and fell to the floor. With him out of the way, Bolling pulled the cabinet back from the door a couple feet. It was all happening so quickly Samples didn't know what to do. The Russian edged sideways, sliding his shoulder along the wall to the door frame as he pulled Crystal along with him. Bolling, who was crouching by the cabinet, unexpectedly jumped to the pair's left side, then turned and pushed them toward the cabinet. The Russian's knees collided with the top edge of the cabinet and started to buckle, causing him to release his hold on Crystal's neck in order to reach out to the door frame for support. Bolling grabbed Crystal's arm and jerked her way, sending her flying to the floor.

"Shoot him!" Bolling yelled.

The Russian immediately regained his balance and spun to shoot Bolling. At the same time his pistol went off, Samples fired the .45 Gaither had given him. Bolling spun around from the impact and crashed to the floor on top of Crystal, while the Russian stumbled backwards out the door. He tried to aim the pistol back into the room, but multiple M-16s fired and peppered his body with 5.56mm bullets until he crumpled to the ground on his back. There was a brief moment of shocked silence.

*****

Lieutenant Carr just stared at the doorway, reconstructing what had happened in his mind, since it had all occurred so quickly. With the Russian dead, the entire situation was changed, and mostly not for the better. He no longer had to make a decision about releasing the Russian to the NVA, nor did he have to worry about guarding the man. On the other hand, they had just lost what could have been a valuable resource for American intelligence and international diplomacy. More importantly, however, they had lost their only ace in the hole to negotiate with the NVA in the woods. The gooks no longer had any reason to limit their fire towards the Americans.

The voice in the woods shouted out questions in Vietnamese, pausing every few seconds in anticipation of an answer, but none came. They had no way to know what had occurred within the temple, and apparently could not see the body of their fallen advisor. Carr knew that this respite wouldn't last. When the gooks figured out the Russian was dead, the firefight would be on with a vengeance. A few feet away Crystal was wailing in terror as she pushed Bolling off her. Doc Allman and Captain Gaither ran up; Gaither knelt beside the young deserter, probing his body and rolling him over onto his back, while Allman tended to Pastorini, who had crawled over to the wall at Carr's feet.

"You idiots!" Colonel Tarreyton hollered. "He was our ticket out of here, and you shot him! Lieutenant, I'm going to have you and your sergeant court-martialed for gross negligence and insubordination."

"Colonel!" Carr shouted back at him in as menacing a tone as he could manage. "Shut the fuck up!"

The tone of the Vietnamese outside changed from questions to a command, and gunfire erupted all around the temple.

"Everybody down!" Carr yelled, jumping across the room behind the askew cabinet to tackle Captain Gaither and push her out of the line of fire.

Almost instinctively she slapped him, and then muttered a reluctant "Thanks" as she scooted over to the north wall next to the reunited Girlfriends who cowered in the corner.

Around him Carr's own soldiers began returning the fire, the blasts echoing in the room almost deafening him. Reyes pushed the cabinet back into place and began firing the M-60, sweeping the spray of bullets across the narrow open area in front of the building. Carr could feel more than hear the enemy rounds whacking the outer walls of the building, and some that flew through the openings to crash into the inner walls. Carr looked around, and as far as he could tell in the dark, everyone who wasn't firing out an opening was prone on the floor. Whether any of those people lying down were wounded or dead was impossible to tell. Carr himself was on his stomach near the middle of the room, unsure what to do next. He felt a hand on his ankle, and then heard Samples say, "Anne?"

"What are you doing, Aaron?" Carr demanded. "You're wounded."

"Where's Anne? Captain Gaither? Is she okay?"

"Over by the Girlfriends," Carr told him, turning to face Samples, who was crawling on his stomach across the dirt floor. "She's okay so far."

Samples stopped low-crawling and scooted over closer to Carr so he could be heard over the cacophonous gunfire. "What are we gonna do, Eltee?" he asked.

"Hold out until the cavalry arrives, I guess. You got any better ideas?"

"Not at the moment," Samples replied.

"Fuck!" Hicks yelled from atop the crate at the back of the room. "I'm hit."

Doc Allman jumped up from where he had just finished bandaging Pastorini and ran to the back of the room, asking "Where? How bad?"

"Left leg. I don't know." Hicks kept firing out the opening as he answered Doc's questions, using one leg and his elbows to keep himself upright.

Carr looked out the doorway, above where Reyes was continuing to pound away with the light machine gun, its red tracer rounds plunging into the dark forest, and saw green tracers zipping past the front of the building before the gunner corrected his aim and the rounds began to impact in a staccato rhythm against the outside wall. So the gooks have a machine gun, too, Carr thought glumly.

"Hope they don't have any RPGs with them," Samples yelled over the noise.

A whoosh from the north side was followed by a flash in the window and a crunching explosion that shook the building. Bits of concrete showered the room.

"You had to say that," Carr chided Samples, like it was his fault for mentioning the rocket propelled grenades.

"Listen!" Samples said, and Carr raised his head to do so. There were shouts in Vietnamese coming from all around the building, and the gunfire from outside quickly abated.

"Cease fire!" Carr ordered his own men, and a moment later the whole area went quiet.

"Americans!" the familiar voice outside called. "You surrender. Or you die."

"Eat shit and die, motherfucker!" Reyes roared defiantly.

"At ease, Reyes!" Samples angrily commanded him. In a calmer voice he turned to Carr and asked, "What do you think?"

Carr was torn. Here was another life or death decision being forced on him. Here they were, surrounded, probably outnumbered, with any help still at least an hour away, and with rapidly diminishing ammo for their weapons. And he had the non-combatants and wounded to worry about. How long could they hold out? How many casualties would they suffer while doing so? Conversely, what would happen if they did surrender? Would the females be treated fairly? Would the enemy follow the Geneva Conventions, or would the Americans be abused or even tortured? And, on a more personal level, how would he, First Lieutenant Stephen Carr, be viewed by the Army for surrendering his men?

"We have no choice, Lieutenant," Colonel Tarreyton intoned officiously. "We cannot risk having more people killed or wounded. We need to surrender. It will be my decision."

The very fact that this obnoxious senior officer wanted him to surrender swayed Carr in the opposite direction. He was convinced that if Tarreyton wanted him to give up, then the only permissible course of action was to continue to resist, because anything the colonel favored was obviously wrong. He could also feel the stern gaze from Sergeant Samples that was warning him not to accede to the colonel's demands.

"I'll tell you what, Colonel," Carr told him in measured tones with only a bare hint of sarcasm. "Why don't you go out there and negotiate a truce. Work out the details, come to a mutually satisfactory resolution, and get suitable guarantees. Kind of a mini Paris peace talk."

Tarreyton spluttered. "Me? No, no. We'll send a representative."

"And who would that be?"

"Well, uh, as the junior officer here, I think you would be the most appropriate choice."

Carr couldn't believe the dumpy colonel was seriously considering his suggestion, and worse, pushing the job off on Carr. "Colonel, I'm in charge of the men here, and frankly, I'm in charge of the situation as well. You can file charges against me for insubordination, if we survive, but I am not allowing any of these people to be taken captive without a fight. The NVA and the Viet Cong do not have a stellar reputation for their treatment of prisoners, and I hate to even think what they would do with the women. No, we are not surrendering. You, however, as a senior officer, are free to follow your own conscience. If you want to surrender on your own, be my guest."

"But, but, but," Tarreyton burbled, unaccustomed to being defied like this.

"It's your choice, sir," Carr informed him calmly. "If you're going out there, now is the time, because shortly hostilities will undoubtedly resume."

Tarreyton huffed and puffed, but didn't move toward the door. Finally he took a deep breath and warned, "All right, Lieutenant, have it your way for now. But this will certainly go in my report."

Carr rolled his eyes, but saw no point in continuing the conversation. Instead he turned to the door and used his command voice to announce, "We will not surrender. In the immortal words of General McAuliffe at the Battle of Bastogne, 'Nuts'." Carr doubted the NVA officer had ever heard of McAuliffe, and had no idea what the word 'nuts' meant in this context, but he hoped it would inspire his own men. He wished he could have come up with his own memorable response, but nothing better had come to him.

"What?" the man in the woods asked, clearly confused. His command of English was limited, Carr assumed, and probably had no idea what Carr had meant. So he decided to clarify his response in simpler language that even the NVA officer could understand.

"Fuck you!" Carr yelled. "And the horse you rode in on!"

Carr heard echoes of a baffled discussion out in the woods. It sounded like the enemy officer was consulting with some subordinates. "Get ready," Carr told the men in the temple. A moment later there was a command in Vietnamese, and the firefight was back on. AKs and a machine gun opened fire, and another RPG was launched, exploding against a tree trunk just outside the doorway. Reyes returned fire with the M-60, and now Pastorini was beside him, preparing to load a new belt of ammunition. The men at the windows popped up and down, firing their M-16s at anything that looked like it might hide an enemy soldier. Crosby fired his M-79 grenade launcher out the south window with a percussive plomp, and managed to avoid hitting any of the nearby trees. The grenade impacted somewhere out in the woods, with unknown effect, but at least it gave notice that the men in the temple were just as dangerous as the men outside.

Carr stood up behind Reyes and fired a series of shots out the door, exposing himself just for the satisfaction of fighting back. Samples reached up and grabbed his pistol belt, pulling him back down. "Don't be stupid, Eltee," the sergeant warned. "Do you want the colonel to end up in charge?" Carr nodded, mostly to himself. Samples was right—he had a responsibility to his men to stay alive and make the right decisions. If only he knew what the right decisions were.

"Sir!" Eberhart yelled over the roar of the guns, "they're coming!"

SIXTEEN

Even though the trees were smaller and more easily crushed by the weight of the armored personnel carriers, it was still slow going. Sometimes the front of the vehicle would ride up a bending trunk and then plop down when the tree broke or became uprooted. The diesel engine roared and the treads gnashed with an ominous grinding noise that worried Masters. They needed to hurry, but he didn't want to have a mechanical breakdown of some sort that would delay their arrival. There had been a couple bursts of gunfire up ahead, each followed by periods of silence, but the third round of the firefight had just started, and it was a crescendo of explosive noise that indicated it had gotten out of hand. With that many guns firing, Masters knew that the NVA must have arrived at the temple, which meant the men inside were in grave danger of being overrun.

PFC Gunn was guiding the track with fantastic expertise, finding the best path between the bigger trees and mashing down the saplings and bushes between. Masters had trouble keeping himself oriented, despite—or perhaps because of—the bouncing headlight beams, but Gunn kept to the abandoned roadway with apparent ease. Behind them the other tracks followed, their own headlights illuminating the backs of Purdey in the 50-cal turret and Handleman holding on to his seat like it was a bucking bronco. Looking straight up, Masters was surprised to see that he could actually distinguish patches of the heavy cloud cover through the gaps in the canopy made by their track's smashing of the trees. The night was no longer pitch black; it was charcoal grey. Looking to their left and right, Masters could make out individual trees with growing clarity. It was time to report in.

When they had left Dau Tieng Masters had made sure to have the porkchop mike of the track radio looped out of the machine gun turret and clipped where he could find it again. Now he pulled it free and held it up to his mouth, pausing as he tried to remember the call signs and figure out what to say.

"Yankee three-three, this is Yankee X-Ray, over," he said, holding down the button on the side of the mike. He released the button and waited for a response. He thought he heard a break in the static, but couldn't make it out.

"Purdey, turn up the radio," Masters said to the gunner. Purdey ducked down inside for a moment then popped back up in the turret.

"It's up all the way, sir."

Masters called again, and this time heard a response. "Yankee X-Ray, this is three-three Romeo, over." That meant Masters was talking to the platoon radio operator.

"Three-three, be advised we are approaching your location from the north, over."

"Say again, over." The RTO seemed baffled by the call.

"This is Yankee X-Ray. I have four papa charlies en route to your location. We should arrive within fifteen minutes. Please advise on how you want us deployed, over."

"Wait one," the RTO said, his elation unmuted by the static and background noise.

A moment later a new voice came on the radio, one Masters recognized as Lieutenant Carr. "Yankee X-Ray, this is three-three Lima. You have four papa charlies, over?"

"Roger that. These are your tracks and men, augmented by walking wounded and FNGs, over."

"How did you find us, over?"

"Old maps, over."

Before Carr could ask another question, a third voice broke in. "This is two-niner Tango. What the hell is going on?" It was the battalion commander, and he didn't sound pleased. Masters grabbed at the side of the machine gun turret as the track lurched to one side

159

while going around a tree and into a ditch. It was time to face the music. Masters had refrained from telling Battalion what he was up to, so that he couldn't be ordered to stop, but it was now too late for that.

"Two-niner Tango, this is Yankee X-ray," Masters said into the mike. "We are reuniting the Yankee papa charlies with their dismounted element, over."

"I didn't authorize that!" the colonel yelled into his mike.

Masters didn't have an acceptable answer for that, so he kept silent.

"Two-niner Tango, this is three-three Lima," Carr interjected. "We are in heavy contact. Those tracks are vital to our defense and will allow us to withdraw our wounded and civilians, over."

Masters was glad Carr had intervened. No matter how annoyed the battalion commander might be by his actions, there was no way he could countermand them now. The radio stayed silent for a minute, undoubtedly because the colonel was conferring with his staff.

"Yankee X-Ray," the colonel finally radioed, "how many men do you have with you?"

"Sixteen, plus myself, over," Masters replied.

"And three-three Lima, how large is your attacking force?"

"Estimate company strength, NVA, over," Carr answered.

"Elements here are mounting up," the colonel told them. "I need coordinates."

Masters had memorized them earlier, and passed them on proudly. He kept thinking how things might have been different if the battalion staff at Dau Tieng had listened to him hours earlier.

"Yankee X-Ray, keep me posted on your progress. Three-three Lima, I'm alerting Division arty. Give 'em hell, guys. Out."

*****

Lieutenant Carr felt a surge of hope well up inside him. His tracks, with their additional firepower and protective armor, were on the way, bringing additional troops to reinforce his beleaguered redoubt. Meanwhile, however, he had to deal with the continuing onslaught surrounding them. From his position beside the doorway he could leaned forward enough to see the bright red tracers of the M-60 flying into the trees, and the glowing green tracers of the enemy machine gun piercing the air from somewhere over to the right, seeming to be aimed directly at Carr, only to bounce crazily into the air when they hit the side of the building. White sparkles glittered among the trees of the dark forest as enemy AK-47s fired in their direction, only their muzzle flashes visible.

Young Crosby darted over and knelt behind Reyes. "I'm right behind you," he yelled at Reyes, then raised his M-79 grenade launcher and fired, sending the grenade arcing out through the upper door opening in the direction of the NVA machine gun. The grenade exploded among the trees, and the green tracers stopped. "Got him!" Crosby crowed, but his elation was short-lived. The machine gun opened up again, splattering bullets around the doorway and forcing Carr back against the inside wall and making Reyes and Pastorini duck. "Shit!" Crosby complained, and hustled over to the north window.

Carr was frankly a little surprised by Crosby's actions. The kid was fairly new to the platoon, and had always struck Carr as kind of a wimpy guy, one who had probably been in the high school band playing a clarinet. He had soft features and wispy blond hair, and spent most of his free time reading science fiction novels. But here, in this situation, he was showing a different side of himself, bouncing from opening to opening to fire his bloop gun, seemingly unconcerned about the bullets flying in through those openings.

To Carr's lower left Reyes had sat back up and was again firing the M-60 in measured bursts, swinging the barrel from left to right and back, while between Carr and Reyes Pastorini sprawled on the floor with an open can of ammo, stretching the belt out toward Reyes. In the pre-dawn greyness Carr could see Sergeant Samples on the other side of the cabinet, his legs stretched out behind him, his

161

pistol belt and helmet now back on. He was firing his M-16 across to the northeast, his gun barrel tucked beneath that of the M-60's, which was elevated on its bipod. Carr peered around the edge of the doorway and fired a few shots of his own toward the area where the enemy machine gun was located, then ducked back, pressing his spine against the wall. He took a quick survey of the situation inside the temple.

To his immediate right Eberhart crouched in the corner, monitoring the radio. Montoya and Vasquez were on either side of the north window, popping up and down to fire out the opening. They paused long enough for Crosby to launch another grenade, before resuming their suppressive fire. Just beyond Vasquez Colonel Tarreyton cowered on the floor, his briefcase pulled tight against his chest. At the back of the room Chief Whitmore lay on his stretcher with Reyes' M-16 in his hands, unable to move but ready to respond if the gooks made it inside the building. Captain Gaither sat low in the corner at Whitmore's head, prudently staying low but alert for any request for assistance. Johnson had taken Hick's place at the high ventilation hole and was firing his M-16 with metronomic regularity. Hick's was on the floor below, his leg being tended to by Doc Allman. Greenberg had joined Sorenson and Reedy at the south window, and the three took turns firing out the opening. Sweet alternated between trying to calm the three Japanese girls who were huddled in the corner and shooting his rifle out the doorway over Samples' head.

The brick walls of the temple were providing protection from most of the incoming bullets, and those that made it through the openings were too high to hit those who were sitting or prone within. Still, those who stood up to fire out the openings were vulnerable, as were those in the back of the room, who could be hit by rounds flying through the doorway just above the cabinet. There was no place totally safe, Carr realized, but the doorway was the most dangerous point of entry.

"Crosby," Carr hollered at the young man as he headed over toward the south window. The rolling thunder of gunfire pounded at his ears. "You got any smoke rounds?" The M-79 could be loaded with a variety of ammunition, and Carr didn't know what Crosby had chosen to carry in his ammo vest.

Crosby knelt down by the end of the stretcher carrying the dead copilot. "No, sir," he shouted back. "Just HE and canister. Oh, and a couple CS."

CS was tear gas, and while it did produce a brief white cloud, it wasn't enough to really obscure the enemy's vision. And in these wet conditions, the gas would have little effect on the enemy's eyes and breathing, because water quickly dissipated the powdery gas.

"We've got smoke grenades," Samples yelled.

Carr was trying to preserve his supply of smoke grenades, in case they were needed later to mark their positions for any aircraft that came to their aid.

"Use your CS," Carr told Crosby. "Who's got smoke?" he shouted, addressing all the men in the room. He had realized that marking their location for choppers only mattered if they were still alive when the choppers came.

"Here!" Montoya responded, stepping over to hand one of the canisters to Carr before returning to the north window.

Crosby fired his M-79 through the opening, and then broke the barrel down to eject the smoking cartridge and insert a new one. Carr leaned his rifle against the wall and grasped the smoke grenade canister in his right hand, holding down the thin metal spoon while he pulled the pin. He waited while Crosby fired the second CS round, then spun around and tossed the grenade out in front of the building about ten feet. The handle flew off in mid-air, and when the grenade hit the ground purple smoke began billowing out of the end of the grenade. Carr jumped back from the doorway and retrieved his rifle. By the time he looked back outside, the smoke was filling the air, obscuring everything but the red and green tracers that continued to pierce the cloud.

"Star shells!" Samples suggested as he continued to fire his M-16 through the murk. "Fire them low, blind them."

Carr remembered that he had two star shell launchers in his cargo pockets, and reached down to pull one out. It was a thin aluminum tube with a cap, shaped kind of like the cold medicine capsules he had taken a few times. He slid off the cap, revealing the open end, and slid the cap on the opposite end. Inside the cap was a sharp metal projection that would strike a primer cap embedded in the rounded end of the tube. Carr again leaned his rifle against the wall and stepped forward, aiming the launcher almost horizontally out the doorway. Holding the launcher firmly in one hand, he slapped the back end as hard as he could with the other, feeling the recoil as the star shell burst out of the tube and flew through the smoke into the woods beyond. As it was designed to do, the projectile separated into several burning elements, each extremely bright, like a scattering of brilliant stars. Unaffected by the rain, the stars bounced among the trees and temporarily destroyed the night vision of the NVA out there. The gunfire from the woods in front abated, albeit only for the few moments the star shell lasted until the glowing lights burned out.

Taking a cue from Carr, other men in the temple brought out star shells and parachute flares to fire out the windows and the ventilation port. Soon the woods outside were bright with pyrotechnics.

"RPG!" Vasquez screamed, and began firing as fast as he could, then dropped to the floor as the rocket slammed into the building just above the north window. The explosion shattered the wall, and pieces of cinder block scattered across the room, leaving a gaping hole above the lintel of the window. Before the dust could settle Montoya and Vasquez went back to the window and fired furiously into the woods. Crosby, who had gone to the south window a moment before, jumped over the dead copilot and pushed his way between the other two men.

"Where?" he demanded, shoving the barrel of his M-79 out the window. Vasquez pointed, and Crosby fired. Carr heard the muffled explosion of the grenade out in the woods, but there was no way to tell yet if Crosby had gotten the guy with the launcher. Carr had hoped to hear the secondary explosions of RPG rounds set off by the M-79, but no cigar.

"Anybody hurt?" Carr yelled out.

"I've got something in my eye!" Tarreyton cried out. Carr wearily shook his head.

"I got it," Doc Allman said, scrambling over the bed to crouch beside the colonel.

Crosby fired another grenade out the window, with the same result, and then scuttled closer to Carr to reload.

"How're you doing on ammo?" Carr asked him.

Crosby patted the pockets of his ammo vest. "Seven more HE, five canister."

The HE, or high explosive, were the standard rounds he had been using, ones which hurled what was essentially a small fragmentation grenade. The canister rounds were glorified shotgun rounds, with BB-sized pellets; they were effective only at close range. If the gooks assaulted the temple and got inside, Carr thought, they would be useful, but he certainly hoped it didn't come to that.

The M-60 stopped firing, and Carr glanced over, expecting to see Pastorini feeding a new belt of ammunition into the weapon. Instead he saw Reyes slumped down, his helmet resting on the shoulder stock. "Reyes!" Samples yelled at him, reaching out to shake the man's shoulder. There was no reaction. Samples pushed back on Reyes' shoulder, pulling him away from the machine gun, and the man fell backwards limply, his helmet clunking onto the floor and rolling away. His legs were askew, with one knee bent and raised, the other canted sideways. At first Carr couldn't see what the problem was. There was no blood on his shirt, and no visible wounds. But his face somehow looked different. In the extremely dim light, it was hard to make out details, but Carr noticed that one eye seemed darker than the other.

Doc Allman was there almost instantly, kneeling beside Reyes and feeling his neck for a pulse. When he turned Reyes' head to find the artery in his neck, Carr saw that the reason one eye was darker was that it was totally missing; where his right eye had been was now just a bloody hole. Doc shook his head. Carr was momentarily stunned. Dark thoughts flashed through his head. He had known Reyes for months, and suddenly he was gone. Carr felt responsible,

165

even knowing there was nothing he could have done to prevent the young man's death. Now he would have to write a letter to Reyes' folks, and that would be really hard.

"Sweet!" Samples yelled, "get behind the sixty." Carr was glad that Samples was keeping his head and not being distracted like Carr was. Shaking his head to clear it, Carr helped Allman drag Reyes' body over next to Bolling's while Sweet sat down behind the M-60 and began firing. Around them the firefight raged on, the cacophony of multiple gun shots reverberating inside the small building, pounding against Carr's ears and drumming his abdomen. Where were the tracks?

SEVENTEEN

The track lurched to the right side as it pushed over a small tree, and Masters had to shift his weight to stay on his seat. Up ahead they could now hear the constant gunfire, and even caught glimpses of tracer rounds, both red and green, and, strangely, brilliant white glows that lasted for several seconds. Masters picked up the mike and thought about what he would say to Carr on the radio, now that they were almost there.

"Ow! Ow! Ow!" PFC Handleman was in a frenzy, slapping at his arms and legs, and then Purdey, in the TC hatch, was swiping at his right arm with his left.

"Mogators!" Purdey shouted.

"What? What are they?" Handleman screamed in pain, trying to crawl across the track behind the turret to get away from them.

Masters felt the track slowing. "Keep moving!" he yelled at the driver.

"They're just ants," he told Handleman, grabbing the young man's arm to steady him, and to keep him and his infestation away from the left side of the track. "They bite, but they don't sting." Handleman was new, and this was his first experience with the red menace. Masters knew it must be both terrifying and agonizing, but they had a more important mission right now. "Just brush them off and pick up your weapon."

"Yes, sir," Handleman squeaked, apparently on the verge of tears. He moved back to his ammo crate, holding on to the edge of the turret with his left hand as he swept ants off the seat with his right, and then plopped down and picked up his rifle. Purdey picked one off his neck and flicked it into the woods, while Handleman squirmed, swiped, and yelped next to him.

Either it had been a small nest, or most of the ants had missed the track, for only Handleman and Purdey had been attacked. Purdey was now concentrating on the woods in front of them, his hands gripping the wooden handles of the 50-cal, and Handleman was cursing quietly as he swatted at the remaining insects. With that crisis averted, Masters again tried to gauge the distance to the temple. The wet forest tended to muffle the reports of weapons, and the occasional flashes of gunfire were hard to zero in on. As best as he could determine, they were still several hundred meters out, and closing in at what was not a rapid pace.

It was definitely getting lighter now. Masters could see about twenty feet into the forest on either side, when he wasn't being blinded by the headlights of the track behind them. And those lights, he realized, made them excellent targets. "Douse the lights," he yelled at Jamison, grabbing him on the shoulder. Jamison looked around at Masters, then nodded and spoke into the CVC helmet mike. A moment later the track lights blinked out on each of the tracks.

"That's better," Purdey commented. Masters agreed. Without the glare and moving shadows of the headlights, it was now easier to see deeper into the woods and pick out the best route between the trees.

"Three-three Lima, this is Yankee X-Ray, over." Masters held the mike close to his mouth and tried to speak as distinctly as possible. He was about to repeat the call when he got an answer, the track radio below whining as the fan spun up and the voice crackled through the small speaker.

"This is three-three Lima, go."

"We are approaching your location. Where do you want us, over?"

"Wait one."

Masters had been so concerned about finding the temple and pushing their way through the forest that he hadn't really thought about what they would do when they arrived. Now that such decisions had to be made, he was foundering. He considered various options, such as splitting his force into two pairs and sweeping around either size of the temple, or bringing the other tracks up on line and assaulting across the front of the temple, but he realized there were flaws with such plans. He would be placing the tracks between the firepower of the men in the building and the enemy besiegers, making his troops even more vulnerable to enfilade fire. He was a little ashamed of himself for pushing the decision onto Carr, but rationalized that Carr was the senior officer on the scene, and knew the situation better. While he waited, Masters wondered if the gooks attacking the temple were yet aware of his presence.

As if in answer, an RPG whooshed out of the woods to their left, slashed across the bow of the track, and ricocheted off the right front corner, spinning up through the trees and exploding when it came down far off to the right. Purdey rotated the barrel of the 50-cal as far to the left as the turret would allow and fired off several booming bursts of machine gun fire over Gunn's head. Behind them Pratt, the gunner on the one-two track, opened up as well, his red tracers ripping into the woods toward where the RPG had been launched.

Masters heard the engine rpm begin to drop, and punched Jamison in the back. "Don't stop!" he yelled over the noise of the 50-cals. "Keep it moving!" Standard practice in this sort of situation was for the men to dismount and the tracks turn toward the attackers, but Masters couldn't lose any time getting the temple and joining up with Carr's force. Jamison passed the word to Gunn over the intercom, and the track immediately accelerated again, crashing through the underbrush. In seconds the track had traveled forward so much that Purdey could no longer swivel the machine gun far enough to shoot toward the suspected RPG launching site, but the guns on the tracks following kept up their fire as they came abreast of the area. Masters was able to hear snatches of the radio conversations as Jamison relayed the plan to the other three vehicles. Then Jamison raised his rifle and began shooting randomly into the woods to their left. Taking that as a cue, Handleman began firing to the right. Purdey appeared frustrated, because he dared not fire forward for fear of hitting the people in the temple, a building still hidden by the intervening trees.

169

To Masters it seemed like a naval battle in the age of sail. The line of APCs was plunging slowly through the forest firing broadsides at unseen enemies lurking in the darkness. So far, he noted, they had only been the target of a single RPG; he had not noted any incoming rifle or machine gun fire. Yet. But as they approached the embattled temple, he knew, that would rapidly change.

"Yankee X-Ray, this is three-three Lima, over." Masters just barely heard the radio call over the noise of the gunfire. The porkchop mike was still clutched in his hand.

"This is X-Ray, over."

"You're taking fire?"

"Affirmative. So far just one RPG. Over."

"Have you stopped, over?" Masters could hear the worry in Carr's voice.

"Negative. Full steam ahead." Masters thought, after he said it, that the remark seemed trite, but he didn't have time to worry about it now.

"Outstanding! When you get here, deploy in a semi-circle around the front of the building, and back in as close as you can get. Over."

"Good copy," Masters replied. "On our way. Out."

All four personnel carriers had now passed the area where the RPG attack had occurred, and the roar of the 50-cals had died, to be replaced by the sharp barks of M-16s laying down a suppressive fire. Masters twisted around to check on the other tracks, to make sure they were all keeping up. There was a metallic whang, and Masters' first reaction was to wonder if something in the machine gun turret had just snapped loose, but he saw Purdey ducking down inside the turret, and Jamison was pointing to a bright silver scar on the dark green turret side. It was only then that Masters realized an enemy bullet had just missed him and ricocheted off the steel plate of the turret.

"Inside!" Jamison yelled, and pushed Masters toward the open cargo hatch behind the 50-cal. Masters jumped in the black hole, stumbling over the stacks of ammo cans and falling onto the bench seat beneath the radio. Jamison and Handleman followed him in, but both men remained standing, firing their rifles between the ammo crates and cans that comprised the upper seats on the vehicle. Purdey was squatting on the ammo cans below the TC hatch, unsure what to do. Without unlocking the turret ring, the machine gun wouldn't traverse all the way to the left or right, so he couldn't use it to return fire. Instead he reached up and retrieved his M-16, which he had left lying beside the hatch cover, checked to make sure the magazine was seated, and then rose up through the hatch far enough to fire through the gap between the steel plates of the angular turret and the pintle for the 50-cal.

In the driver's compartment Gunn had lowered the seat so that his head was below the rim, and was trying to see through the prismatic vision blocks, a difficult task at the best of times. He kept his foot to the floor, but the progress became more erratic and bumpy, since he couldn't really see where he was going. The track hit one of the larger tree trunks and slammed to a halt. Gunn backed away and pulled on the right lateral to swing around the tree, only to hit again with the other side of the glacis. "Fuck it!" Gunn screamed, and raised his seat enough that he could see over the rim of the driver's hatch. He was wearing his CVC helmet, which offered virtually no protection from bullets, and Masters admired his courage. Once again Gunn backed the track up a few feet, then stomped on the accelerator as he guided the lumbering beast between trees and onward toward their goal.

A voice Masters didn't immediately recognize came on the radio. "Pratt's hit!"

Jamison keyed his helmet mike. "Carl, how bad?" Masters now realized that the call had come from Specialist Tenkiller, the driver of the one-two."

"His arm's messed up," Tenkiller replied. "Wilson's taking care of it."

Jamison looked over at Masters and shrugged. They both knew there was nothing they could do about Pratt right now.

A flash lit up the interior of the track for a microsecond, and it took Masters a couple moments to register what it represented. Another RPG, and this one had flown right over the top of the track, somehow missing the machine gun turret and the ammo cases strapped to the roof. An explosion off in the woods to their right signaled where the rocket had ended up. Masters held on to the bench with one hand as the track bounced and swayed through the woods, the sharp cracks of M-16s combining with the roaring diesel to create a chaos of sound in the tight confines. Masters started to stand up, planning to squeeze in beside Jamison in the cargo hatch opening and add his rifle to the mix, when the radio crackled right beside his head.

"Yankee X-Ray, this is two-niner Tango, over." It was the battalion commander calling. Masters didn't want to deal with the man right now, but military protocol demanded it. Sitting back down, he found the coiled mike cord and followed it to the mike.

"This is Yankee X-Ray, go."

"I need a sitrep, over." With all the noise, and the poor radio reception, it was hard to be sure, but Masters thought he detected actual concern in the colonel's voice.

"We are under fire, and approaching the temple, over."

Presumably the commander could hear the gunfire in the background when Masters spoke, as well as the lieutenant's level of anxiety, for he asked no further questions. Instead he signed off, saying only, "Good copy, out."

Glad that the colonel didn't want to prolong the conversation, Masters stood up and stuck his head out the cargo hatch, poking his rifle between two ammo crates strapped to the roof. Jamison was to his right, banging away with his rifle from behind the metal ammo can he normally used as his seat. Masters was surprised by how much better he could see now. Despite the clouds and constant drizzle of rain, the darkness was retreating, revealing the dense trees and bushes around them. He could almost pick out colors—mostly greens and browns—glistening with water, interspersed with the deadly sparks of muzzle flashes. He could also hear better with his head outside the walls of the vehicle, with the sound of heavier gunfire coming from the front. Masters peered around Jamison's shoulders, looking out over Gunn's helmet, and through the trees he caught glimpses of purple smoke and glowing sparks he finally recognized as star shells. He even caught a brief glimpse of a rectangular shape that he assumed was a corner of the temple building.

Purdey had apparently seen it, too. He put down his M-16 and stood up enough to once again grab the handles of the 50-cal. Since he now knew where the friendly troops were, he could resume laying down a base of covering fire with the big machine gun. With a jarring whump-whump-whump, the machine gun sent large-caliber lead flying into the forest, shredding leaves and breaking off branches, its glowing red tracers arrowing into the brush in a violent stream. Although Masters knew it was mostly illusory, the clout of the 50-cal and heavy metal bulk of the APC gave him a feeling of invincibility and strength, and hope surged through his body like a tidal wave. He was leading the cavalry to the rescue!

*****

His leg felt like someone was pounding it every two seconds with a baseball bat. Samples tried shifting his weight, but nothing seemed to bring relief. He had refused morphine for fear it would cloud his judgment; now he was beginning to regret that decision. With agonizing slowness he pushed himself erect, sliding his back up the wall next to the doorway.

"Short bursts!" he yelled at Sweet, who, in the fever of combat, was leaving his finger on the trigger for far too long for the good of the barrel. Too many rounds in too little time would get the barrel so hot it would warp, or even cook off rounds before they were fully seated in the chamber. The M-60 had a barrel that was easily swapped out for a cooler one, but that only worked if you had a second barrel handy, and they didn't. Sweet nodded obediently and let the barrel cool for a couple seconds. On the other side of the

173

doorway Lieutenant Carr was leaning over the seated Pastorini to fire his M-16 into the woods. Crosby came over and crouched behind Sweet to fire his M-79 over Sweet's head. Samples heard the crunching explosion of the grenade, but because he was facing the inside of the temple, he didn't see the flash. He hoped it had landed somewhere useful.

"Last HE," Crosby announced loudly as he moved back to the south window.

Samples cursed himself for being in the wrong place. With his right leg throbbing, he couldn't lean out enough to fire his M-16 through the doorway opening, nor even peer out to see what was happening. He needed to be on the other side of the doorway, where Carr was, but getting there without exposing himself seemed far too daunting a task at the moment, and would interfere with Carr's shooting position. He reached down to gently rub his right thigh, and felt the bulge in his cargo pocket. He still had another star shell—or parachute flare, he wasn't sure which—he could launch. Setting down his M-16 and pulling the tube from his pocket, he slipped off the cap and placed it on the opposite end. Holding the launcher in his right hand, he extended it into the opening, pointing it directly out to the east, and pounded the end with the heel of his left hand. Because he was balancing mostly on his left leg, with his arms outstretched, the recoil nearly spun him around, but a hand caught his bicep and kept him from falling.

"Easy there, Aaron," Anne Gaither said, pushing him back against the wall for support.

"I'm okay," Samples insisted, perhaps a little more defiantly than the situation called for, and he instantly regretted his tone.

"I know," Anne soothed him.

He looked over at her, and marveled at how beautiful she looked in the dim light streaming in through the doorway. He wanted to say something, but he didn't know what, so he just stared.

"The tracks are coming," he finally managed. He cocked his head to listen. "I can hear the fifties."

"Yes," she agreed. "And then what?"

Despite the fact that a firefight was raging all around them, Samples oddly felt like he and Anne were alone, in a bubble of silence. "Well, that's, uh, that's up to the lieutenant, but probably we'll load up in the tracks and bust our way out of here."

"That's sounds pretty dangerous. Shouldn't you be helping the lieutenant plan how you'll do that?"

"Well, yeah," Samples admitted, but winced when he tried to put weight on his right leg, trying to show her how difficult it was for him to move.

"I'll help," she said, and pulled on his arm, gripping it with both hands. Samples quickly grabbed his rifle and hobbled alongside her, the two of them hustling around behind Sweet to the opposite corner while bullets whizzed past them from outside. The two of them crowded in between Eberhart and Carr. Anne pushed him against the wall and then pressed down on his shoulders until he slid down into a sitting position, both legs stretched out in front of him. She tugged at Carr's shirt tail and motioned for him to kneel down beside Samples. "You two need to talk," she told them loudly and forcefully. While she stepped over Samples' legs and crouched down to check his bandages, Samples and Carr exchanged glances with raised eyebrows.

"What's the plan?" Samples asked, grimacing as Anne gently pressed on his wound.

"I told the tracks to form a defensive perimeter around the front of the temple."

"How close in?" Samples asked.

Carr shrugged. "I said close, but didn't specify."

"We need to have them back in as close to the front of the building as possible," Samples said. "Drop the ramps, put up heavy suppressive fire. Then we can move the cabinet out of the way and load up the women and wounded—and dead."

"Okay," Carr agreed. "Then raise the ramps and maybe lock open the personnel hatches. The rest of us can jump in as the tracks start pulling out."

175

"Pop all our remaining smoke out the windows and back," Samples suggested, "and some out front, too."

"Yeah," Carr agreed, nodding. "I'll see who still has some." Carr stood up and began circulating around the room, seeing how much smoke and other ammo the men had, and giving them the basic plan for the withdrawal. Samples felt somewhat useless; that would normally be his job.

"So, we're going to make it?" Anne asked.

"Yes, ma'am," Samples assured her, sounding more confident that he really felt. While loading the tracks they would be far more vulnerable than inside the temple, and the unmoving vehicles would be sitting ducks for RPGs. And then they would have to fight their way back out of the forest, forced by the foliage into a slow-moving single file.

A few feet away Samples saw Vasquez jerk back from the north window and grab at his neck. "I'm hit!" Vasquez hollered, more in surprise than in pain. Anne jumped up and ran to him, sitting him down on the bamboo bed so she could inspect his wound. Doc Allman joined her, but after taking his aid bag, she shooed him away.

"It's just a nick," she called out to Samples. Doc Allman came over and knelt down by Samples.

"So why am I here?" Allman complained quietly. Samples didn't want to hear any bitching about Anne, so he changed the subject.

"How's the colonel?" he asked, nodding toward the man who huddled between the end of the bamboo bed and the wall. His eyes were both completely covered by bandages.

"He's fine," Allman told him, keeping his voice low enough that Tarreyton couldn't hear. With all the gunfire, that wasn't a hard thing to do. "I covered both eyes just to keep him quiet."

"Good idea," Samples told him. "The less involved he is, the better."

176

Allman tilted his head back a little. "I can hear the tracks. Never thought I'd be so glad to hear diesel engines."

"Bet that," Samples agreed whole-heartedly.

EIGHTEEN

Around Masters was a bewildering swirl of noise and vibration. The diesel engine throbbed, its rpm cycling up and down as PFC Gunn worked the accelerator. The treads clanked and rumbled over the drive and road wheels, and the entire vehicle surged and dropped as it crushed the bushes and saplings before it. Above him the fifty caliber machine gun thumped away in short bursts as Purdey pierced the surrounding woods with a deadly stream of bullets the size of your thumb. Beside him and behind him Jamison and Handleman peppered the forest with their small caliber M-16s, the sharp cracks of the rifles blending with the somewhat deeper reports of the AK-47s returning fire. Leaning against the edge of the cargo hatch coaming so he could fire his own M-16, Masters felt the little jolts as bullets pranged into the vertical sides of the personnel carrier. He had been told that the aluminum alloy armor of the M-113 APC would stop rifle rounds, but could be pierced by heavy machine guns, and was extremely vulnerable to the shaped charges of RPGs. Still, the illusion of protection was reassuring.

Masters felt his bolt lock back, indicating his magazine was empty, so he dropped down inside to put in a new one. As he pulled a full magazine from his ammo bag, while simultaneously pressing the release to drop the empty one, he marveled at the fact that the hail of bullets being sprayed into the forest by the four tracks didn't seem to be diminishing the volume of return fire from the gooks hidden there. For that matter, he thought, it was surprising that none of the American soldiers, other than Pratt, had yet been hit. Mentally he crossed his fingers while he jammed the fresh magazine into the rifle, pressed the bolt release, and then stood back up to resume firing.

"There's the building!" Jamison said excitedly over his left shoulder, and then nodded toward the front, still firing his M-16 out to the side. Masters fired a couple rounds at random between the ammo crates, and then leaned back a little to see around Jamison. There was yellow smoke billowing straight ahead, and to the right red smoke swirled through the trees. Between them he could see the corner of the building, and saw red tracers spitting out from the front. It was still dark enough that he could barely distinguish the colors of the smoke, but the red tracers glowed with deadly brightness. He looked up to see green tracers flying overhead, but couldn't track the source. Which made sense, he realized, because the tracers were designed to be seen primarily by the gunner himself, not the person they were aimed at. One of the incoming rounds hit the sloping front glacis of the track and ricocheted straight up, its green streak disappearing into the leafy canopy. Purdey's red tracers now concentrated on the area from which the enemy machine gun was suspected to be firing.

For the last few minutes Masters had been so immersed in the chaos of the battle that he felt more like a participant than a leader. He knew he had to get his act together and start making things happen. Crouching back down inside, he found the porkchop mike and began issuing orders to the platoon. He was glad he had made the four tracks line up in numerical order, for otherwise he would have been at a total loss in giving commands to the unfamiliar platoon.

He keyed the mike, took a deep breath, and gave the orders. "One-one, this is Yankee X-ray. Proceed to the southeast corner of the building, and take a position facing south. One-two, pull up in front of the building to the south of the doorway, facing east. One-three, you'll be just north of the doorway, and one-four, take the northeast corner. How copy?"

One by one the four drivers radioed their understanding. Masters again raised his head above the coaming and looked around. Wisps of smoke were drifting over the track, and the smell of cordite permeated the air. Looking back over the cargo hatch cover, he could see the one-two, and caught glimpses of the others behind it. He was just thinking how lucky they had been so far when another RPG roared out of the woods, and this one smacked into one of the ammo boxes strapped to the top of the one-two track with a blinding flash. The track faltered, but kept moving.

"One-two, one-two," Masters called frantically, "anybody hurt?"

There was only a clicking as the mike button was pushed somewhere, but no one spoke. Finally a voice came on. "We got a man down. Need a medic ASAP."

"How bad?" Masters waited for an answer, and the seconds dragged out.

"He's talking," the response finally came. "Says he'll be all right for a while."

"Medic's in the building," Masters radioed. "Let's get there."

Turning to look forward again, Masters peered through the smoke, stepping on the bench seat below to raise his head higher. The abandoned road they had been following actually continued on south, passing about twenty feet from the front of the temple, leaving what used to be a clearing between the two. Like the road, the clearing had been taken over by bushes and small trees, but in the dim pre-dawn light Masters could just make it out. He dropped down to yell at Gunn in the driver's compartment. "You see it?"

Gunn nodded, but was too busy guiding the track to respond. They had reached the edge of the clearing, and Gunn pulled back on the right lateral lever to swing the track to the right. Masters stood on the bench seat and the stacks of ammo cans to make sure Gunn was placing the track correctly. Ignoring the snap of bullets flying past his head, Masters yelled and pointed where he wanted Gunn to go, and Jamison relayed the directions on the intercom. Smashing down the saplings and bushes, the track roared past the doorway of the temple, where Masters could see the now-quiet M-60 machine gun smoking on top of some sort of box blocking the lower part of the opening. He saw a couple faces looking out at him, and waved.

When the track stopped just beyond the southeast corner of the building, Masters yelled, "Cover me!" and climbed up on the cargo hatch. He reached out to grab a slender tree limb with his left hand

and jumped down from the track, swinging on the limb like Tarzan until his boots slammed into the soft leaf-covered earth. High-stepping and stumbling over the broken foliage left by the one-one's passage, Masters rushed over in front of the one-two track and waved his arm to guide that vehicle into position. He darted in front of the track as it turned to face out from the doorway of the temple and held up his fist to show the driver, Specialist Tenkiller, where to stop. In the back of his mind Masters knew he was exposing himself to enemy fire, but he didn't let that interfere with doing his job. The men on the tracks were firing all their weapons, and their noise drowned out any evidence of the enemy shooting back, giving him an undoubtedly false sense of security. When a shiny scar suddenly appeared on the flank of the one-two, he chose to ignore the implications.

The one-two rocked to a halt and the engine went to idle, but Masters was already moving again. He rushed over to place the one-three, and then the one-four. Someone, possibly Sergeant Jamison, must have passed a command over the radio, because several smoke grenades arced out from the cargo holds of the tracks and began spewing a festival of colored smoke across their front. Red, yellow, and purple, the smoke quickly obscured the forest and swirled around the tracks, further adding to Masters' spurious feeling of invincibility. If he couldn't see the enemy, then they couldn't see him either, and thus couldn't shoot him. He knew that wasn't really true or realistic, but he took comfort in the idea anyway.

After positioning the one-four, he ran back to the front of the building, where he met up with Lieutenant Carr and his radio man, who were just coming out of the building. The box that had blocked the doorway had been removed, and two other soldiers followed Carr out and deployed between the tracks to lay down a base of fire. Carr motioned to Masters and led him to the back of the one-three track, where they and the RTO crouched down, seeking the protection of the boxy armored vehicle.

"Good to see you," Carr shouted over the noise.

"Glad I found you," Masters replied.

"I've got civilians, wounded, and dead to evacuate," Carr informed him. "How about we back the tracks up a little more and then drop the ramps?"

Masters was pleased that Carr was asking his opinion. After all, this was Carr's platoon, his men and vehicles, and he outranked Masters, so it was entirely his right to completely take over the operation from Masters. Yet it seemed he was treating Masters as his equal. Masters really appreciated that. "Good idea," Masters told him, nodding. He started to stand up and go around the side to tell the driver, but Carr pulled him back down.

"Earnie," Carr said to his RTO, "tell the drivers to back up as close to the building as they can and drop the ramps." While the radioman relayed the orders, Carr tugged at Masters' sleeve. "Let's go inside." The three of them sprang for the doorway, and Masters nearly stumbled over the body lying on the ground just outside the entrance. "Dead gook," Carr explained succinctly as they entered the building.

*****

Carr pulled Masters over into the corner, out of the line of fire. Eberhart crouched nearby. "How many men do you have?" he asked the young lieutenant. He had heard Masters report that to the battalion commander, but wanted to confirm the number, in case someone had been killed or wounded. Masters was shaking, but the glint in his eyes told Carr that the shivering was due to excitement and adrenaline, not to fear.

"Your guys, plus four walking wounded and four new guys. What have you got here?"

Carr had to stop and think. "I had thirteen of my guys, but one's dead, and two are wounded. I've also got a colonel from G-4, a nurse, a wounded chopper pilot, a dead copilot, a wounded door gunner, and three female USO singers. Oh, and one dead truck driver. I'll tell you about him later."

"Shit!" Masters cursed, slapping his helmet. "One of the guys in the one-two is wounded. No, two. Pratt and somebody else. Can your medic take care of them?"

"Doc!" Carr called out into the room. Allman came running over. Outside they could hear the tracks backing up and the rear ramps slamming down. "A couple wounded in the one-two," Carr told the medic.

"That one," Masters said, leaning forward to point out the door. Allman nodded and scooted away, scrambling through the door and up the ramp into the dark interior of the APC.

Carr watched Masters lean back and survey the room. There was now just barely enough light coming in through the windows and doors to make things out. The cabinet had been moved to the right of the doorway, and Pastorini sat on it, the M-60 across his lap and one arm hanging limp by his side. Beyond him the three Japanese girls hugged each other in the corner, while Crosby stood in front of them for protection. Since Crosby had used all his HE rounds, his M-79, now loaded with canister, was only good for close-in defense. Sorenson and Rancy were still at the south window, taking turns firing single shots out the window through the smoke that hung in the damp air outside. In the middle of the floor lay the body of the copilot on a stretcher, and next to him lay Bolling and Reyes. All the bodies had been covered by ponchos and the old clothing that had been there when they arrived. Carr had sent Sweet and Greenberg outside when the tracks arrived, leaving Johnson on the crate at the back, still firing out the high ventilation hole.

Chief Whitmore's stretcher had been pushed into the northwest corner to make room for Hicks and Samples, who both sat on the raised floor with their legs stretched out in front of them. Captain Gaither squatted beside Samples, one hand on his shoulder. Tarreyton, his head swathed in bandages, sat on the end of the bamboo bed, his arms wrapped around his briefcase. Vasquez and Montoya were on either side of the north window, maintaining a slow suppressive fire into the woods.

"Well, this is bizarre," Masters commented.

183

"You got that right," Carr agreed. "Let's get them all loaded up and get the hell out of here."

"How do you want to do it?"

Carr had been thinking about that for a while. "We'll put all the bodies in the one-three first, because that will take the longest. Then load the pilot into one-two, along with the colonel, the nurse, and the rest of the wounded. The girls can run to the one-four, and my guys will go wherever there's room. You can lead out in the one-four, and I'll ride drag in the one-one."

"Sounds good. Let's get them loaded."

Carr began yelling orders. "Sorenson, Johnson, Vasquez, you stay where you are and keep firing. Sergeant Montoya, have Crosby and Rancy take the copilot out and load him in the one-three. We'll help you with Reyes and Bolling."

Montoya directed Crosby and Rancy to pick up the ends of the stretcher and led them out the door to the open ramp of the one-three track. While they maneuvered the stretcher inside and secured it, Montoya rushed back in and handed his rifle to Masters. "Hold this a minute, sir," he said, and squatted down beside the poncho-covered body of Bolling. Tossing the poncho aside, he grabbed Bolling's arms and pulled them around his own neck. With a mighty grunt he stood up, the body draped across his back, and ran through the door. As soon as he was gone Crosby and Rancy raced back in, without the rifles they had presumably left inside the track. Shoving the poncho from both ends toward the middle, they exposed Reyes' head and feet. Crosby wrapped his arms around Reyes' knees, and Rancy stuck his hands in the body's armpits. With a nodded signal, they lifted the limp form and shuffled to the door.

Montoya rushed back in, and Carr nodded approvingly when Masters, without being asked, headed to the back with Montoya to get Chief Whitmore's stretcher. Laying their rifles on either side of the wounded pilot, the two lifted the stretcher and maneuvered it around the foot of the bamboo bed, with Masters in the lead.

"Aaron," Carr called out to Samples, "you, Hicks, and Preacher are next. Can you make it to the one-two?"

"I'll help 'em," Pastorini rumbled, laying aside his M-60 and rising from the cabinet to offer his one good arm to Samples. In the back Hicks pushed himself erect and used his rifle as a make-shift crutch to hobble forward, but Captain Gaither immediately ran over to him and gave him support. Crosby and Rancy dashed back in and looked to Carr for orders.

"Crosby, you help Pastorini and Free. Then load up on the one-three." Mentally counting heads, Carr realized the one-two was getting pretty full.

"What about me?" Tarreyton demanded, his voice quivering.

"You're next," Carr told him. "Rancy, help the colonel out to the one-two. Then join Crosby on the one-three."

Carr watched impatiently as the walking wounded shuffled out the door and made their way up the ramp of the one-two, maneuvering around the stretcher that filled the center of the floor. Rancy went over to the bed and took Tarreyton by the bicep to help him stand up, saying "This way, sir." At that moment an explosion rocked the building, and it took Carr a couple seconds to process it. He finally realized that an RPG had hit the back of the building, and there was a small hole in the wall near the ceiling a few feet from the northwest corner. The blast has caused everyone to duck or go prone.

"Johnson," Carr yelled, "you hit?"

"Don't think so," the soldier replied, and resumed shooting out the ventilation hole.

"Anybody else?"

"My briefcase!" Tarreyton screamed. Carr looked down and saw the colonel sprawled almost at his feet, his briefcase a few feet away. While Rancy helped Tarreyton get back on his feet, Carr reached for the briefcase, finding the thick leather handle and lifting it. When it was dropped the latch had come loose, or broken, because the top flap lifted free and some of the contents spilled out onto the floor. The case was filled with small white boxes, cubes about four inches on a side. Carr went to his knees to gather them up and stuff them back in the case, where they had been neatly stacked

185

before. They were all jumbled now, and he had to repack the entire case, which held about thirty of the boxes.

"What happened?" Tarreyton cried. "Is my briefcase okay?"

"It's fine," Carr reassured him in the tone of a parent calming a petulant child. "What is this stuff?"

"None of your business," Tarreyton said sharply. "Give it to me."

Carr, annoyed by the colonel's antics, picked up the last box and paused to examine it. Holding it up to catch what little light was streaming in through the doorway, he slowly turned the box in his hand. On one side, printed in gold letters, was the word "Rolex." He couldn't believe it. Despite the urgency of their situation, he took the time to pry open the box and examine the contents. Inside was a leather case, and inside that was indeed a very fancy watch. Shaking his head in disgust, Carr resealed the box and finished packing the briefcase. He wanted to confront the despicable man, but this was neither the time nor the place. Instead he shoved the briefcase at Tarreyton and growled at Rancy, "Get him out of here." With his eyes covered by the bandages, Tarreyton probably didn't know that Carr had discovered his secret, and that might be a useful bargaining chip later.

As soon as Rancy and Tarreyton were out the door, Montoya and Masters re-entered and stopped in front of Carr. The room that had been so crowded before was now almost empty. The three Girlfriends waited in the corner, and three men fired out the openings, leaving just Carr, Eberhart, and the two men waiting for orders.

"Take the girls to the one-four," Carr told Montoya and Masters. "You all stay there and get ready to move out. The rest of us will load up in the one-one. Harry, you'll lead us out of here. Got it?"

"Roger," Masters said. Motioning with his head to Montoya, Masters went over to the three girls and began talking softly to them. Carr watched the young lieutenant and Sergeant Montoya coax and herd the frightened girls to the door and encourage them to run to the open ramp at the northeast corner of the building. He

186

followed them to the doorway and made sure they made it safely to the track.

"Sweet, Greenberg, mount up in one-four." The two men who had gone out when the tracks first arrived scrambled up from their prone positions and ran to the track, crowding inside with the Girlfriends. Carr ducked back inside.

"Earnie," Carr said to his radioman, "tell everyone except one-one to raise their ramps." Eberhart spoke into his handset, and over the din of the continuing gunfire he heard the unmistakable whine of the motors lifting the heavy metal ramps. "Sorenson, Johnson, Vasquez, go to the one-one, on the far right. Johnson, grab the sixty on your way out." The three men pulled back from their firing positions and rushed out the door, with Johnson pausing just long enough to pick up the M-60 machine gun from the cabinet and heft it onto his shoulder. Carr took one long look around the room to make sure he hadn't forgotten anyone or anything; for a second he wondered where Doc Allman was, but then remembered he was already in the one-two taking care of the wounded men there. Satisfied they were ready, Carr turned to Eberhart. "Let's go."

NINETEEN

The ramp of the one-four thumped into position and locked, cutting the dim light in the interior in half. Masters took a quick look around and made sure everyone was accounted for. In the rush to load the tracks, he wasn't even sure exactly who was supposed to be here. He could see the silhouette of someone up in the driver's compartment—Knox, wasn't it?—and Delaney was in the TC hatch, crouching down enough to keep his head below the rim of the turret while he fired the 50-cal. One of the new guys, the thin soul brother whose name Masters soon remembered was Dubois, was standing in the cargo hatch firing his M-16 around the right side of the machine gun turret. Montoya had pushed his way forward to the left front of the cargo hatch and was shooting over the driver's head. Greenberg was on Montoya's left, his rifle pushed between the ammo boxes on top, firing in to the woods north of the temple. Sweet had lined the three Japanese girls up on the bench seat along the right side of the track, just below where the 90-mm recoilless rifle was strapped to the wall, alternately bending down to say soothing things to them and then popping up to fire his rifle into the trees to their east.

For a moment Masters wasn't sure what to do next. Trying to stay out of the way of the other men, he held on to the edge of the cargo hatch and kept his head just below the coaming. Was he supposed to go ahead and move out, or was he supposed to wait for Carr's order? He tried to remember what Carr had told him just a few minutes ago, but with all the noise and confusion, and his lack of sleep, his mind was a jumbled mess. Fortunately the track radio blared at that moment, and he heard Carr's voice: "Move out! Follow the one-four."

It was the command Knox had been waiting for, because the track immediately jerked into motion, nearly throwing Masters to the floor. Regaining his balance, the grabbed Dubois by the shoulder and yelled into his ear. "Move over there, next to Sweet." He pointed to the right rear corner of the cargo hatch. Dubois nodded and the two men scooted past each other, so that Masters could take Dubois's position behind the turret. He needed to be where he could see what was going on, and at least appear to lead the column out.

Knox steered the track back onto the roadway, the trail blazed earlier by the four APCs clearly visible now in the growing light. The problem, Masters now realized, was that when the tracks had been on their way south to the temple, they had pushed down trees and brush ahead of them. Some of the smaller trees had partially sprung back up after the last track had passed over them, and now the one-four faced the tops of the trees leaning in their direction. They were literally going against the grain here, and the rapid trip back up the trail that Masters had envisioned now appeared to be far more difficult than he had thought. Leafy branches poked at them as the track ground forward, making everyone duck to avoid being stabbed in the eye. The slope of the track's glacis eventually pushed the trees upright and then over and down in the other direction, so the tracks behind them would have less trouble, but for this track it was slow going.

The rain, Masters noted belatedly, had increased again, a steady downpour washing over the vehicle. Water dripped from his helmet, and his uniform was soaked. They were still taking fire from gooks in the woods, but Masters imagined that it was less intense than before. The other men on the track kept up a steady suppressive fire, spraying the woods randomly with bullets to keep the gooks' heads down. Looking back, Masters could see the one-three following close behind, but it blocked his view of the other two. He hoped they were moving along with the rest. He was a little dispirited when he saw the corner of the temple only a hundred yards back, for they had clearly made less progress than he had hoped.

"What's the hold up?" Carr asked on the radio. Masters grabbed the mike and explained briefly about the trees. The diesel engine roared as Knox pushed his way through the brush, the leaves flinging their accumulated rainwater onto the track, further soaking Masters and the others.

The radio came on again, and Masters heard the battalion commander calling for a sitrep. Carr answered him, giving him a succinct report on their slow progress away from the temple.

"Can you confirm the grid coordinates of the temple?" the colonel asked.

Masters squeezed the push-to-talk button on his mike. "This is Yankee X-Ray, I have those. Are you prepared to copy? Over."

"Send it," the colonel replied. Masters again gave the coordinates, this time slowly and distinctly, and then repeated them to be sure.

"Good copy," the colonel said. "Let me know when you are clear enough for an arty strike on that location."

"Roger," Carr replied. "We are still too close. I'll let you know."

"Standing by," the colonel told them. "The rest of your company is departing this location at this time. ETA the intersection of your road and the highway is twenty mikes. Air support is on alert, but grounded by the weather."

"Roger," Carr replied. "We are still under fire, over."

"Understood," the colonel said. "Do your best. Out."

Masters involuntarily ducked as a bullet pinged of the side of the machine gun turret. He hoped Knox could see where they were going better than he could. The swath of broken trees blocked his view forward, and it was only the open sky above that reassured him they were still on the right road. An explosion rocked the woods somewhere ahead of them, followed closely by another. Masters' first thought was that the artillery strike had already begun, and it wasn't where it was supposed to be. Had he gotten the coordinates wrong? He started to panic, and clutched the microphone to call a cease fire. A third explosion occurred, and Masters caught a glimpse of the flash.

"That's not arty," Sergeant Montoya announced, shaking his head. He apparently knew what Masters had been thinking, or maybe he had just had the same thought and was now retracting it.

"What is it?" Masters asked, frowning with worry.

"Bad news," Montoya told him.

*****

Sergeant First Class Samples was extremely frustrated. His platoon was in heavy contact, and he was relegated to the role of witness. He needed to be in the thick of things, taking charge, making decisions. The one-two track was extremely crowded, with Whitmore's stretcher filling the center, and the other wounded packed together on the benches, trying to find someplace to put their feet. Whitmore's stretcher had one end propped up on the ammo boxes that filled the front of the interior, leaving him to hold on to keep from sliding down the stretcher and piling up at the raised ramp. Some guy Samples didn't know was in the TC hatch, pounding away with the fifty-cal, and a new guy was sitting on the ammo boxes behind the driver, ready to hand a fresh box of ammo to the gunner. The new guy had no helmet, and his head was wrapped in bandages. Samples was sitting on the bench next to the ammo boxes, listening to the radio chatter between Carr, Masters, and the BC. Captain Gaither—Anne—sat beside him, one hand on his wounded thigh. Pratt, with his arm in a sling, was on the other side of Gaither. Hicks was curled up on the ammo boxes at the right front, his back pressed against the engine access panel, trying to avoid the machine gunner's feet. Directly across from Samples was the obnoxious Colonel Tarreyton, now blessedly silent, with his eyes covered in bandages and his briefcase in his lap. Next to him was Pastorini, and at the left rear Doc Allman rummaged through his aid bag.

Rain poured in through the open cargo hatch, and the track rocked and swayed as it moved slowly over the bent trees and broken stumps. Samples took the rifle from between his knees and with grunt of pain pushed himself erect, twisting around until he could see out between the ammo crates fastened to the roof of the track.

"Aaron, no!" Anne cried, clutching at his shirt. "Stay down!"

191

"Can't," he told her. He brought his rifle up and fired a couple shots into the woods. Up ahead of the track he could see the one-three, with Merrill behind the fifty-cal, swinging the gun back and forth to alternately fire bursts to the left and right. He couldn't see the one-four, but had heard on the radio the problems that track was encountering. Behind him he saw the snout of the one-one following close, several helmets crowding the cargo hatch as the men on that track fired to the sides and rear. Samples let his right leg hang free, supporting himself on his left leg and his elbows. The pain in his thigh was a constantly throbbing annoyance, and he wished he was more mobile. Still, he admitted to himself, there wasn't much he could do at this point to influence the firefight one way or another. All they could do was keep moving and keep shooting.

He, too, heard the explosions to their front, and he immediately recognized their significance. He knew by their sound they weren't artillery rounds. It was the distinctive boom of demolitions, either American C-4 or the North Vietnamese equivalent. And that could mean only one thing: a barricade and an ambush. Most likely the gooks had used explosives to cut through tree trunks and cause the trees to fall across the trail, hoping to bottle up the convoy and trap them in a zone of fire.

Grabbing the radio mike Samples yelled into it, "Ambush! Don't stop!"

*****

When he heard the blasts up at the front of the column, Lieutenant Carr quickly reached the same conclusion as his platoon sergeant, and totally agreed with Samples' instruction. They simply could not afford to slow down or stop, not with all these wounded and civilians on board. It was some consolation that the gook's plan was a hasty ambush, quickly improvised based on changing conditions. Many of their troops were still surrounding the temple, and none had had time to dig spider holes or bunkers along the trail. In theory that gave the Americans an edge: shielded by armor, they were both more mobile and possessed superior firepower. Their

192

armor and mobility, however, funneled them into narrow lanes between the trees, denying them the advantages of fire and maneuver. If they were forced to stop, the wide and tall sides of the APCs would become barn-door-size targets for RPGs. And then the NVA would have the advantage of maneuver, for their soldiers could filter around in the thick forest, virtually unseen in the still dim light of early morning with the rain permeating the atmosphere.

"One-four, keep moving," Carr barked over the radio.

"Roger," he heard Masters reply. "So far, so good."

The column was still moving forward, but not at a great speed. Carr knew that the one-four had been slowed from the start by the condition of the trail, and the explosions had sounded like they were several hundred yards ahead, so Masters had probably not yet reached the area of the ambush yet. The one-one track was crowded, and Carr realized he perhaps had deployed the platoon poorly, for most of the able-bodied men were here with him in the last track of the column. Some guy he didn't know was manning the fifty, and a new guy, small and wiry, was firing his M-16 from the right front corner of the cargo hatch. Sergeant Jamison was in the front left corner where he could talk to Knox, the driver, and Vasquez, Sorenson, and Johnson were shoulder to shoulder along the back of the cargo hatch, firing over the locked-down cover. Eberhart was on the bench below, monitoring the radio, and Carr could only stand up in the center of the cargo hatch, peering around the helmets of the other men and the ammo crates strapped to the roof. Looking back, Carr could still see the temple, which meant that artillery was as yet too risky a proposition.

The fifty-cal, which had been booming away, went quiet. Jamison yelled at the little guy on the right side of the hatch. "Handleman, get Purdey more ammo." Handleman dropped down inside, grabbed a can of ammo, and passed it up to Purdey behind the fifty. While Purdey tossed the empty can over the side and opened the new can, Handleman picked up his rifle and resumed shooting. Carr had never met Purdey and Handleman before, but was pleasantly surprised by their competence and confidence under fire. Especially Handleman, because Carr could tell by his new uniform and boots that the young man had just arrived in country.

This was almost certainly his first taste of combat, and he was dealing with it admirably.

All of the men on the track who could find a place to aim their rifles were banging away, firing single shots at a measured pace to conserve their ammo. While there was plenty of 5.56mm ammo inside the track, it was still in the metal ammo cans. It couldn't be used until it was fed from the clips in which it was packed into the magazines that fit in the rifles, a tedious process that wasn't practical under fire. Practical or not, Carr looked down to see Eberhart doing just that. He had an open can of ammo on the floor between his feet, and was using the metal loading device that allowed him to push a clip of bullets into a magazine five at a time. While Carr watched, Vasquez released an empty magazine that bounced off the bench and clattered to the floor. Eberhart reached out and picked it up with one hand, while handing a full magazine to Vasquez with the other.

It was hard to be sure, with all the weapons firing inside the track, but Carr didn't think they were getting much incoming. He saw only an occasional wink of muzzle flash from out in the dark forest, and no green tracers from a machine gun. He guessed that most of the gooks were running ahead to take part in the ambush. It was vital that the tracks maintain their forward movement, hopefully fast enough to outrun the enemy, or at least prevent them from taking up good positions.

*****

"Oh, shit!" Delaney cursed as the one-four rode up and over one of the small saplings in the middle of the trail, revealing what was ahead of them. Masters had to agree with Delaney's pithy assessment. Fifty meters ahead of them a large tree laid across the trail, the trunk at about a thirty-degree angle as its upper branches propped it up. Behind it Masters could see another tree blocking the trail, this one leaning the opposite way. The two logs formed a shallow X, and Masters knew just what that meant, both figuratively and literally. His body shifted forward as Knox slowed the track down, but kept it inching forward as his head swiveled, looking for

194

an alternate route. Masters looked to Montoya for advice, but the burly sergeant had disappeared inside the track, shooing the Girlfriends toward the back. A moment later the long black tube of the 90 millimeter recoilless rifle was pushed up through the cargo hatch by Montoya.

"Knox, quarter turn left and stop!" Montoya yelled over the noise. Knox looked back over his shoulder, saw what Montoya was doing, and responded. Locking the left lateral, the armored vehicle slewed around and stopped, now pointed northwest. Montoya pushed the ninety between the ammo crate seats, screaming, "Sweet! Load me." There was a scramble below as Sweet unstrapped the cardboard tubes containing the recoilless ammunition and extracted a round. During what seemed like an interminable wait, Delaney kept up a constant stream of heavy machine gun fire, and Greenberg poured M-16 fire from the left side of the turret. Dubois got out of the way, bumping into Masters as he sought to avoid the back end of the recoilless. Masters had seen one fired on a range back in the States, and was well aware of the danger the back blast presented when the weapon was fired. He ducked down inside and watched Sweet slide a round out of the cardboard tube and slip into the end of the launcher. The round looked like a huge .22 Long Rifle bullet, thin and about two feet long, but the brass cartridge was perforated like a sieve. Sweet swung the rear door of the tube closed and made sure it was latched in place.

"Ready!" Sweet shouted, tapping Montoya on the helmet, and he ducked down inside, along with Greenberg, Dubois, and Masters. Montoya looked back over his right shoulder, making sure the back blast would clear the cargo hatch cover, and then took aim.

"Hold your ears!" Montoya shouted, and Masters stuck fingers in both ears while Sweet demonstrated to the three frightened girls how to cover theirs. A tremendous boom shattered the air around them and the interior of the track was lit up for a microsecond.

Masters jumped up beside Montoya and looked down the trail. The round had struck the first tree trunk right in the middle, splintering it in half. As Masters watched, the trunk collapsed in the middle. Meanwhile Sweet was busy loading another round. A glance over his shoulder told Masters that the other tracks had halted as well, with the one-three pointed to the northeast. Although he couldn't see them, Masters presumed the other two tracks had stopped pointed left and right as well.

"Hold your ears!" Montoya yelled again, and everyone complied. Masters ducked down inside again just as the launcher banged, the shock wave causing him to slip and fall to his knees. Scrambling back up, he looked forward to see the second tree smoking but intact. "Gimme another one!" Montoya yelled to Sweet. Masters could hear the snap of bullets flying overhead, and the thumps as some of them hit the sides of the track or the turret. The gooks were now concentrating their fire on the one-four, and Montoya was in mortal danger. Masters poked his rifle between two of the ammo crates and began firing rapidly into the surrounding woods. Greenberg and Dubois joined in as well, and Delaney kept up a steady stream of 50-cal fire, while Sweet fumbled with the 90mm ammo.

"Shit! Beehive!" Masters heard Sweet complain loudly. Glancing inside, Masters saw Sweet put one of the tubes back and grab another one. He remembered being once told that the weapons track carried both high explosive and beehive rounds for the 90mm. While the beehive rounds, which launched a cloud of dart-shaped flechettes, were very effective against personnel, they wouldn't do much against a fallen tree.

"Hurry the fuck up!" Montoya shouted at Sweet.

Sweet finally withdrew the proper round from its protective tube and jammed it into the back of the launcher. When he latched it shut, he slapped the back of Montoya's helmet and shouted "Clear!" Everyone but Montoya collapsed inside the track and covered their ears, just in time. Another percussive blast pounded the interior, and Masters immediately jumped up to observe the results. This time Montoya had hit the second tree dead on, and the two halves had been blown apart with enough force to leave a ten-foot gap between them.

"Go!" Masters and Montoya both yelled at Knox, and the driver was ready. Instantly the engine revs zoomed and the track lurched forward, slewing around to head directly for the gap in the barricade. An RPG flashed by just behind the track, missing it by inches, and exploded off in the trees to the left. Masters hoped it had hit some of the gooks that were attacking them from that direction.

By the time they reached the downed trees the track was going a good thirty miles an hour, and when it hit the splintered trunk of the first tree it shoved the two ends aside, the wood scraping down either flank of the APC with a horrible screech. No sooner were they through that gap than they came to the second obstruction, but in this case the remains of the tree trunk were far enough apart that Knox sailed through without even touching them. Masters looked back and saw the other three tracks following close behind, guns blazing in all directions. Another RPG burst out of the woods and slammed into the side of the one-three, directly behind the one-four carrying Masters.

"Oh, shit!" Masters exclaimed as the one-three track slowed to a halt right in the middle of the breach in the obstacles, trapping the other two tracks on the other side.

*****

When someone in the one-four track up ahead had used the 90mm to blast a hole in the enemy's impromptu barricade, Lieutenant Carr had congratulated himself on his totally lucky decision to have that track lead them away from the temple. Now the platoon was moving again, rushing forward to soon emerge from this cauldron of enemy fire. Or so he thought. The booming flash as the RPG hit the one-three track shocked and dismayed him completely, especially after the flash of hope the opening of the obstacles had engendered. The track stopped right between the two halves of the second tree, effectively blocking the two tracks behind it. His mind raced as he tried to come up with alternative actions. Could the one-two push the one-three forward, out of the way? Could the one one-four hook up a tow cable and pull it on down the road? In theory, yes, but under heavy fire, who would be willing to jump out and hook up the heavy steel cables? Carr's eyes darted around them, looking for a way around the barricade, a place where the trees were spaced far enough apart that they could bull their way through. But then, he realized, he would be leaving the men in the one-three, assuming any were still alive, to be killed or captured by the enemy.

"Grenade!" someone shouted, and the next events happened so quickly that Carr couldn't actually process it until after it was over. A hand-grenade, an American-made type shaped like a large green egg, was flying through the air toward the track, clearly destined to drop right inside the cargo hatch. Almost miraculously Handleman's right hand let go of his M-16 and shot up snatching the grenade out of the air and immediately flinging it back into the woods. Everyone ducked down as it exploded a few yards away.

Handleman looked at Carr, his eyes wide with surprise, and said, "I can't believe I did that! I sucked at baseball."

Carr patted the young man's forearm. "Good catch." Handleman stood back up to resume firing into the surrounding woods, while Carr peered forward to try and find a workable solution to the impasse. When the one-three had halted between the fallen trees, the drivers of the one-two and one-one had automatically swerved left and right to give their fifties a better sweep of fire, so Carr could clearly see the one-three, squatting in the brush with no sign of movement. No one was in the fifty-cal turret, but wisps of diesel smoke indicated the engine was still running.

"Cover me," Jamison said loudly, stripping off his pistol belt, ammo bag, and helmet.

"What are you doing?" Carr demanded.

Jamison looked into Carr's eyes with fierce determination. "I'm going to go up there and get it running."

"No, I'll do that."

"Sir," Jamison said, shaking his head wearily, "you don't know shit about driving a track."

Carr was a little offended, but had to admit his mechanical skills were not that great.

"They're moving!" Purdey yelled from behind the fifty.

Carr and Jamison both turned their heads to see around the turret, and Carr felt a surge of relief as he saw the diesel smoke billowing from the one-three's exhaust as the track began crawling forward. A head popped up in the fifty-cal turret and began firing wildly to the right side of the gap.

"Yeah!" several of the men on board the one-one yelled simultaneously. PFC Gunn stomped on the accelerator and jerked forward, slewing around in line with the one-two as the tracks raced for the opening. In moments all three of the remaining tracks were through the barrier and plunging ahead down the trail they had blazed earlier. One last RPG swooshed over the one-one as it cleared the second downed tree trunk, but after that the incoming fire quickly diminished and faded away, and the men on the tracks ceased their fire.

Exhilarated by their narrow escape, Carr yelled "Yee-ha" and burst out laughing. The other men looked at him strangely, and Carr decided his joy was perhaps premature and inappropriate. Nonetheless, they were on their way. It was now full morning, the rain had stopped, and the clouds seemed to be lifting.

The radio scratched and crackled, and a voice Carr didn't recognize blared from the speaker. "Uh, this is, uh, Alpha one three, over. We've got wounded, over." Although the guy had said "over," he kept the mike key pressed so no one could answer him. Carr could hear background noise, mostly the rumble of the one-three's engine and disjointed speech. Finally the key was released and the radio went silent. Carr picked up his mike.

"One-four, this is three-three Lima, hold up a second. Doc, can you switch over to the one-three?"

All four APCs slowed and stopped, closing up until they were only about ten feet apart. The personnel hatch at the back of the one-two opened and Doc Allman jumped out, stopping to swing the door closed again and latching it. He waved at Carr in acknowledgement and quickly picked his way around the track through the broken foliage, heading up to the one-three. A single rifle shot came from behind them, reminding Carr they were not out of the woods yet, both literally and figuratively. Looking over the top of the one-two, he caught a glimpse of Doc Allman leaping up and into the cargo hatch of the one-three. A moment later someone shouted "Go, go!" over the radio, and the convoy resumed its slow headlong rush through the forest.

One by one the men on the tracks climbed out of the holds and took seats on the ammo boxes and crates. Carr waited for Jamison to get situated behind Gunn's head, then clumsily pulled himself up on top of the bucking vehicle and plopped down on the crate behind the squad leader. With his rifle across his lap, Carr held the porkchop mike in front of his face. It was time to report to Higher. And that's when he heard the helicopter.

TWENTY

Carr and Masters stood beside the one-three, staring at the shiny hole in the hull, low on the left side. The RPG's shaped charge had burned through the aluminum alloy armor like butter, spraying the inside of the track with molten metal.

"Could have been worse," Masters commented.

"Definitely," Carr agreed. The hot shrapnel had mostly been absorbed by the three dead bodies on board—SP4 Reyes, the deserter Bolling, and the chopper copilot whose name Carr had never learned. Two guys Carr had not previously met—SP4 Karper from Bravo Company, and a new guy named Kirk—had suffered minor leg wounds. Fred Aiello, the track's driver, had somehow been hit in the back of the helmet by flying debris that had knocked him unconscious, which was why the track had stopped when it was hit. PFC Merrill, who had been behind the fifty-cal, had been untouched by the blast, and was able to extract Aiello from the driver's compartment and take his place to get the track moving again.

The platoon was now deployed in a rough semicircle on the north side of the highway, facing the rubber plantation and staying out of the way while the rest of Alpha Company, along with the just-arrived Bravo Company, lined up on the south side of the road in preparation for making a sweep south to the temple. A constant rumble of explosions from that area was the result of a heavy and extended artillery strike. Overhead two Cobra gunships and a Huey slick circled, ready to launch rockets and fire miniguns into the area when the arty ended. The sky had almost completely cleared, and bright sunshine beat down on the men and tracks of First Platoon.

A few minutes earlier medevac helicopters had taken off all the wounded to the MASH unit at Dau Tieng, including Sergeant

Samples, with Captain Gaither accompanying him. Aiello had woken up just as they had emerged from the forest, and had insisted he was now okay. He refused to be evacuated, not wanting to leave his trusted but injured APC. Before the dustoffs had arrived, Doc Allman had removed the bandages from Colonel Tarreyton's eyes, and "discovered" that miraculously his eyes were fully recovered and working fine. The colonel had been typically unappreciative. Tarreyton had tried to hitch a ride on the medevac chopper, but had been politely refused due to space limitations. He had been so self-absorbed that he had never even noticed the presence of Lieutenant Masters, much less recognized the man whose career he had tried to ruin. Now he sulked in the back of the one-two track, his arms wrapped around his briefcase, waiting for some other opportunity to get away from the action.

A chopper came and collected the three bodies, but Tarreyton didn't even ask if he could ride on that one. Over by the one-four the three Girlfriends had removed their baggy jumpsuits and were modeling their sparkly sheath dresses for Sweet, Crosby, and Rancy, smiling and giggling as they combed their hair with their fingers. The rest of the platoon was standing guard, but Carr could already see heads nodding as the men fought off sleep. He didn't blame them. He felt like he could sleep for a week.

"They're moving out," Masters said, and Carr turned to see the line of tracks enter the forest, muscling their way through the trees. Most of the men had dismounted and were spread out between and behind the tracks, ready to engage any enemy they might encounter. The artillery barrage ended, and the choppers took over, firing rockets into the woods far to their south. If any NVA or Viet Cong were still in that area, they were getting pounded.

"The gooks have gone by now," Carr said pessimistically.

"Probably," Masters agreed. "But I guess they've got to make sure."

"Gotta get the body count," Carr remarked sourly. Masters just shrugged.

Carr watched as Lieutenant Colonel Duran, the battalion commander, turned away from the departing formation and strode over to where Carr and Masters stood. Duran was a short stocky man who kind of reminded Carr of the Fred Mertz character on "I Love Lucy," although not as bumbling. He actually seemed pretty competent, albeit not, perhaps, inspiring.

"Sir," Carr greeted him, observing the policy of not saluting in the field.

"Gentlemen," Duran responded, coming to a halt in front of them. Carr couldn't help noticing how clean and neat the colonel looked, compared to the dirty and ragged uniform he was wearing. It must be nice, he thought, to be able to put on a clean pressed uniform every day.

"All your wounded taken care of?" Duran asked.

"Yes, sir. The dustoffs took my platoon sergeant, the downed chopper's door gunner and pilot, and four other men. Except for the pilot, none are too serious. The three KIA just left, as well." Carr didn't mention Aiello, for fear the colonel would insist the driver be evacuated as well, as a precaution.

Duran scowled as he looked over at the Japanese girls. "Were they dressed like that the whole time?" he asked.

"Uh, no, sir. They had flight suits on most of the time. My men are keeping them company to help them calm down after their ordeal." Carr had added the last to ensure the colonel didn't criticize his men for not being on guard.

"Huh," Duran grunted. He looked at the hole in the side of the one-three track. "How bad?" he asked.

"It's still fully operational," Carr assured him. "Patch the hole and it's good to go."

Duran nodded. He looked sternly at Masters. "So, lieutenant, you figured out where they were, and took it upon yourself to ignore orders and go to their rescue, is that it?"

Masters stammered. "Uh, not exactly, sir. I mean, yes, sir, I guess I did."

"Well, good job. I like officers that take the initiative." Carr could see the relief wash over Masters' face.

Turning back to Carr, Duran said, "Okay, tell me what happened, from the beginning."

Carr took a breath and then related the story of how they had seen the chopper go down and had headed to the crash site, only to get bogged down in the swamp. He told how they had sent the tracks back to Dau Tieng, had the encounter with VC and captured one, and then their arrival at the helicopter. Because of the reported NVA unit to their south, and the sniping from the VC to their north, he had led the group west until they were able to take shelter in the temple.

"At the temple we found Private Bolling, a truck driver who had gotten lost in the woods." Carr didn't mention that Bolling was a deserter, deciding that since the young man was dead, it was no longer relevant. "It was Bolling that figured out our prisoner was a Russian, but then the guy tried to take the girls hostage. Bolling stopped him, but was killed in the process, and my men killed the Russian. We think that the Russian was the reason the NVA were so intent on keeping us there."

At this point Masters took up the story, explaining how he had used the old French maps to locate the temple, and had organized the track crews, walking wounded, and new guys to go to Carr's rescue. Then Carr related the action at the temple as the dead and wounded were loaded aboard the tracks and brought out of the woods.

"I'll need you two to write that all down for an after-action report," Duran told them. "You'll probably want to submit some medal recommendations, I presume." Carr nodded.

"Where is Colonel Tarreyton now?" Duran asked, looking around. Masters pointed to the open ramp of the one-two, where two boots could be seen hanging over the end of the bench seat. After the chopper carrying the dead had left, he had stretched out on the bench seat and fallen asleep.

"I believe he's resting, sir," Masters said judiciously.

"And, uh, sir?" Carr said tentatively. "He's got a briefcase. It's full of Rolexes."

"Rolexes?" Duran said with a puzzled frown. "Why?"

"He wouldn't say, sir. But there's at least thirty of them. He was very anxious to get them back to Cu Chi."

"Strange. Wait, isn't he the one who made the complaint against you, Lieutenant Masters?"

"I believe so, sir," Masters replied cautiously.

"And what is his job again?" Duran was staring at the soles of Tarreyton's boots with one eyebrow raised.

"Deputy Assistant for Logistics is what he told me," Carr answered.

"And what in God's name does that mean?" Duran shook his head in disgust.

"Beats me, sir."

The sound of another helicopter approaching made Carr look up, and he saw the shiny LOH circling to land on the highway.

"Oh, shit," Duran said mildly. "That's the Division Commander. I better go meet him." The colonel turned and jogged away, leaving Carr and Masters standing there wondering what they should be doing next.

"Are you going to tell the general about the Rolexes?" Masters asked.

Carr shrugged. "Probably wouldn't be a good idea. Nobody likes a tattle-tale."

"But you told Colonel Duran," Masters pointed out.

"Yep. I'll let him tell the general, if he thinks it's appropriate. That way, I don't get any shit."

"Good plan," Masters said admiringly.

*****

Masters watched as General Samuels and Lieutenant Colonel Duran strode down the highway together to get out of the downdraft from the general's helicopter and all the dust it was stirring up. Despite all the rain, the dirt road had dried out quickly. When they were far enough away, they stopped and faced each other as Duran spelled out what had occurred.

"Think we ought to wake up Tarreyton?" Masters asked Carr.

"We probably should," Carr replied, but made no move to do so. After a pause he added, "At the appropriate time." Masters looked over and saw the half-smile on Carr's face. Masters decided he could learn a lot from Lieutenant Carr.

He resumed watching the two senior officers, and after a minute or so Colonel Duran motioned toward Masters and Carr, and the two men began walking over toward them.

"Now?" Masters asked.

"Not yet," Carr replied, straightening his body and brushing dust off his uniform. Carr strode forward to meet the general, holding out his hand to shake as he heartily greeted him, "Morning, sir."

Masters stumbled forward and limply shook the general's hand after Carr did so. He was embarrassed that he was so nervous in the presence of higher rank. Samuels was an imposing man, and not just because of his rank. He was a good six feet tall, with an athletic build and rugged good looks complemented by his sandy hair. Masters had heard somewhere that Samuels had been a star player on the West Point football team, and he could believe it.

"Lieutenant Carr, I am very impressed with your actions last night. Outstanding!"

"Thank you, sir," Carr replied modestly. The four men now stood in a loose circle.

"And Lieutenant Masters," the general said, giving him a slightly stern look, "I appreciate your initiative, but you should have gotten permission first."

"Yes, sir," Masters said meekly.

"But all's well that ends well, right?" The general beamed with satisfaction. The other three men nodded, as was expected of them. "Now, where's this Colonel Tarreyton? I know he works for me, but I'm not sure I'd even recognize him."

Carr turned toward the one-two track, where the driver was squatting down to inspect the tread blocks and road wheels. "Specialist Tenkiller," Carr called loud enough to be heard over the continuing buzz of the helicopters, "would you please tell Colonel Tarreyton the general would like to speak to him?"

Masters stifled a laugh. Now he understood what Carr meant about picking the right time.

Tenkiller stood up and went around to the back of the track, stepping up on the ramp and shaking one of Tarreyton's knees. There was some scuffling around as the colonel's boots disappeared inside, and then the man banged his helmet on the top edge of the opening as he scurried out, clutching his briefcase in one hand as he tried to straighten his uniform with the other. He looked around, blinking his eyes in the bright sun, until he spotted the four officers and hurried over to join them.

"General, good morning," Tarreyton said obsequiously when he reached them. Tarreyton glanced over at Masters with a puzzled look, as if trying to place him.

"Colonel Tarreyton," the general replied, nodding at him. "Sorry we had to disturb your sleep." It was said with apparent sincerity, but Master thought he heard a rebuke hidden inside.

"No problem, sir. It was a long night."

"So I hear. As the senior officer on site, I presume you helped direct the defense?" The general's demeanor was calm and pleasant, but Masters had a feeling this was not going to end well.

"Certainly, sir," Tarreyton asserted, puffing out his chest a little. "I let Lieutenant Carr here make the smaller, tactical decisions, while I planned the overall strategy."

"Indeed." General Samuels noted. Maybe he was just imaging things, but Masters felt like he could see the general's face clouding over.

"But I have to say, sir," Tarreyton continued, "that the lieutenant's actions were not always optimal, in my opinion. He made some dubious decisions, and he was not always receptive to my suggestions. As you know, sir, several men died out there."

Masters couldn't believe the slimy little man was taking cheap shots at Carr, after Carr had saved his ass. He gritted his teeth and refrained from speaking up against the colonel.

"I'm well aware of the casualties, Colonel." Samuels' expression was now transforming into a genuine frown, and Masters could see from Tarreyton's expression that he, too, was now aware that the general's attitude was darkening. "I believe Lieutenant Carr did all he could to minimize them, under very trying circumstances. Despite your suggestions."

"Uh, yes, sir. I agree." Tarreyton hastened to change his own approach to meet the general's expectations. What was that phrase, Masters thought to himself? Whichever way the wind blows?

"And I see your briefcase made it through intact," the general observed, looking down at the battered leather case hanging from Tarreyton's left hand.

"Oh, uh, yes, sir." The colonel slowly moved the case backwards, as if trying to hide it behind his leg.

"I understand you mentioned that it contained classified materials, correct?"

"In a manner of speaking, sir."

"And you work in G-4, right?" The general's implication was clear. G-4 was the division's staff section concerned with supply and logistics, one that would not be expected to handle any kind of secrets.

"That's correct, sir. Deputy Assistant for Logistics. I work directly for. . ."

"I know who you work for, Colonel," the general interrupted him. "And I'm not aware of any classified issues in that area. So what exactly is in that briefcase?"

Masters saw Tarreyton's eyes get wider and wider, and he detected a subtle quivering of the colonel's knees.

"Um, uh, I'm redistributing certain, uh, line items that were misdirected to Dau Tieng."

"Uh, huh," General Samuels said doubtfully. "Could I see them, please?"

"Now, sir?" Tarreyton unconsciously took a half step backwards.

"Now, Colonel."

Reluctantly Tarreyton brought the case up to chest level and fumbled with the latch. "I'll need to explain this, sir," he temporized, having difficulty opening the case. "It might be better if we discuss this back at headquarters."

General Samuels just glared at him. "Open. The. Case."

Tarreyton finally released the latch and nearly dropped the briefcase as the leather flap flew up into his face. He tilted the case forward so Samuels could see the neat rows of white boxes inside, and then quickly spun the top flap closed. "These are delicate pieces of machinery, sir, and I don't want them too exposed to the elements."

Samuels hand darted forward and flipped the lid up to take one of the boxes from the briefcase. Rolling it over in his hand, he inspected it closely, especially when he found the Rolex logo embossed in gold on one side. While Tarreyton watched with growing horror, Samuels opened the cardboard box and withdrew the brown leather presentation case, popping open the lid to reveal the fancy watch that glittered in the sunlight. With narrowed eyes General Samuels held the watch up to Tarreyton's face.

"Explain, Tarreyton!" Samuels demanded.

Tarreyton took a deep breath, and Master thought he saw tears forming in the corners of his eyes. "Well, sir," he rambled, "they sent too many of these watches to the PX in Dau Tieng, and I was bringing them back to Cu Chi to see that they were properly distributed."

Samuels snapped the lid of the leather box shut and methodically slipped it back into the white cardboard box. He reached out and put it back into the briefcase that Tarreyton still held in front of him, and then slid his hand deeper inside the case to count the boxes. When he pulled his hand out, a slip of paper was trapped between two fingers. Samuels unfolded the paper and read the small writing on it.

"It says here you bought these watches," he said, scowling.

"Well, yes, sir." Tarreyton was now stammering, and a tear rolled down his dusty cheek. "I needed the proper documentation, of course."

"And you paid twenty dollars each?"

Tarreyton cleared his throat. "Well, uh, that's the wholesale price, sir."

"I don't think so, Colonel. The PX sells everything at wholesale, and I know the average GI cannot buy one of these for twenty bucks. So what were you really doing?"

"Like I said, sir, I was . . ."

Samuels didn't let him finish the sentence. "You were planning to sell these on the black market, weren't you? Don't bother denying it."

"But, sir," Tarreyton begged, unable to come up with a better explanation.

"Give me that!" Samuels said, jerking the briefcase from Tarreyton's hand. He latched the lid shut and then pushed it at Masters, who grabbed it just as it was about to fall on ground. The general's face was now flushed with anger, and he stared with fire in his eyes at Tarreyton until the man visibly cringed and started whimpering.

"What is that CIB doing on your chest?" Samuels almost shouted, pointing at the black metal device pinned to Tarreyton's uniform.

"I was told I could wear it," Tarreyton bleated fearfully. "Since I'm in an infantry division in combat for over thirty days."

"Bullshit! That's only for infantry officers and men, not for supply pukes like you." Samuels reached out grabbed the medal, ripping it off and leaving two ragged holes in the colonel's uniform. "You are disgrace to the uniform! Get out of my sight!"

"But, sir," Tarreyton pleaded again, tears now flowing freely.

"Are you pissing your pants?" Samuels yelled with disgust, looking down at Tarreyton's legs. Masters followed the general's gaze and saw the spreading stain on Tarreyton's trousers. "Fuck me! You can ride back to Cu Chi in the back of one of the deuce-and-a-halfs, one that isn't carrying any real soldiers. God! What is this Army coming to?" Beckoning for Masters to follow him, Samuels stomped off toward his helicopter. Masters exchanged surprised and bemused glances with Carr and Colonel Duran and then scurried after the general, the briefcase dangling from his hand.

When they reached the general's helicopter, its blades still turning slowly, Samuels took the briefcase and tossed it in behind the seat. "Lieutenant," he said loudly to be heard over the engine, "I think you might have a future in the Army. Don't let that asshole discourage you." With that he climbed in and waved Masters back so the pilot could spin up the rotors. Masters scampered a few yards away and then turned to watch as the small helicopter rose up and zoomed away. Then he trudged back over to where Carr and Duran stood talking quietly. Tarreyton had stumbled away, looking for a truck that he could hitch a ride on.

When Masters reached the other two, the three men looked at each other and chuckled. "Justice does sometimes prevail," Colonel Duran remarked.

"What do you think they'll do to him," Masters asked.

"Psh," Duran scoffed. "He'll be allowed to retire with a full pension. It would make too much of a stink if they court-martialed him. But I'll say this, Lieutenant Masters: your reprimand will be removed from your records. I'll see if I can't find you a different position in the battalion that better suits your capabilities."

"Thank you, sir," Masters told him with sincere appreciation.

211

"Lieutenant Carr," Duran continued, "why don't you load up your men and take to the Fires Support Base. Looks like they could use a little rest and maintenance. Take Masters here with you. For now."

TWENTY-ONE

They were outposting again, for what seemed like the millionth time. Sergeant First Class Aaron Samples sat on the bench at the back of the one-one track, his right leg stretched out across the open ramp, absently massaging his thigh. Lieutenant Stephen Carr sat on the opposite bench, his rifle across his knees. Both men were taking advantage of the only shade available on yet another hot sunny day in Viet Nam. From this location they could see the other three tracks of the platoon parked in a rough semicircle beside the dusty road, waiting for the supply convoys to pass by. Flooded rice paddies stretched out in all directions, with little old men and women tilling the flourishing rice plants while young boys tended to the occasional water buffalo. This was Samples' first day back out in the field, and the experience was met with mixed emotions.

He was glad to be away from the REMFs, the clerks and jerks in the base camp, and back out in the countryside, doing something useful. On the other hand, he was already missing a certain nurse.

"So how was your R&R?" Carr asked casually. While recovering from his wound in Cu Chi, Samples had asked to take his long overdue Rest and Recreation leave. Normally R&R had to be requested weeks ahead of time, and you rarely got your first choice of location. Most of the guys wanted Tokyo, Melbourne, Honk Kong, or Bangkok, but Samples had chosen Vung Tau, the South Vietnamese version of Miami Beach, which was much easier to arrange. Carr and Colonel Duran had pulled a few strings and gotten it approved in record time.

"Good," Samples replied simply. "Nice beach. Nice hotel."

"Uh-huh. So what did you do there?"

"Oh, you know, just goof around, take it easy." He didn't want to tell Carr what had really been going on, both out of a sense of maintaining his personal privacy, and out of a desire to avoid any lectures. At the Cu Chi hospital Nurse Gaither and he had developed a very close relationship, and she had been able to finagle a week in Vung Tau the same time as his. While they were technically housed in separate hotels—one for officers, one for enlisted—they had managed to spend a great deal of time with each other. More time, and more intimately, than Army regulations allowed. He smiled as he remembered some of the nights they had spent together, either in her room or his.

He had never met a woman like her. She was strong, independent, intelligent, and totally unlike the airheads he had previously been involved with. With Anne he didn't have to be in charge all the time; he enjoyed having her make the decisions half the time, and taking the lead when they made love. Maybe, he thought, it was just a reaction to his usual oppressive daily responsibilities as a platoon sergeant, but whatever it was, he liked it. And he really liked her. They had both avoided discussing the future, however. There were too many possible complications to even think about establishing a real relationship, what with the war, the Army, and her being an officer. Nonetheless he had grown really attached to her, and he had to admit he was falling in love. He wasn't sure if she felt the same, but he hoped it was so.

Carr interrupted his reverie. "So, have you heard anything from Captain Gaither?" Carr had a look of feigned innocence on his face.

"Well, I've got her address. Thought I might write to her, you know. To thank her for taking care of me and all." Samples looked around for some reason to change the subject. He saw one of the new guys, PFC Kirk, stroll out to the road where a gaggle of Vietnamese on bicycles waited to sell sodas and trinkets to the GIs.

"Kirk!" he yelled, "where's your helmet?"

"In the track, Sarge," Kirk replied sheepishly.

"Get it! And stay away from the Coke kids."

214

With his shoulders slumped, Kirk turned around and trudged back to the track.

"It's always something," Carr remarked with a chuckle.

"Yep," Samples agreed. "So we're going into Dau Tieng tonight?"

"Yeah. I guess I ought to tell you now." Carr looked over at him with a sly grin.

"Tell me what?"

"Sweet didn't really go in to do Finance paperwork. Colonel Duran has arranged something for us tonight at the EM Club."

Samples gave him a puzzled look. "What's Sweet got to do with it?"

"They specifically asked for him."

"Who did?"

"The Girlfriends. They're going to put on a show just for our company, and Sweet is setting it up."

"No shit?" Samples wasn't sure if this was a good thing or not. Sweet could be a fuckup sometimes.

"Don't tell the men yet. Wait until we get back to the company area and they've done all their maintenance. Otherwise nothing will get done right."

"Definitely," Samples agreed. "The whole company's going to be there?"

"That's the word. The colonel, too. Kind of a reward for what we did in the Boi Loi two weeks ago."

"Hmph. About time our guys got some recognition."

"I don't know for sure," Carr added, "but there might be an awards ceremony. I put Handleman in for a Silver Star. There are some other guys recommended for medals, too. Purple Hearts, Bronze Stars. They probably haven't all been approved yet, but you never know."

"You didn't put me in for anything, I hope." Samples scowled at Carr.

"Why not?"

Samples shook his head. "I've got enough of that shit. And I didn't do anything special."

"You got wounded. That gets you another Purple Heart."

"I guess. Like I need another reminder that I was too slow or stupid to get out of the way of an incoming round."

Carr started to say something, but they both heard the distant rumble of trucks, and leaned out to look down the road. Approaching quickly was a plume of dust that marked the afternoon supply convoy. Once it passed, they were through for the day. Samples got up to start getting the men ready to pack up and move.

The Enlisted Men's Club was filled with raucous noise and cigarette smoke. Wooden chairs scraped on the concrete floor, beer bottles clinked, and loud laughter reverberated in the wide room with a fairly low ceiling. Bare electric bulbs hung from the rafters, and at one end a small stage had some Asian men setting up band equipment. Samples held the cold can of beer in his hand, enjoying the cool wetness of it, while keeping an eye on his men to ensure they didn't get out of hand. He had insisted that all of First Platoon put on clean and complete uniforms—no cutoffs—and at least wipe the mud off their boots. This was their first real break from the field in over a month, and they were living it up. Even the new guys were mixing in well. FNGs were often shunned at first, because no one wanted to be friends with someone who might get killed before they finished their first month. But these guys had already proved their worth in combat, on their first day in the unit.

Sitting at the table with Samples were Lieutenant Carr and Lieutenant Masters, both sipping moderately at their beers, presumably to maintain proper decorum. "What's Rancy doing up there?" Carr asked, pointing toward the stage. Sweet and Rancy had both stepped up on the stage and were in discussion with the guys who had been hooking up amplifiers and a drum set.

"God only knows," Samples remarked, not terribly concerned. Sweet and Rancy were always up to something, but never anything really bad. As they watched, one of the Asian men opened a case and withdrew an electric guitar, plugged it in, and handed it to Rancy. Rancy got a pick from the man and strummed the guitar strings, sending a blasting chord that temporarily shut everyone up. The Asian man made an adjustment to the amplifier, and Rancy carefully placed his fingers on the fret and strummed again. This time it was barely audible, but it sounded pretty good. Rancy played a few more chords, and then handed the guitar back to the man, who was now smiling.

"I didn't know he could play guitar," Carr remarked.

"Me neither," Samples said. "I hope he plays better than he shoots." There was movement over by the door, and Samples glanced over and saw Colonel Duran coming in. Shooting to his feet, Samples bellowed, "Room, atten-SHUN!" Despite the free-flowing beer and the relaxed atmosphere, Army training kicked in and all the men in the room jumped up and stood at attention.

"As you were, gentlemen," Duran announced with a broad smile, and most of the men sat back down and began talking and drinking again. Duran was followed in by Captain Raymond, the Alpha Company commander, and then Samples saw something that made his heart leap in his chest. There was Anne Gaither, her orange hair framing her radiant face, and her eyes swept the room until they locked onto Samples, when her mouth split into a gleaming smile that made Samples go all gooey inside. The new arrivals wove their way around the tables to join Samples, Carr, and Masters, who had remained standing. So focused was he on Anne that Samples only noticed as they began pulling up chairs that Staff Sergeant Pastorini was with them as well. Everyone shook hands, and Samples and Anne did their best to pretend there was only military protocol involved in the process, despite the meaningful glances they exchanged. Once everyone was seated, Samples finally remembered his manners and took everyone's orders. Because it was an EM Club, the only choices were beer and sodas. While Samples went to get their drinks from the bar, he heard Carr thanking Duran for setting up the evening.

After he returned and passed out the refreshments, Samples turned to Pastorini and said, "So how you are doing, Preacher?" While he was indeed curious about the big man's recovery, he was even more anxious to distract everyone—and himself—from his reactions toward Anne.

"Getting better," Pastorini told him. "Be back on flight status next week, the docs tell me."

"And Chief Whitmore?" Carr asked, leaning forward to see around Samples.

"Back in the World," Pastorini said.

"He'll be in Walter Reed by now," Captain Gaither elucidated. Samples forced himself to refer to her, even just in his mind, by her rank.

The conversation around the table ebbed and flowed with tales of recent humorous incidents, personnel changes, and the seemingly perpetual peace talks. Samples pretended to be interested, but mostly we was stealing glances at Anne and reminiscing about their time in Vung Tau. The approach of PFC Sweet didn't really register until the young man stopped next to Colonel Duran and awaited permission to speak.

"What do you need, Sweet?" Samples asked him.

"I just wanted to let the colonel know that we are ready whenever he is."

"That time already?" Colonel Duran said, smiling up at Sweet. "I'll be right there."

Samples saw Carr look questioningly at him with a raised eyebrow, and Samples could only shrug in reply. Captain Raymond saw their expressions, and spoke up.

"PFC Sweet came to me with a special request that he wanted to keep from you two as a surprise. I hope you don't mind."

What could they say? He was their company commander. "Certainly not, sir," Carr answered for both of them. He and Samples again exchanged brief worried glances. Sweet was generally regarded as a harmless goofball, a jokester who never quite stepped over the line. Conspiring with the battalion commander, however, took his shenanigans to an entirely different level.

Colonel Duran took one last swig from his beer can and pushed back from the table. "Duty calls," he joked, standing up and weaving his way through the tables toward the stage. As he did so, three Asian men in frilly white shirts and tight black trousers came on stage, one taking his place behind the drum set and the other two picking up guitars. Rancy, with a third guitar, joined them.

As the colonel stepped up on the stage, Sweet bellowed, "At ease!" The room quickly went quiet. There was a microphone on a tall stand, and Sweet showed the colonel had to switch it on. After a quick squeal of feedback, the colonel tapped the mike, sending loud thumping noises across the room. Nodding with satisfaction, the colonel began speaking.

"Men of Alpha Company, are you having a good time?" He was rewarded by applause, whistles, and hoots of pleasure. When the noise died back down, he continued. "I thought your actions two weeks ago in the Boi Loi deserved some recognition, and I also had a request from the USO to show their appreciation. So tonight, live on stage, we have. . . The Girlfriends!" With great showmanship the colonel swept his arm toward the curtains and out came the three Japanese girls, wearing cropped red blouses and white miniskirts. Dark blue go-go boots reached nearly up to their knees. All had their hair teased into giant bouffant hair-dos, and more make-up than perhaps was really needed. The room erupted into cheers and wolf-whistles. The girls moved to center stage, lining up behind the colonel. He patted the air to calm the crowd down.

"It was one of your fellow soldiers that came to me with this idea, and I think you all owe him a debt of gratitude. PFC Sweet, take a bow." He gestured to Sweet, who was standing at the edge of the stage. At the same time the band began playing softly while the three girls sang, "Soldier boy, oh, my rittle soldier boy, I'll be true to you." Sweet visibly blushed, but grinned and bowed theatrically as the men in the room roared with laughter.

Duran let the room settle down. "I'd like to recognize each of you individually for your actions, but we'd be here all night. I do want to point out one young man in particular. He had been in the battalion only one day, but he volunteered to go out in the woods and help rescue his fellow soldiers. And then, during an intense firefight, he snatched an enemy grenade out of the air and threw it back, undoubtedly saving the lives of the other men in the track. PFC Handleman, would you stand up, please?"

At a signal from Sweet, the band played and the Girlfriends began singing again: "Ooh-wah, ooh-wah, ooh ooh, Kitty. Tell us about the boy from New York City."

There was some scuffling in the middle of the room, and then Handleman was pushed to a standing position by the other guys at his table. He kept looking down, too embarrassed to acknowledge the approving shouts of "Yeah!" and "Mr. Baseball!" His friends finally let him sit back down and the room settled again.

"Although he isn't part of our battalion, we would certainly welcome him. I really want to thank Staff Sergeant Pastorini for his support and firepower during that long night. Sergeant Pastorini, would you please stand up?" Samples nudged Pastorini, but he wasn't averse to being recognized in this way. With a wide grin splitting his dark face, he stood up and waved at everyone. Up on stage the Girlfriends sang, "The only boy who could ever reach me was the son of a Preacherman, yes he, was, yes he was, oh, yes he was." Next to them Sweet was beaming, obviously pleased with himself. Samples wondered how much time Sweet had spent on making all this work out. And then it occurred to him that he could be next, something he really didn't need.

When Pastorini sat back down and the noise abated, Duran looked over the heads of the crowd at the table where Samples sat with the officers. "And of course, I want to mention your leaders, who made the right decisions at the right times. First off, there is your remarkable platoon sergeant, Sergeant First Class Aaron Samples." Behind him the singers belted out, "My boyfriend's back, and you're gonna be in trouble, hey, ra, hey ra, my boyfriend's back." Pastorini forced Samples to stand up, and he felt his face flushing as he tried to maintain a suitable scowl of disapproval. The men applauded, and someone shouted "Welcome back, Free!" which drew a round of laughter. As quickly as he could, Samples sat back down and with forced nonchalance took a drink from his empty beer can.

"And then there is Second Lieutenant Harold Masters," Duran said, looking sternly straight at the man. Even Duran was obviously caught unawares when the girls began singing, "Don't say nothin' bad about my baby." He looked back at Sweet with an odd expression, and then shook his head slowly. He started to speak again, but the girls segued into, "He's a rebel and he'll never ever be any good. He's a rebel 'cause he never ever does what he should." And that started Duran guffawing so hard he stepped back from the microphone to catch his breath. The soldiers in the room were laughing equally hard, and Samples looked over at Masters. The young lieutenant had his hands over his face, but the redness of his complexion shone through.

Duran finally went back to the mike and said, "I guess I don't need to say anything else about him. I do have an announcement for him, though. Lieutenant Masters, you have been reassigned as the platoon leader of third platoon, Alpha Company. Also, I have requested that you be frocked as a First Lieutenant, and that should be coming through shortly. You will also be getting your CIB, which you have truly earned. Congratulations." Everyone clapped, and Masters dropped his hands and looked to the ceiling with his eyes closed, silently mouthing the words, "Thank you." Carr reached over and gently punched his shoulder.

"And next, I want to thank First Lieutenant Stephen Carr, who did such an outstanding job of rescuing the people in the helicopter and bringing his platoon through a nasty firefight."

Behind the colonel, the Girlfriend named Crystal, the one with the blond hair, took one step forward and sang acapella, "I met him in the Boi Roi Woods, he kinda smiled at me, you get the picture?"

The other two girls responded, "Yes, we see."

"And that's when I fell for. . ." The other two girls join in: "The Reader of the Pack."

And virtually every soldier in the room responded with "Vroom, vroom!" and other raucous engine noises. The band, with

Rancy joining in, played loudly the opening bars of the song, but tapered off at Duran's upraised hand.

"And finally," Duran said when the noise died down, "I want to recognize Captain Anne Gaither, who took care of all our wounded and soldiered through with great strength and determination. Anne, could you stand up, please?" Samples was glad the situation allowed him to watch her stand up and gaze at her for a minute. But then the singers on stage started up again.

"Tell him that your never gonna reave him, tell him that your always gonna rove him, tell him, tell him, tell him, tell him right now."

Anne's face turned bright red, her freckles disappearing, and she abruptly sat back down. Samples stood up and glared at Sweet, then realized his actions only reinforced the message, and hastily sat back down. The men in the room snickered, and Colonel Duran assumed a look of mild innocence. He clearly knew of Sample's relationship with Captain Gaither, and he wasn't disturbed about it. Samples sighed with relief.

"Okay," Duran said, "I've got to get back to work. You men have a good time." He stepped off the stage and headed for the door, the crowd of men parting before him like the Red Sea. On stage the band began playing the Animals' song, "We've Gotta Get Outta This Place."

"Another beer, Aaron?" Carr asked him, pushing back from the table. "I'm buying."

"Sure." He looked over at Anne, and she winked at him. He couldn't help but smile. "That would be really good."